Everything Within AND In Between

Everything Within AND In Between

NIKKI BARTHELMESS

HARPER TEEN
An Imprint of HarperCollinsPublishers

For my grandma—
Te quiero mucho, Abuelita

HarperTeen is an imprint of HarperCollins Publishers.

Everything Within and In Between
Copyright © 2021 by Nikki Barthelmess
All rights reserved. Printed in the United States of America.
No part of this book may be used or reproduced in any manner whatsoever
without written permission except in the case of brief quotations embodied
in critical articles and reviews. For information address HarperCollins
Children's Books, a division of HarperCollins Publishers, 195 Broadway,
New York, NY 10007.
www.epicreads.com

Library of Congress Control Number: 2021941132
ISBN 978-0-06-297690-1

Typography by Jessie Gang
21 22 23 24 25   PC/LSCH   10 9 8 7 6 5 4 3 2 1
❖
First Edition

Chapter ONE

Act natural, I tell myself as Mrs. Viola peers down at my transfer application. The scribbled forging of Grandma's signature practically pops off the page, at least to my eyes.

"Are you having problems in French?" The guidance counselor's long fingers intertwine on her desk where she sits in front of me. "We're only a few weeks into the new semester. I'm sure you can make it work if you stick with it."

I shake my head as I tap the wood in between us. "I'm not having a hard time in French." I can't quite meet Viola's eyes. Instead I stare at the wall behind her, decorated with posters sporting the usual clichés of *The future starts with you* and *Every morning is a new beginning*.

"French is great. It's just that there's this program in Mexico, through my church, that I'm hoping to do this summer." The lie slips off my lips easily. "I figured now would be as good a time as ever to brush up on my Spanish."

Viola pushes her slipping glasses back into place and looks down at my transfer form. "Miss *Fernández*, if you ask me, you'd be better off staying in French. You could practice Spanish at home, with your familia."

My stomach lurches at the way Viola says my name, overly dramatic—smug, even.

Her assumption crawls over my skin. Like this woman knows a *thing* about me or my family. I want to shake my head or wiggle my shoulders to get this feeling off me, but instead I stare at her blankly. Viola clicks at her keyboard and stares at the computer screen in front of her.

She glances at me. "You do speak *some* Spanish, right?"

"Yes," I rush out. "But I think it's really important for me to transfer. I realized that even though I've studied some French, the standards for fluency are much higher than what I'm learning. I doubt I'd become proficient by the time I graduate, starting from scratch. Since I have a much stronger foundation in Spanish, I'd rather make the switch, where I'm much more likely to actually become fluent, like by school standards. I think it would help with college applications."

I smile innocently. My grandparents never *actually* taught me, but they spoke it to each other and my mom when I was young. So that probably wasn't the right thing to say, but I need to sell Viola on this. Wanting to be fluent in any language, whether I should already be or not, is something a guidance counselor won't argue will help me get into college. It still won't be enough to get me into the kind of college Grandma has her hopes set on, I'm sure, but it's a reason Viola can wrap her head around at least.

Viola nods. "Well, it's good to hear that you're so focused on your future. I'll put you in Spanish Two, then, and if you have any problems, you can let me know."

Like that's going to ever happen—I don't ever want to tell her or anyone else how little Spanish I speak. I'll just pick it up quickly. I'll have to.

Viola signs the yellow piece of paper allowing me to switch classes. But just as I'm about to grab it, she rests her hand on the transfer slip. "Just try not to get in trouble, Maria. The kids in Spanish class . . . a lot of them take the class for the easy A, since most of them already speak it. It'd be a shame to see such a good kid like you pick up any bad habits."

Like me.

So the other kids, the ones who aren't like me, are lazy? Not good kids? Grandma's voice bursts into my thoughts. She's telling me Brittany is a good girl and Nina isn't.

I narrow my eyes at Viola. "It's Ri," I say coldly.

The bell rings and hundreds of students push through the classroom doors into the hallways of Riviera High School. School's out for the day.

Seeming to notice my change in demeanor, Viola fidgets. She looks to the door behind me. "Good luck in Spanish." She nods in the direction of the hallway.

I don't thank her, not after what she insinuated. Did she think I'd take that as a compliment, her not throwing me in the same "category" as them? I snatch the paper from her and rush to the door.

My irritation at Viola grows as I visit the Spanish classroom and pick up the textbook from Señora Almanza.

Down the hall, I blink several times and stare at my locker. So much has felt off-kilter since I found my mom's letter. Realizing Grandma lied. Realizing I have a lot less in common with my own family than I ever thought.

My eyes have been closed to so much. And I wonder. *Has Viola always been like that, and I'm just noticing now?*

My locker door slams into the one next to it after I fling it open, the sound reverberating mercilessly, just as Edgar Gómez approaches.

With a tentative smile, he lifts his notebook in between us, as though it's a shield. "Permission to approach?"

"Sorry," I exhale, before pulling my locker door out of his way. "It's been a day."

Edgar nods as he opens his locker.

"What kind of day are we talking here?" He puts his notebook inside and shifts a couple of books around, apparently looking for something. "Like you stubbed your toe or you just found out you're allergic to puppies, killing your long-held dream of running a corgi farm?"

I can't help but laugh. "That was oddly specific."

Edgar shrugs. "My mom loves watching *The Crown* and is way into those little dogs the Queen has. If our apartment allowed pets, she'd for sure get one."

That gets me to pause. "That's really sad."

"It is, but"—Edgar's face brightens as I turn to face him—"I got her the next best thing." He grabs his phone from his pocket and scrolls through until he hands it to me.

On the screen, there's a picture of a very fluffy, very cute, nearly life-sized corgi stuffed animal.

I laugh, hard. Edgar beams. "Now she's gotta share her queen-sized bed with that, but she's good with it!"

I shake my head at Edgar, feeling lighter. He and I don't talk much more than the nods or the casual pleasantries we exchange whenever we run into each other at our lockers. But today, this was nice.

I lift my Spanish book to put it away, smiling.

"Hey, are you in Spanish Two? I thought there was only one period for that."

I pause, the book suspended in midair.

"There is," I say slowly. "I just transferred."

Edgar scratches his head full of thick and wavy black curls. "Me and a few of my friends are in there. It's a pretty good class. You should sit with us. My friends and me, that is."

Sit with Edgar? I've seen him with Nina, and I'm sure she doesn't want me around. Since she and I stopped hanging out in middle school, though, I haven't really hung out with any other Mexican American kids.

I stare at Edgar for probably a second too long without answering.

Edgar's dark brown eyes hold my gaze. "If you want to, I mean."

I find my voice, though it comes out much higher than

intended. "Of course, yeah, that would be great. Thank you!"

Before I can think too hard on the fact that I don't have any Mexican friends anymore, Brittany appears next to me—benefits of having a locker near your best friend's.

"Just saw you leaving Mrs. V's. What's going on there?"

I look back at Edgar as he closes his locker. "See you in class," he says.

I wave as he walks away, before bringing my focus back to Brittany's question.

"It's nothing. I'm just transferring to Spanish class. Remember that thing I told you about with my church's trip to Mexico?" Without thinking, the lie I told to Viola comes out. My stomach sinks; I don't want to lie to my best friend too.

Brittany's light brown hair cascades over her shoulder as she sweeps it out of her face. "Yeah, but I didn't think that meant you were transferring. What about French?"

I hold my locker door for a moment, readying myself. "I'd rather practice my Spanish."

Brittany's eyebrows lift in disbelief. "You speak Spanish? Since when?"

"I know some, you know." My locker slams shut, and I wince. I did it again. My voice comes out calm, apologetic. "I picked it up at home, when my grandparents used to speak it to each other."

Brittany watches me quietly for a moment. No doubt trying to figure out what the actual eff is wrong with me. I've been *off* in other ways too, lately. I know it.

"Viola gave me a hard time about it, and I'm just annoyed." I exhale slowly. "I'm sorry."

Brittany keeps her eyes on me, not noticing a couple of senior guys checking her out as they walk past. "It's cool."

"You ready to go?" I ask. "There's something I want to talk to you about."

Brittany insists on driving me home most days, even though I only live a few blocks away. It's mostly because we run together, after I quit cross-country and she quickly followed suit.

"Right behind you, *señorita*. Should I start calling you Maria now too?"

I push her backpack, nudging her forward with a smile.

We follow the crowd through the hallway—everyone making a beeline out of the building.

"So, what's so important that you can't wait for our run to tell me?" Brittany asks.

"I can't run today," I sigh. "My grandma ended up getting the night off and she'll want to spend time together."

Grandma's a personal assistant to a seriously rich family in Montecito. Not like the kind of personal assistant that takes phone calls and schedules stuff, though she does that too. She does everything. Cooking, cleaning, grocery shopping, errand running, phone answering, bill paying, you name it. She works twelve-hour days, often, five to six days a week. With rent prices in Santa Barbara sky-high, even for our tiny house, we couldn't afford to live here otherwise.

I know Grandma works hard and thinks that everything

she's doing is what's best for me. But she's wrong. I grit my teeth, thinking about the letter.

"Her boss should go easy on her," Brittany says, shaking her head. "Your grandma's not getting any younger. I mean, that woman can afford to hire more help. Why doesn't your grandma say something?"

"Money," I deadpan. *As in, some of us need it.*

There's a tense second when I stare at Brittany and she flushes, looking away.

"I get it," Brittany says, even though we both know she doesn't. Or maybe it's just me who knows that.

Brittany sighs as we walk through the front doors and out onto the expansive lawn. "Although if I'd known you were going to bail on running," Brittany says, in a singsong tone, "maybe I wouldn't have quit cross-country."

Even though I know she's teasing, I can't help but glare at her. It's not like I asked Brittany to quit when I did a few weeks ago. I wanted more time to babysit and make money to help my grandma.

Brittany puts her hands up. "I got it, I got it, not your fault. I know I could have stayed if I wanted to, but it wasn't the same without you. Who would I even hang out with at the away meets? You know us, we're not great with other girls."

But that isn't exactly true, at least not for me. I used to have other friends.

As if on cue, across the school's front lawn, I hear the once familiar sound of Nina laughing. I glance in her direction. The crowd around her is hanging out under the shade of one of the taller, thicker trees on campus, less than the distance of a classroom away. But we might as well be on other planets.

Brittany digs into her bag for her car keys as we approach the parking lot full of luxury cars, like her Mercedes—a hand-me-down from her grandmother, as she likes to remind me—and beaters, like I would have if I could afford my own wheels.

As we close in on Brittany's car, silver and sleek, she turns to me, so close I could count the light freckles spotting her nose. "We'll run tomorrow. I could use the time for studying tonight anyway. But you said you wanted to talk, so spill."

"Not here." I open the car door, and once Brittany's inside, I tell her to drive.

I've been working up to this moment for weeks, since I found Mom's letter. I wanted to tell Brittany, but I just couldn't. Doing so would make it more real, would make me feel like I'd have to do something. And I just wasn't ready. Not until today, when I forged Grandma's signature and lied my way into Spanish class.

"I didn't tell you what happened on my birthday," I finally say.

Brittany stops at a red light and I take a deep breath. "Early in the morning, when she thought I was asleep, I saw my grandma. There was a box that I'd never seen before next to her. She was looking at a picture, sitting on the floor rocking back and forth, crying."

Brittany's eyes widen. We both know how stoic my grandma

is, so she's probably about as shocked as I was. My grandma never shows emotion like that.

"I knew she'd be embarrassed if she realized I'd seen her, so I didn't say anything about it when we had breakfast together." I keep talking as Brittany pulls onto my street. Selena's "Dreaming of You" blasts from the Navarros. Mrs. Navarro always keeps the windows open when she's cleaning inside.

"She was acting like everything was fine. Which was dumb since her eyes were all puffy but whatever. After she left, I snuck into her room and found the box with the picture hidden inside."

I turn to look at Brittany, who I can tell is totally wrapped up in my story. "My grandma had been looking at a photo of my mom when she was pregnant with me. She was seventeen at the time."

Brittany parks in front of my house. Like ours, our neighbors' homes are small, with varying levels of upkeep. Chipped paint, dead grass—we're practically always in a drought in Southern California.

I don't make a move to get out of the car.

"Seventeen," Brittany repeats quietly. "Like you are now. Maybe that's why she was crying."

I peel my eyes away from the kids playing on the other side of the street, to look back at Brittany. "Under the photo there was an envelope addressed to her. The return address, the name, it was my mom's."

Brittany's shocked face is as I expected. She knows I've

googled Marisol Fernández probably a thousand times. My mom's not on social media. She's not online anywhere. It's like she was a ghost until now.

"My mom wrote my grandma this letter two years ago— two years!—saying she wanted to be in my life. She lives in Oxnard, less than an hour from here," I say out loud for the first time.

Every time Brittany and I shopped at the outlets, I was only minutes away from her. For all I know, she could have been at a nearby store. I could have been mere feet away from my mother and never have known.

I think of all the time lost. The moments I had with my mom when I was young that I took for granted, forever seared into my mind now, into my heart—the place that aches at the absence of her.

I touch the ends of my hair. Images of Mom brushing and braiding it before I went to bed come to mind, hollowing out my chest. I remember sitting on the floor, leaning up against her on the couch, feeling safe and loved.

Feeling wanted.

I've had a mom who wanted to be in my life all along. And Grandma never told me.

Brittany reaches for my shoulder and squeezes it. "That's a lot," she says.

I shake my head, because that's not all. It's like a rock drops in my gut as I admit the next part.

"The letter was in Spanish," I finally say. "I couldn't even read it myself, not without looking stuff up."

Recognition dawns on Brittany's face. "Oh."

Silence stretches between us until Brittany recovers. "Why didn't you tell me? I mean, not just about the Spanish and why you *really* wanted to transfer. But about your mom?"

Brittany looks more confused than offended, her light brown eyes staring at me with concern.

I offer a sad smile. "I was embarrassed."

Brittany scoffs. "You know better than to be embarrassed about family drama with me. Helloooooooo." She draws out the last syllable. "I mean, have you met my mother?"

A laugh bursts out of me. Brittany's mom is hardly ever around. And when she is, she's a bottle of wine deep with a mission to get Brittany to hang out more at the country club with her. She's always trying to get Brittany to be some perfect image of what she thinks a daughter should be. But this is more than just family drama.

I couldn't understand the first words I've heard from my mom since she left when I was a kid. I had to look it all up on Google Translate. Grandma's never wanted me to learn Spanish, even though it's her first language—Mom's, too, since my grandparents didn't speak English well when she was a kid. Not being able to understand Mom's letter made me wonder what she would think of me growing up completely isolated from something that must have been a big part of her life—her heritage.

Because it's not only about not speaking our language.

Whenever I try to ask Grandma about any of it—anything at all related to her being Mexican or me being part Mexican American—she shuts me down. A few clipped sentences and a shut door. End of conversation.

Grandma won't talk about her past. She doesn't want us to hang out with anyone in our neighborhood. And every time I've even come close to bringing up anything that could be remotely tied to learning about Mexico, Grandma quickly shuts it down by reminding me that I'm American. Which is exactly why I didn't ask her to sign the transfer slip. I imagine her disapproving face, eyes narrowed, mouth puckered. *We're in America and need to act like it.*

I don't have any other family who can teach me Spanish, no less other parts of our culture. Learning the language feels like the only piece of my heritage, not to mention connection to my mother that I can carve out for myself, the only thing I can control. Because with Grandma keeping such a massive secret on top of everything else, I've never felt more alone. She has lied to me every single day for the last two years by pretending she doesn't know where Mom is. She must never want me to see Mom again.

So I haven't told her about Spanish class. Or that I know about Oxnard. And I definitely am not going to tell her about my plans, but I should stop keeping this bottled up inside. I can tell Brittany. I just need to say the words, make them real.

"I want to see her."

Brittany leans a hand on my knee. "I will literally do anything and everything I can to help. I'll drive you myself." Brittany's words quicken, as though she's excited. "Need an alibi? I'll lie to your grandma. Anything you need, I'm your girl."

I smile, a real one. "I'm so glad I have you."

Chapter
TWO

I tell Brittany I still need some time before we go to see my mom. It's been so long, and I just want to make sure it goes well, that I know what I want to say to her. And then there's the thing I'm afraid to say, even after I told Brittany everything else.

There's still the glaring question, the one I'm scared to learn the answer to.

Why did Mom leave in the first place?

After Brittany drives off, I can't seem to move my feet from the sidewalk outside my tiny salmon-colored house. I suck in a breath. I can't avoid Grandma forever.

I'm about to take a step when someone says my name.

Tommy, the ten-year-old who lives across the street, waves to me from atop his bike in his yard. He's shirtless and smiling. "¡Hola, Ri!"

"Hey." I don't bother saying hola, even though I obviously know what it means. I don't want people in my very bilingual neighborhood forgetting I don't speak Spanish and trying to talk to me. Expecting me to speak it back. *It's embarrassing that I don't.* With all of Grandma's efforts to make us more

"American," it's just one more thing that makes me different from everyone else around here.

Not speaking Spanish is the final nail in the coffin. The thing that puts me over the edge. I can't help that people I've grown up around know I don't speak Spanish. But if I keep my mouth shut as much as possible in Spanish class until I learn more, maybe I can keep Edgar and his friends from knowing. From thinking of me as I see myself—an outsider.

Tommy's mom waves from behind him, bringing me out of my thoughts.

"Tell your abuela that we say hello," she calls to me. "We miss her at church. If I didn't see her at the market from time to time, I'd think she'd moved away."

Abuela. Such a normal word for pretty much every grandmother in my neighborhood but mine—who would never, ever let me call her that. I nod and smile, acknowledging Mrs. Sánchez's words without actually agreeing to anything. She used to stop by our house and ask for my grandma, invite us over for Sunday brunch after mass for months after we stopped going in favor of attending the nondenominational church that meets in another part of town. Now that it's been a few years, basically everyone else has given up on trying to socialize with my "abuela." The one exception are her friends from the church we go to now, who she meets every week for their Bible study and knitting club. Always at one of their houses on the Riviera or the Mesa, or sometimes downtown, but never at our tiny place on the Eastside.

But even after all that time, sometimes I see that little flicker of hope in Mrs. Sánchez's eyes. I can't bear to squelch it.

My shoes crunch over the yellow, brittle grass of our front lawn. I jam my key in the door and wrestle it unlocked. Drop my backpack on the brown love seat—I've given up on trying to talk Grandma into getting a new one because it clashes with the pink carpet. Just another thing she won't listen to me about.

"I'm home," I mutter.

The smell of chicken enchiladas wafts over to me as Grandma opens the oven to check on the food.

"Hi, baby! I hope you're hungry. Enchiladas are almost ready!"

I unclench my teeth, preparing myself for the usual pretending-I'm-not-infuriated-with-Grandma act I've been perfecting since I found out the truth. "Yeah, I'm hungry."

Grandma smiles, revealing the gap in between her front teeth. The imperfection made her even more beautiful in a photo I saw of her and Grandpa in Mexico when they were young and in love. She stood tall and thin, dignified, like a model. Now she hunches her back from years of hard work. But she still has the same smile.

"Come on," Grandma calls from the kitchen. "Sit down already."

I stare at the hallway, my feet still planted on the doormat, yearning to be in my bedroom with the door closed. Writing in my journal about Mom and all the things I can't say to Grandma. Seconds tick by. Slowly, I walk toward her.

The kitchen air is warm with the smell of chicken and melted cheese. Grandma bends to take the enchiladas from the oven. From this angle, with her black hair cropped short and her bony figure, she almost looks like a little old man. Her womanly curves have long since left her.

I sit at the table, squeezed in the spot of tile in between our kitchen and living room. Grandma dishes two massive enchiladas onto my plate, covering them in sour cream, along with beans and rice, filling my plate to its limit. She halves one of the smaller enchiladas with a knife and puts it on her own plate, along with a spoon-sized helping of beans and rice.

"Eat up!" She sits across from me. "We'll save the leftovers. I'd say you can take them for lunch tomorrow, but I know how you and Brittany like to go out. Which reminds me"—Grandma reaches into her pocket and pulls out a ten-dollar bill—"here. For lunch this week."

She grins as she hands it to me, not realizing that it would only cover lunch for a couple of days, not the week. She never eats out. Maybe if Mom were around, she would know these kinds of things.

I push the money back to her side of the table. "Thanks, Grandma, but I don't need it."

Grandma purses her lips and begins poking at her food. "Well, you might change your mind about that because I spoke to Mrs. Tanner and suggested she find a new babysitter."

I blink. Set my fork down carefully. "What?"

Grandma's eyes don't leave her plate. "You've been so busy

lately with babysitting, I thought you'd be relieved to have more time with Brittany. More time for school. And you can rejoin the cross-country team. You've seemed so upset lately, so I took care of it. I am doing you a favor."

"You're not," I push out through gritted teeth. "I want to babysit, and I wanted to quit the team—"

"I talked to Mrs. Tanner, and we both agree that she should find someone else," Grandma interrupts. "Your studies are most important. And so are school activities. They're an important part of your applications for universities."

"Grandma—"

"It's done." The cross Grandma wears every day dangles from her neck as she nods emphatically. "Mrs. Tanner already found someone to replace you from the youth Bible study group. You don't need to worry about work until you're older, baby. Trust me, you have your entire life after high school for that."

It's as though the air is being sucked out from my chest. I sputter, but words don't come out. Because I know before saying another word she won't listen. Grandma's word is law and has been since Grandpa died.

"You should rejoin cross-country."

My eyes stay on my plate. "I don't want to."

Grandma huffs loudly. "You have time, and you love to run. That's all you do when you're not studying or writing in that notebook you love. You should at least be letting it count for something, for helping you get into a university. That is why I work so hard and sacrifice *so much*, Ri." The annoyance in

Grandma's voice falters for an instant. "So you can get into a good university, one of the best, and do better for yourself, more than I ever could."

I look away and try to control my anger. The blanket Grandma knitted for me about a month ago lies atop the couch. She handed it to me proudly and said, "It's Yale blue," after our most recent argument about me getting into a "good" college; this variation was about her wanting me to do volunteer work so that it would look good on my applications.

I didn't tell Grandma it takes a lot more than volunteering—although that's when I got my brilliant idea for telling her I want to go on the Mexico service-learning trip—to get into Yale or Harvard. Kids who get into schools like that are often prodigies or geniuses. They're usually rich, which gives them the ability, from birth, to learn any hobby or skill to basically look perfect for college apps. They are legacies whose parents donate money to the school. Or they have a compelling personal story about *saving people* in a "third-world country" or something.

But there's no telling Grandma that. She thinks I've got the same chance at the American Dream as anyone else and won't hear a word that says otherwise.

"I have good grades, but it's not like I'm going to get into an Ivy or anything," I say. "And playing one sport isn't going to make a difference."

I set my fork down. I don't want to fight with Grandma, but it's getting close to college application time next year, and she needs a dose of reality before it's too late. "Grandma, what do I care if I go to Stanford or Yale? It's so much money, and it doesn't even really matter anyway."

Grandma slams her hand on the table. "It does matter. It's the only thing that matters. Getting into the best university you can is how you get a good job, Ri. You know that."

My laptop with tabs open on the writing program at UCSB comes to mind.

"My grades are fine, Grandma, and I'll get into a good school," I say, averting my eyes. *Maybe not the school you'll want me to go to, but a good one all the same.* "I promise."

Grandma's eyes soften and she gives me a small smile. "Good girl."

She takes another bite of enchilada, and I feel the room cooling down in response.

Grandma eyes me for a moment before wiping her mouth with a napkin. "Eat, Ri, the food's getting cold."

We eat in silence. I know I should tell Grandma about Spanish class, but the words don't come easily. Especially given how worked up she already is about cross-country and college. I rehearsed what I was going to say to Grandma about transferring in my mind so many times, though.

"So . . ." I begin, my voice unaffected, "there's something I'm interested in at church."

Grandma sits up in her chair, her cross necklace swinging as she does.

"The youth group is doing a service-learning trip to Mexico City, and I think it would be really awesome if—"

Grandma sets her water glass on the table. Hard. "I know about that trip." She gives me a pointed look. "They're going to have some art classes and sing 'Kumbaya.' They're not going to do any real work."

I open my mouth, but Grandma holds her hand up to silence me.

"It's not safe in Mexico." She shakes her head. "We send you kids there, with your iPads and cell phones, and you meet some new friends and sing songs. And you're a target for anyone who is poor, who has nothing to lose."

I sit up in my chair, my face burning. "Grandma, *you're* the one who said I should be volunteering for college applications. It would be a great learning experience, and anyway, it would be totally safe. We'd have chaperones and—"

"I meant you should serve food at a soup kitchen or clean up a park." Grandma huffs. "Where I grew up, people stole; they hurt others if they wanted what they had. And it's only gotten worse. If you're in the wrong place, people will harm you. You're a pretty young woman, so you'd be putting yourself even more at risk."

Grandma reaches over and squeezes my shoulder softly. When I stiffen, hurt flashes in her eyes, and she pulls her lips back into their familiar tense line.

"I'll just wrap these up for tomorrow," she says, before heading to the kitchen.

I stare at the long scratch down the center of the wooden table.

I didn't *want* to go, not really. I just wanted an excuse, a reason. My mouth opens and the truth tumbles out before I can stop myself. "I transferred from French to Spanish class today."

Grandma stops walking but doesn't say anything. She's still, her back toward me. I can't see her face, but I know she heard me.

"It's already done, Grandma. Please don't fight me on this." Like a gust of wind, the words rush out of me. If I don't say them now, I never will. "I just want to have some of my culture in my life. It's ridiculous that we're Mexican, but you don't want me to speak Spanish."

Grandma puts the enchiladas in the fridge and closes the door. "You're. Not. Mexican." She turns to face me, her mouth set. "Ri, you're white. Your father was a white man. Your mother was born in this country. *I am Mexican.* You are not."

I flatten my hands against the table, my chair screeching against the tile as I stand. I walk toward her in the kitchen. "Fine, I have Mexican heritage, or I'm of Mexican descent, a Mexican American, a Latina, whatever. My point is I'm probably one of the only kids who doesn't speak Spanish in this neighborhood, and I want to."

Grandma sighs deeply before closing the distance between us. "Look in the mirror, baby." She reaches a hand to pull a piece of hair from my face softly.

And I deflate.

"Do you think anyone would even consider the idea that you're Latina without a second glance? Your skin is nothing like mine. Yours is fair—you have dark hair, sure, but what does it matter? To the world you're white," she says, standing so close that in her eyes, I see my reflection. I see me as she sees me.

Even though my tone is more of a cool fawn, it doesn't change where our family came from or our history. That doesn't change who we are, *who I am*.

"My name is *Maria Fernández*, Grandma."

She puts her hands on my shoulders, and under her touch I become smaller. "I know you've always wanted to fit in, and maybe this is you trying to do that." She sighs and shakes her head to herself, like I'm a silly child she has to keep reminding not to do something obviously stupid.

I open my mouth but nothing comes out. How can Grandma brush this off like it's about fitting in? It's about my identity. My family—her, Grandpa, *Mom*.

Unable to form words, I just glare at her.

"Fine, if you care so much, stay in Spanish. But if you get anything less than an A, that's it for you. No más." Grandma stops, realizing she spoke Spanish, and says, "I've had a long day."

Though I should be celebrating this victory, my heart is still pumping wildly. I shouldn't have to beg her to let me learn a language.

"I will get good grades in Spanish," I say through gritted teeth. "But I wouldn't even have to be taking this class if you and Grandpa had taught me in the first place. You taught Mom."

Grandma blinks several times, her eyes wide as orbs. "Watch

your tone with me, young lady."

My cheeks flood with heat. I never talk to Grandma like that. But maybe if I did, I'd get more answers.

"Ri, you want to take Spanish class in school; I already said that is fine," she says curtly. "But in this house, you will remember one thing: We are in America and we speak English."

"Grandma, that's so backward. You know—"

The dishes clang as she piles them in her arms. They clatter as she plops them in the sink, and I walk my plate over to her as well. As I turn, Grandma mutters something in Spanish under her breath.

"Grandma?"

She shakes her head. "Ri, we share a last name, but you look how you do, and you sound like you do, and that will go a long way for you in life. Be grateful for that. There is no reason for you to make problems for yourself."

I open my mouth to tell Grandma that's not what I'm doing when she releases a few more words, sharp as daggers. "Don't try to be someone you're not."

Grandma walks past me to the hallway, to shut herself in her room. And all I hear for the rest of the night is our argument on a loop in my mind. Grandma's words about me not being Mexican, about how white I look. The worst part is, she thinks of it as a good thing.

I massage my jaw. It hurts from clenching it so much. Grandma always says Mom left because she wasn't ready to be a parent. It bugs me that I don't know for sure. A part of me, the part that hates that I'll never be what Grandma wants, has worried Mom had felt that I wasn't good enough for her. But after tonight, I wonder if my mom left because Grandma was so controlling and stubborn.

She practically blew a gasket because I had the nerve to transfer to Spanish class. There's no way I can tell her about wanting to go to UCSB to study journalism now. What if Mom left because Grandma was going to squash her dreams too?

Chapter

THREE

I wake up before sunrise. Unable to get back to sleep, I stare up at the air bubbles in the ceiling for a long time. My chest feels like someone's squeezing it. Today is the day, my first class in Spanish. I want to look good for it.

After yanking my closet's sliding door open, I reach for my favorite striped shirt and throw it on over a pair of tight jeans. Grandma's gone to work by now, as always, so it's not like she'll be able to make any comments about what I'm wearing.

I want to make a good impression because I know Nina will be there. I haven't been around her, like really around her, in years. When she passes me in the halls, I make sure I'm busy looking at something else, or that I'm smiling at whatever Brittany has just said. I act as though I don't care we're not friends anymore. As if sometimes I don't watch her at lunch time, wonder if she's happy, if she misses me. I want Nina to see that I'm doing perfectly fine without her when I walk into class.

Nina and I were close, until one day she stopped taking my calls and then wouldn't even say hi to me at school or at church. Grandma thought it was for the best. *Nina isn't a good girl, like*

Brittany, she said. Even though Nina went to church—what Grandma used as a qualifier for being a good girl, usually—and Brittany didn't.

I used to do all the same things Nina did, hung out at the same places, grew up in the same neighborhood. I thought that made me less of a *good girl* to Grandma too. But I wanted to be one. I wanted her to see me the way she saw Brittany back then. I wanted to be enough.

Despite Nina ghosting me, I can't forget what she meant to me back then. She was the first person I told that I wanted to be a writer. She got how I can't understand the world around me until I write about it. I remember how we rode our bikes around the Eastside and she sketched pictures of me climbing the jungle gym at the park. We hung out at the beach, rolling our jeans up to dip our toes in the ocean as we walked alongside the waves.

Out of my makeup bag, my fingers graze the palette I rarely use, unless it's a special occasion. I apply eye shadow before I lengthen my lashes with mascara. I squint at myself in the mirror. From far away, maybe, just maybe, I wouldn't look that different from Nina.

At school, each thud on the carpet brings me closer to Señora Almanza's classroom. My heart rockets in my chest, yet I try to look like this is any other day. Like what I'm about to do isn't terrifying.

Next thing I know, I'm standing in the doorway of Spanish.

Indecipherable voices talk and shout at one another. A couple guys shove each other back and forth. They're smiling, and other people are laughing. A handful of girls sit in front of them, including Nina and Cassie, Nina's best friend—the girl she seems to be inseparable from, like she and I used to be.

"Miguel, do you always have to be the loudest person in any room?" Nina laughs at her boyfriend, her straight black hair falling over her shoulder.

Miguel opens his mouth to respond to Nina, before the guy he was messing around with knocks him into his chair with his backpack. "Yeah, Miguelito. Sit your ass down, before your mommy over there makes you."

"Ooh," a few of the surrounding guys say. Nina's eyes—beautifully accentuated with multiple colors of eye shadow—narrow at the guy with the backpack.

Miguel jumps to his feet so he's looking down at the backpack thwacker. "You wish you were so lucky as to have a fine woman like Nina boss yo' ass around, Jorge! Don't hate."

Nina, who hasn't yet noticed me lurking by the door, cuts Miguel with a look.

"I mean, not boss, but make suggestions to." He gives Nina an over-the-top pleading look. "Carefully thought out, wonderful suggestions!"

Nina holds the glare on her boyfriend for an instant before both of them bust up laughing. She leans up in her chair and kisses Miguel softly.

My eyes flit to the back row by the window where a few

white kids who take this class sit. Next to some sophomores whose names I don't know, there's Carrie Leslie, Kelsey Ford, and Blaine Todd. We're not friends, exactly, but I'm not seeing Edgar anywhere. . . .

I lock eyes with Kelsey, and she smiles as if she's welcoming me. Like I'm one of them. Even though we've barely said a few words to each other.

Is she inviting me to sit with them because I look like them? Or is she just being nice and I'm the one overthinking it? I shift from foot to foot, my heart racing, as Edgar passes by me.

"You're here! I forgot to mention I sit up front." Edgar chuckles. "Still want to sit with me?"

I feel eyes on me, and I look to see Nina has finally noticed that I'm here.

Nina's gold hoop earrings bounce as she tilts her head toward the seat. She smiles, and my chest tightens. "Hey, Ri. Didn't know you were taking this class."

I blink, stare at her welcoming face, and then remember to answer Edgar. "Thanks." I drop into the chair, back turned toward Kelsey. And Nina.

Nina, who was just so *nice*. Not like just a few years ago, when she conveniently forgot about all the good times we'd had when she basically dumped me as her best friend, leaving me with nothing but memories. Like making forts in my living room, using anything and everything we could find to hold the sheets up, even a vacuum cleaner. Turning off all the lights in the house and using flashlights to brighten our faces as we told scary stories. Sharing our secrets too. Our dreams.

A couple more kids file into the classroom. I catch a few odd looks; maybe it's because I'm transferring after the semester started. Or maybe they're just wondering what the hell I'm doing in here. We've gone to school together for years, but I've been in other classes. Classes mostly full of white kids.

My friends take other languages for the countries their parents take them on vacation, like Italian, French, and German. They make up the bulk of the AP and "enrichment" classes, like Multimedia. My stomach wiggles a little. Because until recently, I've acted like I was one of them just like Grandma wanted me to.

"Hey, you new here?"

My head snaps up and I see a tall, broad-shouldered guy in front of me. I recognize him from the football team. Though we've never spoken, he'd be hard to miss, looking like that. Buzz cut. Broad shoulders. Probably abs by the look of him.

He squints his eyes dramatically, like he's trying to place me. "Actually, you know what? I think I do know you. I've seen you before, somewhere."

My eyes narrow, annoyed. Just because we've taken other classes doesn't mean I don't exist. "I've been going here since freshman year. And I grew up here, like you, I'm guessing."

The football player takes the seat to my left. His eyes linger on me a little longer than what's considered normal for people who don't know each other. My gaze falls over his broad chest and then rises quickly back up to his eyes.

"Hey, Carlos," Edgar says. "This is my locker neighbor, Ri. She just transferred into Spanish."

Carlos doesn't take his eyes off me as he gives what feels like a flirtatious smile. "Obviously."

At that moment, the second bell rings and Señora Almanza glides into the classroom.

"Buenos días. ¿Cómo están?"

"Estoy bien," the class answers in unison. All but me, of course. "¿Y usted?"

"Bien, bien," she says, before continuing in Spanish.

My grandparents sometimes spoke Spanish around me, before Grandpa died, when I was six. My mom too. And I hear it in the hallways and in my neighborhood. I know some, but not enough to keep up with whatever Señora Almanza is saying super fast.

I touch my neck and feel cold sweat on the back of my hand.

Señora Almanza pulls out her teacher's book, and the rest of the class begins to shuffle their textbooks out as well. I look at Carlos beside me. He turns to page twenty. I do the same. He, along with everyone else in my line of vision, seems to be keeping up just fine as they read along.

My chest tightens. I clench and unclench my sweaty palms. Look at the hands moving slowly on the wall clock as time practically grinds to a stop.

When the bell finally rings at the end of the period, it couldn't be more welcomed. My chest remains tight, cramped. I'm going to have to learn Spanish fast if I don't want Grandma to kill me for my GPA dropping.

Carlos stands beside me. "At least she moved the test to Wednesday—"

I whip toward Carlos. "We have a test Wednesday?"

He leans back slightly, away from me as my backpack almost accidentally whacks him. "Yeah," he says slowly. "Didn't you hear her just say that?"

Nina and Miguel brush past us, Nina even smiling at me as she does, and Carlos reaches toward Miguel to stop him. "You busy after school?"

Miguel turns to him. "I'm around. Come by if you want. You too, Edgar."

Edgar puts his hand on my desk as he stands. "I was actually going to shoot some photos of my little cousin's basketball game at the middle school." He lifts a camera—an expensive, professional-looking one—off the side of his backpack, then takes a step toward the door.

"You coming, man?" he asks Carlos.

"Hold up a second. I wanna talk to this chava hermosa here."

I can't help but grin, lifted by the compliment.

Edgar raises an eyebrow at me, as if asking me if I'm buying his friend's game.

I can't keep smiling like an idiot, so I look elsewhere, anywhere, so they won't see me blush. "Señora Almanza," I say, seeing my chance to kill two birds with one stone. "Given that I'm new to this class, I was wondering if—"

"If you have to take the test?" Señora Almanza gives me a

knowing look, somehow correctly guessing that I was going to try to get out of it. She strides from the podium to her desk, stacking her notes on top of a few books, and smooths her hands on her full skirt before addressing me.

"Yes, Maria, you do. But I'm sure you'll be fine with whatever Spanish you already know. Or if you don't," she says, seeming to register my face falling, "it'll be a good way to glean where you have room to improve."

I swallow, words escaping me, as Señora Almanza cocks her head at the boys. "And it looks like you've made a few friends who might want to study with you." She gestures to Carlos and Edgar, waiting for me. Carlos's face lights up and Edgar chuckles.

I blink a few times, fast. Studying with them, they'd realize super quick that I don't speak Spanish. Or at least that I can't speak it like they can.

I grab my bag. "Maybe another time."

By the time the bell rings for lunch, I've mentally run through the thousand ways I could have handled the first day of Spanish differently. I should have been smoother with Carlos. Maybe asked Señora Almanza if I could study privately with her. I could have said something more to Nina, or maybe I should have not acknowledged her at all. *Let her see how it feels.*

Brittany's at my locker waiting for me. "Okay, tell me all about it." Her mouth turns down just a little too sympathetically and her voice sounds wary. Like she expected the first day to be a disaster.

"It's just class, Brittany." I snap. "You don't have to make it such a big deal."

Brittany's face falls, her light beige skin turning pink.

I sigh. "I'm sorry." *For the second time this week.* "I know I've been weird about all of this."

Brittany shakes her head quickly. "You've got a lot on your mind. No worries at all."

I hesitate, searching for the right words. "I guess I didn't want it to be a big deal, and pretending like it isn't made me feel like . . ."

"Like you're in control," Brittany finishes.

"Exactly."

I smile at Brittany as she squeezes my arm. We fall in step together. The conversation turns to Multimedia, which we have later this afternoon. Yesterday we got saddled with an assignment where we have to make a short film about something that has shaped us as individuals. I'd consider doing something writing-related, but then I'd have to present it to the class, and I'm just not about that. So I think I'll play it safe and do something about being in nature. Maybe incorporate how I like to run by the beach in there somehow.

Brittany starts ranting about how she should choose the country club her mom attends. "Without it, she wouldn't be able to hear all of her friends talk about how great their daughters are doing at *everything*." Brittany's voice gets louder as she gets more worked up. "And then my mom wouldn't come home on a tirade about how I need to get better grades, make more of an effort on my appearance, and do just about everything else *better*."

She imitates her mother's sickly-sweet lecturing tone. "Because, you know, *honey*, everything you do is a reflection of us."

I laugh as Brittany makes gagging noises, miming vomiting all over herself. Brandon Reid shoots her a confused look before walking past us in the hall. Brittany ignores him. "What she really means is damnit, *why can't I just be prom queen and student body president just like her?*"

The words shoot out of her mouth faster as we walk through the school's front entrance. "What I'll never be able to understand is why anyone would want to subject themselves to that kind of popularity contest when it has nothing at all to do with being smart or a good person and everything to do with who's the biggest bitch in school or who gives the best blow jobs!"

"I have no idea what you girls are talking about, but sign me up." Carlos appears behind us, pushing through the double doors, with Edgar behind him. Brittany's eyebrows shoot to the top of her head and she flushes, mad or embarrassed, I can't tell.

Carlos takes in Brittany's expression. "I'm kidding. Relax," he says, before turning to me. "Ri, long time no see."

Much to Brittany's apparent alarm, I step aside so people can keep walking in the usual rush to their cars for lunch.

"I'm Edgar, by the way." Edgar reaches a hand out to Brittany. Her lips shift from a tense line to a small smile as she shakes his hand. "I always see you talking to my locker neighbor, but this might be our first official meeting."

Brittany offers an awkward laugh. "I guess I mostly hang out with the same people."

"Same, but no time like the present to change that, right? Who doesn't like more friends?" Edgar asks.

Carlos looks right at me. "Especially fine ones."

Brittany rolls her eyes so hard, I'd be impressed if she weren't embarrassing me. Sure, Carlos is laying it on pretty thick. But I like it. She seems to like Edgar well enough, at least.

A thought comes to mind and I blurt it out before thinking to check with Brittany. "You guys have plans for lunch? Want to come with us?" I may not have been friends with people who share my culture since Nina, but this is a chance to change that.

I look at Brittany, hoping she'll say what a great idea that is. Instead she just stares at me blankly.

Before I get the chance to say something, Carlos jumps in. "Yeah, seeing as how we're a few of the only juniors in Spanish Two, we might as well get to know each other, right? It's mostly freshmen and sophomores except us and Cassie, Nina, and Miguel. You know them, don't you?"

I ignore the fact that Carlos didn't acknowledge Kelsey and the other white juniors in our class. I doubt they acknowledge him either.

"Exactly," I say. "Do you want to walk somewhere for food?"

Edgar and Carlos agree as Brittany slides closer to me. She mutters under her breath. "Ri, it's usually just the two of us for lunch."

My face warms as I look to Carlos and Edgar, who are walking a couple of paces ahead and didn't seem to hear. "Shaking things up a bit won't kill anyone," I whisper back.

Brittany opens her mouth to argue, but I shush her as we follow the guys out of the parking lot.

Inside Jack in the Box, Carlos sits by me, his body warm against mine. Across from us, Edgar offers Brittany some of his fries. Brittany smiles sheepishly before raising her fork to her salad. "I'm good, thanks."

Carlos laughs. "You white girls and your diets. We're at Jack in the Box and you're eating a *salad*." He shakes his head.

Brittany's eyes narrow at me as I swallow a chuckle.

"I like burgers just fine, just not whatever processed garbage you'd call that." She eyes Carlos's burger with contempt.

I look to Carlos before jumping in. "Lighten up, Brittany. Just because it's not on the menu of Honor Bar in Montecito doesn't mean it's not good."

Brittany's face flushes, so I quickly add, "But no one grills a better burger than your dad on Fourth of July."

Edgar looks down at his food rather than at the conversational landmine that is my best friend. Why does this have to be so awkward? I quickly stuff a few French fries in my mouth.

"You guys are runners, right?" Edgar asks, before taking a drink of his soda. "I've seen you jogging on the beach before."

Brittany turns to him, a look of amusement on her face as her eyes dart to me and back to Edgar. "Well, next time say hi. No need to be a creeper." She laughs and then Edgar laughs, and I feel the tension in my gut ease.

"I go to the wharf on the weekends a lot," Edgar says. "Mostly for taking pictures." He looks at me and then back at Brittany. "It's something I've done for years. I even did a film on the wharf's history for my Multimedia project last year."

Brittany's eyebrows shoot up. "*You* were in Multimedia as a sophomore?"

The smile slides off Edgar's face. He blinks several times and I stop breathing. What the eff does Brittany mean by *you*?

I swoop in. "That's, like, impressive. Multimedia isn't easy, I mean, not for me anyway."

Edgar's relaxed grin returns as he looks at me. "I can help you with your project this year, if you want. I love that kind of stuff."

Carlos raises an eyebrow at Edgar and smirks at him. Edgar rushes on before I have the chance to reply. "Anyway, what were we talking about? Running, yeah. Have either of you ever run the marathon in town? One of my cousins does the half-marathon every year and my family usually watches on the sidelines."

"We haven't," Brittany says, looking at me with her fork

suspended over her salad, "but we really should. I think it could be fun."

I open my mouth to agree, but next to me, I feel Carlos pulling out his phone to check a text. He turns his shoulder away slightly to get a better look at his phone. I bite into my burger and try to steal a look.

Brittany sees me watching Carlos. She rolls her eyes—which he doesn't see since his head is down. She's not even giving Carlos a chance. But why? And what the hell kind of reaction was her shock about Edgar taking Multimedia last year?

Brittany turns to Edgar. "So, you like photography?"

I release a breath, relieved that the conversation keeps moving along, but I don't hear the rest of what they say. Instead my thoughts race as they land on the same question I had yesterday. Only then it was about Viola. *Has Brittany always acted like this?* My stomach clenches, because if she has, she's said those kinds of things to my face, and I never thought a thing of it.

Never cared about who she was insulting.

Never realized it was also me.

Chapter

FOUR

After school at my locker, I see Edgar before he sees me, so I stay put, waiting for him. He grins in greeting, readjusting his camera strap as he puts some stuff away.

"You've always got that thing on you. How come?"

Edgar lifts the camera so it's in front of his face. The camera shutter clicks. He laughs at my mock horror and looks at the picture. "This—I'll call it Girl Who Doesn't Want Picture Taken."

I roll my eyes. "Cute. Now delete it."

Edgar hits delete and then shows me the camera screen to prove it. "Done."

I smile at him, but his eyes shoot behind me.

"Incoming," Edgar says, nodding at Brittany. My stomach drops as I remember how rude Brittany was at lunch.

Edgar shuts his locker and looks at me. "See you later," he says. As he walks by Brittany, he says hi to her, and he's friendly enough, but it looks forced.

"Hey, Ri!" Brittany says, oblivious.

I cut right to the chase. "You didn't have to be such a jerk to Edgar and Carlos at lunch, you know."

Brittany's eyebrows furrow and she lifts her chin, taken aback. "I wasn't."

My jaw tenses.

Brittany's laugh comes out breathy. "Look, I didn't want to say anything before, but those guys just aren't our scene. Well, Edgar was okayish, but Carlos—"

"*Our* scene?"

Brittany shifts her weight and adjusts her bag strap. "Yeah, no offense, but we have like nothing in common with them."

I blink, several times, not sure how to respond.

Brittany laughs again, this time high-pitched. "What's up with you, Ri? You seem pissed. It's not like we have to be friends with everyone—"

My words come out hard and clipped. "*You* might not have anything in common with Carlos and Edgar, but *I* do. And it's not just . . . just . . ." I don't want to say our ethnicity. "Because we're in Spanish together. *I* like them, Brittany."

Brittany throws her hands up. "Whoa. I'm sorry." She stumbles over her words a bit. "I didn't mean anything by it."

I take a deep breath, and then another, before trying to talk again. "Okay, sorry. I'm just . . ." I don't really want to apologize because I don't know what I would be sorry for, so I let the words trail off.

Behind Brittany, Finn Wesley's tall and tanned frame becomes visible. She's been crushing on him for a while and has even talked me into going to the beach he surfs at to "hang out," but really, she's just been looking for a chance to run into him.

Brittany's eyes follow Finn as his wavy, light brown hair flops while he walks by us. He stops a few paces later and turns to head back. "Brittany, Ri, you coming to the beach later?"

Just then, Carlos approaches us, either not noticing or not caring that Finn asked a question. The two boys nod at each other. "Glad you're still here," Carlos says to me. "I thought I might have lost the chance to walk you home. Nina mentioned you live nearby."

Brittany's mouth opens like she's just about to say something, but she catches my glare and beams at him instead.

"I was actually going to head to the beach, work on my tan," Brittany says to Finn before looking at me. "Are you coming? Or do you want to . . ." Brittany eyes move between Carlos and me as she trails off, waiting for my answer.

Carlos slips an arm around my waist. My breath catches. I hardly know Carlos, but I can practically feel my skin tingle underneath my clothes where he's holding me.

I swallow. "Go without me. I'm walking home with Carlos. But we'll hang out later."

Brittany looks like she wants to say something until Finn answers. "Sweet. Some other time, then. Brittany, you still coming?"

"Yup, just give me a second."

Finn nods at us before taking off.

"Maybe we can go for a run later?" Brittany asks me. "I don't mind driving back to meet you."

"Yeah, text me when you're on your way over."

A relieved smile takes over Brittany's face. "Okay, well, have fun! And I really am sorry."

I want to believe her, but part of me wonders if she even knows what she's sorry for. I guess now isn't the best moment to figure it out, though. "Don't worry, Brittany. I'll see you later."

"Yeah, see you later, Britt," Carlos says.

Brittany's face flushes. She hated that he called her *Britt*, I'm sure.

Rather than giving Brittany the chance to ruin her apology, I quickly start walking away.

"What's she sorry for anyway?" Carlos asks. His hand trails down my back to my arm, and I pause, considering the tingly feeling I'm getting where Carlos's hand meets my skin. Thinking about Brittany can wait.

"Oh, nothing, just a girl thing." Time to change the subject. "I normally ride home with Brittany, even though I live so close."

I don't address the fact that Nina and Carlos were talking about me, though I find that very interesting. I smile up at Carlos. "I guess I could use the exercise, though."

"Nah, you look perfect. But it's nice out for a walk."

Carlos leads us down the hallway. I feel eyes on us as we walk outside together. We pass a few of Carlos's football friends and he nods at them.

"Wait. Don't you have practice?"

Carlos's fingers slide a little lower on my waist. "Nope. I didn't try out this year."

"Why not?"

Carlos lets me go. He puts his hands in his leather jacket. "Not into it anymore. It was more for my dad, anyway." Carlos shrugs. "He always wanted to be a ball player in college, but had to work, since his parents couldn't put him through school and he didn't get a full scholarship. And then my dad and my mom had me before they graduated Cal Poly, so they had to work even more. Now that he's all college educated and a fancy tax lawyer, he wants me to do everything he couldn't. You know how parents are, wish fulfillment with their kids and all that."

I think of Grandma and her insistence that I get an education, get an education, *get an education*, and nod.

"Still, do you miss it? I quit cross-country this year, too, but I can run anytime."

Carlos shrugs again. "I just don't see the point. It's not like I was going pro or anything. Why waste the time? I got other things I could be doing."

"Like what?"

"Like a bunch of stuff." Carlos slows his stride as we walk on the school's front lawn. "My parents have been on my ass about getting my grades up—my dad thinks I have to become a lawyer like him to be successful."

"There are a lot of ways to be successful," I mutter.

Carlos nods.

I don't want him to think my dark tone had anything to do with him. "My grandma—"

"My dad's always—"

We both stop when we realize we're talking over each other. Carlos chuckles. "Go ahead."

"You go." I'd much rather hear from him.

Carlos sighs and I lean a little into him. This is nice. Just talking, walking together.

"My dad's always on me to be grateful for everything," Carlos says. "Because even after he graduated, my parents were still broke for a while. They were sending all the money they could back to my mom's family in Oaxaca. She moved here with my abuela when she was a kid," Carlos adds as an aside.

I look at Carlos, his nice shoes and clothes.

Carlos catches my stare. "Oh, my parents make me buy my own shit. Or they do when they think it costs too much. I have to do yard work and stuff around the neighborhood for money."

I chew on my bottom lip, thinking that one over.

I guess it's not just Grandma who tries to force her will on others. Carlos is dealing with it too. I steal a glance at him. Carlos, a lawyer. I have a hard time seeing it. Not that he's not smart—I mean, I guess I don't know if he is or not—but I can't see him all buttoned up like that.

I want to be a writer, but if I tell him that Grandma doesn't want me to be one, he might ask why. And it's so tied into her backward views—I just can't go there.

As we walk, I notice Edgar, Miguel, Nina, and a few of their friends are standing on the outermost part of the parking lot. Miguel is talking to Edgar about something.

We start to walk by, but Cassie catches my eye.

"Hey, Ri. How's it going?"

My throat dries. I shouldn't be surprised Cassie knows my name. Nina must have told her about me too. I don't know if that makes me feel good or bad. Maybe a little bit of both.

I blink several times. "Hi, Cassie."

Before I get the chance to say anything else, Miguel cuts in. "Carlos, you coming with us tonight to play ball? We need another guy for the game."

Cassie rolls her eyes. "Another *person*," she says. "Maybe if Carlos doesn't show up"—she says *Carlos* full of annoyance—"you'll actually let me and Nina off the bench at the same time."

Nina laughs. "Since we're better than you and Edgar anyway!"

"You guys play basketball after school?" I look at Nina and Cassie. "Is it for a club team?" I know none of them play for the school.

"Nah," Nina says. "Just some neighborhood people."

There's a long pause as we stare at each other, but I finally look away. I shouldn't expect her to invite me.

"You want to come?" She surprises me, and I can feel my whole face light up as I look back at her. "It would be cool to have you around more."

My stomach dips a little. Part of me, completely unbidden,

wants to rush over and hug her, and the other wants to cry. She's the reason I'm not around.

Carlos shrugs off the invitation, like it's no big deal. "We can't today—Ri and I are busy."

Miguel laughs. "N'hombre. You don't have any plans."

"What? We're talking—that's *our* plan." Carlos says.

Cassie raises a black, beautifully sculpted eyebrow. "And you can't *talk* while you play basketball with us?"

I hold my breath and look to Carlos, who doesn't acknowledge the second invitation for me to stay but instead chuckles. "See you fools later." He starts to leave, but I turn back to Nina.

"Thanks . . . for the invite," I tell her. "Another time?"

Nina nods, but the smile feels a little off. I wave to her and the rest of them before rushing to catch up.

Once we're out of earshot, I steal a glance at Carlos.

I think about Cassie, how she seemed annoyed with Carlos. "Cassie will be happy, I guess. That she and Nina can play together."

Carlos says nothing.

"She doesn't seem to like you very much. Or the two of us together."

"Cassie's just jealous."

The wind picks up and whips a piece of my hair into my face as we hit a red light. We stop on the sidewalk. "Why would she be jealous?"

Carlos gently reaches down and tucks my hair behind my ear. "She and I were *talking* a while back, but it didn't work out.

And now she sees me with you, and you're beautiful." He pulls his full lips into a sexy smile. "Don't girls normally get jealous over that kind of thing?"

Cassie was nice enough; I mean, she didn't need to say hi to me. Even still, my heart seems to all but jump out of my body. Carlos called me beautiful.

Carlos grins. "Cassie is just used to how things are, hanging out with the same people, everyone knowing everything about each other."

The light turns green and we start walking again. A line stretches around the block outside La Super-Rica Taqueria, the nearby Mexican restaurant that's always busy, no matter the time.

Carlos glances toward the line of people again. He's smiling, watching a kid bounce a basketball in the street in front of his parents while they wait. The crowd, the noise, everything that sometimes annoys me on my walk home doesn't seem to bother him.

I rack my mind for something to say, wanting to keep his attention on me.

A man and woman pass us walking on the other side of the street, speaking Spanish together. Carlos grins as they walk by, the woman smacking the man playfully on the shoulder as he rapid fires something back at her. My face flushes but I quickly fake a smile, like I'm following along. If Carlos were to ask me what they were talking about, I wouldn't know.

Carlos kicks a pebble away from him with his Air Jordans.

His parents can afford a nicer house on a nicer street than this, I bet, but Carlos seems completely at ease here. Maybe because this neighborhood is where his friends live, or maybe he lived around here when his dad was just starting out his career. Or it could be because Carlos can understand the Spanish spoken by passersby, neighbor to neighbor. Maybe it's because he looks like them, he's one of them. Or *us*. He's one of us.

Carlos turns, and I hold my breath now that his eyes are on me. "What about you? What do you like to do, when little Miss Brittany isn't breathing down your neck?"

My eyebrows furrow. "Brittany comes off a little strong, but . . ." I hesitate, look down at my sneakers, slow my pace. "She's my best friend, the only person who really gets me." The second I say the last part, I realize, for the first time, that I don't know if that is really true anymore.

I stop at the edge of the sidewalk. "This is my street. My house is just down the block."

"You may do everything together"—Carlos pauses and whistles softly—"but I doubt that girl gets you."

Warmth rushes to my face. Even though I was just worrying over the same thing, I can do that. *She's my best friend.* "How would you know? It's not like we've talked much or ever even hung out before this week."

Carlos lifts his eyebrows. "I don't. But that doesn't mean she does either."

I think about how Brittany didn't want to give him or Edgar a chance. I think about how she talks about money like it's nothing, when it's everything in my family. The reason Grandma works so hard. The reason she's never around to see me.

But Carlos doesn't know that either.

I narrow my eyes at him. "Brittany's been my best friend for years. She doesn't put me in a box, or look at me like I'm different, like a lot of the other rich kids at our school do."

The words feel wrong coming out of my mouth, even as I say them.

Carlos's eyes brighten. "So, you do acknowledge you're not like them, huh? You had me starting to wonder."

"Look," I say, shaking my head, "I don't have to hang out with people based on where I live or what my last name is. I don't know what Nina's told you, but she's the one—" I stop, cutting myself off. Not going there.

Silence lingers between us like a puff of smoke.

Carlos finally nods, and his lips twitch as though he's trying to suppress a smile. "You're right, you don't. I don't either. But you seem to only hang out with certain types of people. You don't find that a little odd? I mean, come on."

"Whatever, this is bullshit." I turn back to the sidewalk. "I gotta go."

Carlos touches my shoulder, stepping closer to me. "Hey, don't be mad. I'm sorry, okay?" He drops his hand as I pull my shoulder away. "I just think Brittany might want you to stay in her bubble."

"That's not . . . I don't . . ."

Carlos shrugs. "All I'm saying is you don't seem to go out of your way to hang out with anyone other than Brittany. And, you know, if that's all people have to judge you by . . ."

I purse my lips. The question that has been following me around all day comes back around. *Has Brittany treated other people like she did Carlos and Edgar the whole time we've been friends?* Because then there are any number of things Brittany could have done that would have pissed Nina and her friends off—rightfully so—and I would have been wrong, too, for just standing there and doing nothing. I would've been . . . complicit.

I blink several times as my throat dries.

"Let's not get *too* into it, okay?" Carlos laughs and intervenes when the silence goes on for too long. "But unless I'm completely reading you wrong, and let me know if I'm coming out of left field here, I thought you wanted to be friends. That's what you're doing now—branching out?"

I open my mouth to reply when Carlos gives me a wicked grin. "I can be a really great *friend.*"

"I, um . . ." I trail off, embarrassed. "Sorry. It's not a big . . . Yeah, new friends. Good." I manage a smile. "I'll see you tomorrow."

Carlos licks his lips, and I find myself staring at them longer than I should. "Count on it." He grins. "Later, Ri."

The second my back is turned toward Carlos, I squeeze my eyes shut tight. And it's now, in this moment, after making a fool of myself in front of Carlos, talking about how Brittany doesn't get me, and realizing that I may be remembering my past through rose-colored glasses, I realize it's time to find my mom. She might be the only one who can actually see the real me and be able to help me figure out who that person is. I have to go see her. I'm ready. Because maybe in knowing her, I'll finally know *myself*.

The house is quiet when I walk inside, which suits me just fine. I might have minded Grandma never being around before I read that letter, but I certainly don't now. I eat leftovers Grandma set aside for me and wait for Brittany. Tense. Not sure how to feel about her or about me. But I know that if Brittany says something messed up, I have to speak up. I'm not a kid anymore and I'm not unaware. I have to be more direct, more than I was when we talked about how she treated Carlos and Edgar at lunch.

She finally texts me several heart emojis along with a picture of Finn surfing. I roll my eyes and text her back. You coming over soon?

We usually jog to the wharf or even the harbor and back, or sometimes we run the roads around State Street. But the longer Brittany takes to get here, the less time we'll be able to run. She calls me and without preamble starts telling me how great it went with Finn.

"When I was leaving just now, he walked me to my car! I couldn't wait to see you; I had to call and tell you now," Brittany exclaims.

My shoulders ease. I need to trust that she'll listen if I have to say something to her because Brittany's still the same Brittany, the overeager dork who gets excited about boys but still always makes time for me. "That's great, Brittany."

"It's kind of late to run anyway, and a few minutes ago my mom called me. She invited you over. She reminded me you haven't come to our house in a while."

I agree to go with her, and Brittany tells me she'll see me in a few.

"You're still wearing your running clothes?" Brittany asks as I open her car door to get inside several minutes later.

I shrug. "I didn't feel like changing."

She snorts. "Lazy."

"Says the person who honked the horn rather than texting me to let me know she arrived."

Brittany laughs and hits the gas. Soon we're on the winding road heading up the hill that overlooks the neighborhoods of red-tiled roofs below, surrounded by palm trees and then beyond them, the ocean. The fading sunlight hits my shoulders through the window. I love this part of the day, when the sun streaks through the clouds, the yellow and orange poking through the sea of blue, and the wind rustles the leaves in the trees.

"My mom's being weird," Brittany says. "She said she wanted to hang out with me tonight, and when I told her we had plans to run, she basically jumped at the chance to invite you over. I have a feeling she wants something."

I mull that over. Brittany pretends not to care so much

anymore, but I know she wishes her mom paid more attention to her. She wishes her mom took an interest in the *real* her, rather than the version she thinks she should be. I can relate, of course.

"Maybe she misses you," I offer. "You've said she's been gone a lot lately, always out with her friends. She wants some quality time."

Brittany shrugs noncommittally. I hold off bringing up how I'm ready to plan our trip to Oxnard to see my mom. It can wait until we figure out what's up with Brittany's mom.

The roads become windier and the trees taller and thicker as we near Brittany's massive, ancient house with a pointed roof and stucco exterior. She slows the Mercedes to park in front of the old oak tree out front—her mom's Lexus and dad's Range Rover taking up the real parking spots in the garage.

The car beeps locked as we head for her front door, and we both slip our shoes off in the foyer, per usual.

"Hey, girls!" Brittany's mom, Tara, calls from the den. Brittany nods for me to follow her, even though we usually go straight to her room when I come over.

We pass through the recently remodeled kitchen, the granite island spotless like the countertops and everything else in this house. In the den, the lights are dim, and we find Brittany's mom lazing on the couch. Tara's bare feet are propped up on the glass table in front of her, and she has a glass of red wine in her hand. She's done up like she spent the day out, blown-out hair, perfect makeup. Her red lipstick stains the wineglass in her hand. "It's been soooooo long since I've seen you, Ri. You haven't been hiding from me, have you?"

I laugh awkwardly. Her mom is definitely tipsy.

"Sit, sit," Tara says, gesturing wide with her arm, the faux fire crackling in the fireplace across from her.

Brittany and I sink into the love seat across from her mom.

"Now that we're all together, I have a proposition for you girls." Tara sits up and leans closer to us. Her amber eyes glitter as the light from the fire flicks. Brittany gives me a knowing look and my stomach sinks.

Tara doesn't seem to notice. "Since you both aren't on the cross-country team, I was thinking you might need a productive way to spend your free time," she says, her eyes glazed and animated. "I could sign you up for golf lessons at the club."

Brittany slumps down in her seat. I tense, feeling my best friend's discomfort. She hasn't mentioned wanting golf lessons to me, but her mom is always trying to get her to sign up for stuff at *the club* that Brittany has no interest in.

Tara doesn't notice her daughter's reaction. Instead, she looks at me. Realization dawns. Tara wants an ally, wants to use me to coax Brittany into this.

I plaster on a fake smile. "That is *so* thoughtful of you, Tara, but money's a little tight at home at the moment, so it's just not a good time for me to sign up for any new activities."

"Of course I'd pay for them, Ri," Tara says, brightening as if she's fixed the only obstacle to getting her way, "and if you two like it, you can try out for the team at your school!"

I take a deep breath. Money isn't a concern for Tara. But that doesn't mean Grandma and me would just take her money, like a handout or something. Grandma works hard for what we have, even if it's nothing like the fancy furniture and fixtures all around me in Brittany's home.

Brittany opens her mouth as if she's about to say something. But Tara continues, "I *know* you said you didn't want to take lessons, Britt, but if Ri joined you, wouldn't that be fun? And then we could all play together—we'd even be able to sign up for the big mother-daughter tournament later this year!" Tara reaches her free hand to rest on Brittany's knee. Her eyes are big and round like a silver dollar as she smiles at both of us.

Tara takes her hand back and sips her wine. Brittany twists a piece of her hair, circling it around her finger quickly.

I reach my hand to pull Brittany's down to the couch.

She leaves the hair but then starts picking at her nails roughly. "You know I don't like hanging out at the club. The girls from Cate—"

"Don't be ridiculous, honey, they don't all go to Cate. Amy, Stephanie, and Tasha all go to Riviera High." She smiles at me curtly before looking back at her daughter. "And it would be great if you made an effort to spend time with them."

Brittany watches her mom carefully. Sometimes I wonder if Tara thinks I'm the reason Brittany doesn't hang out with her friends' daughters.

"Ashley, Katherine, and everyone are always saying you should come around more often." Tara's voice comes out flat. "I'm the *only one* who doesn't bring her daughter to club activities." Tara frowns at Brittany, who has gone quiet.

I shift in my seat. This might not be the way Brittany wants to spend time with her mom, but at least she has a mom who wants to spend time with her. Sort of. Maybe I could too, if I went to Oxnard. *When* I go to Oxnard.

I look at Brittany. "Golf might not be that bad." *For you that is, not me.*

Brittany glares at me.

Tara brightens. "Don't knock it until you try it, right, Britt?"

"Mom," Brittany cuts in, "seriously, we don't need to be spending more money on golf lessons, right? You're always talking about how expensive club dues are, and—"

Tara stands abruptly. "I do no such thing, Brittany. *Of course* we can afford going to the club, otherwise we wouldn't."

I purse my lips to keep from smirking. Tara's perfect life isn't as perfect as it seems? She would never want anyone to know their family worries about money too.

"Why don't we spend the weekend together, Mom, just me and you?" Brittany looks hopeful as her mom takes a long gulp of her wine and sets it back on the table, the glass clicking against glass. "Dad's going out of town on that business trip, right? We can watch movies and make popcorn. Or salad, you can eat salad, and I'll eat the popcorn." She laughs too loudly, and I reach my hand out reflexively to keep her from going to town picking at her nails ferociously.

Tara takes the wineglass and strides toward the den's entryway. Brittany and I have to turn to look at her.

"I thought I told you this, honey, but I'll be out of town too. The girls and I are doing a spa weekend in La Jolla. A road trip." Tara seems to sense Brittany's disappointment. "Next time, we can go together. We can get massages, facials, and pedicures. It'll be fun."

Brittany gives her mom a sad smile. Like she wishes her mom would choose her this time.

I suck in a breath. What I would give to have a weekend like that with my mom, or any weekend at all. I keep my hand steady on Brittany's, wishing she'd see how lucky she is, even if her life isn't perfect.

Tara finishes her wine. "You two have fun tonight." Tara disappears down the hallway, toward her bedroom. From a distance, we hear her call out. "And have that popcorn and watch those movies over here this weekend, the two of you. Good seeing you, Ri!"

"Mom, wait!" Brittany calls, shocking me enough that I sit up straight. She looks at me sheepishly. "Maybe golf wouldn't be so bad. If Ri comes, too, that is. You'll come with, won't you, Ri?"

I stare at my best friend, the sadness and loneliness I see in her eyes. The last thing I want is charity from Tara. Grandma has built a good life for us, and I'm proud of that. But . . .

Brittany's my best friend. And she needs me, so I nod. "Of course. Sounds fun."

Tara reappears in the doorway, her eyes gleaming and her lips grinning. "Perfect! Oh, this is going to be so much fun!"

Brittany looks at her hopefully enough that it makes the thought of doing golf lessons worth it. Almost.

"I can't wait to tell Katherine and the girls. They're going to be thrilled!"

Brittany's smile falls off her face as soon as her mom finishes the thought.

As Tara's form retreats, Brittany sighs bitterly. "I guess we know why she wanted me to invite you over now. Golf lessons at the country club." She uses her hands to push herself up off the love seat. "Mother of the year, that one."

I stand too. "She tries."

"Not hard enough." Brittany scoffs. "Honestly, those two should have at least given me a sibling if they didn't want to spend any time with me. If I didn't have you, I'd lose it."

My shoulders sag, seeing how hurt Brittany is. Her feelings about her mom are real, even if I don't always agree with them. I put my hand on Brittany's shoulder. "Good thing you don't have to worry about that. You'll always have me."

Many of the late nights Grandma works and I otherwise would eat leftovers alone, Brittany's with me. Or when she's at home and would otherwise be by herself in her huge house, eating takeout, I'm right here with her. She's been there for me when Grandma wasn't. And I've done the same for her. Even when Brittany doesn't understand me and makes mistakes, we're family.

Brittany exhales unevenly. "Thanks." She pauses a beat before looking at me. "Speaking of moms, don't think I forgot about Oxnard. We need to go. I mean, we can. As soon as you're ready."

She looks at me.

My insides warm. Even with drama in her own family, Brittany still wants to help me with mine.

"Yeah, I am. I was thinking we could go tomorrow, if you don't mind driving me?"

Brittany's eyes widen and she nods aggressively. "Of course I'll take you! There's literally nowhere else I'd rather be."

I hug her. "I'm so glad I'm not alone in this, Brittany. Thank you."

When Brittany pulls away, her eyes are watery, and I can't tell if it's from what I said or what happened with her mom. She looks back toward the hallway. "It looks like my mom is done with anything that isn't that glass of wine for the night, so . . ."

Brittany's eyes meet mine.

"I think we could use something mindless, some trashy reality TV or something," I offer.

Brittany exhales, looking relieved. "Want to go back to your place?"

I nod. "Sounds perfect."

I give her a reassuring smile and Brittany brightens. "Bye, Mom!" she calls, but the TV is already on loud in her parents' bedroom. Tara probably doesn't hear as Brittany slams the front door behind us.

Chapter
FIVE

Before reading the letter, when I thought of Mom, I told myself she'd be with me if she could. Sometimes I wondered how her life turned out, wondered if she missed me. But mostly I tried to focus on memories of bath time and good-night kisses, to remember the good times. But now that I know Mom's back, I can't help but wonder why she left. I'm remembering before, not knowing where Mom was when she was gone for days at a time. Grandpa yelling at her behind a closed door while Grandma said nothing.

I remember one time Mom came home after being gone for weeks. I played with my favorite doll, waiting for their fight to be over. Mom burst into our room, scooped me into her arms, and wiped the tears from my eyes. "Shhh, mija, it's okay. I'm here," Mom said quickly, and I smelled something sickly sweet on her breath. I didn't like it. Mom's eyes were red and puffy. Grandpa must have made her cry, with all that yelling.

Now, all these years later, I'm going to face Mom again. What will I say?

Oh, hey, it's me, your long-lost daughter? Sorry I haven't reached out sooner but Grandma is a liar? Oh, and by the way, why haven't you come for me?

After last period, Brittany and I walk to her Mercedes silently and climb inside. I lean into the leather seat and roll down my window, letting the cool California breeze wash over me. Moments later, once we're on the Pacific Coast Highway, I taste the salt in the air as we drive by the ocean on this short trip my mom could have easily taken to see me.

But hasn't.

I push the thought away.

Brittany's GPS tells us to get off on the North Rose Avenue exit in Oxnard, and after a few turns, we pull into a parking of an old apartment complex, several identical beige buildings standing side by side.

"Number four." I look around until I find it. It's on the first floor, apparently, next to a staircase on one side and an over-flowing dumpster on the other.

As we reach the door, Brittany grabs my hand and squeezes it. I let go to knock, my other hand clutching Mom's letter.

The knot in my chest tightens, tightens, tightens as long, agonizing seconds pass. "Maybe no one's home."

Brittany shakes her head. "Shhh, listen."

I hear it too. A few footfalls on the other side of the door, and then the rustling of blinds. Some short, sausage-like fingers tilt one of them, and a set of narrowed eyes peep through to look at us.

I hold my breath. The door opens a crack.

"Whatever you're selling—"

"We're not selling anything," Brittany cuts in. "We're here to see Marisol."

My voice doesn't work anymore, and my lips don't move.

Brittany nudges me.

I shake my head and let out a weak exhale.

She calls out, "I'm Brittany, and this is my friend Ri, um, Maria. We're looking for her mom."

"Marisol!" I choke out, finally. "We're looking for my mom, Marisol." As I start to push her letter toward the opening, the door swings open.

A short and stocky white man steps outside. His San Francisco 49ers jersey, tight around his belly, hangs low over Dickies. His blue eyes light up as a smile of recognition crosses his face. "Maria! I've heard so much about you!"

I blink. He knows who I am. He knows my mom.

"Y-y-you have?"

"Of course I have. You look like her, you know. Your hair is different and you're a bit lighter, but you've got her eyes. I'm going to call your mom right now."

The man, still grinning, pulls his cell out of his back pocket and makes the call. He waits for an answer but then mouths "voicemail" to us.

"Marisol!" he exclaims as he shifts from foot to foot. "You have to come back home right now. You won't believe this, but your little girl is here! She came and found you and she's here right now. Call me when you hear this."

He hangs up. "She went on an errand but should be back any minute."

I look at Brittany. "We can wait a little while," she says to me, but it comes out like a question. "If it's okay with . . . ?" Brittany trails off.

The man barks out a laugh. "I was so excited I forgot to tell you my name. I'm John, Marisol's boyfriend."

He reaches my hand to shake and then after I do, he takes Brittany's to do the same.

John's light eyebrows furrow as he looks down at his phone. "I'm sorry she's not here. We never heard from your grandma after we moved to Oxnard, so we just figured she wasn't going to let Marisol see you."

John shoots a quick text and then looks back at us.

I look down at my feet. "Oh . . . um, well, she never told me. I found the letter in her room recently."

John shakes his head and chuckles, but there's no humor in it. "Yeah, we thought that might have been the case."

I lift my head, and he gives a small smile. "Do you girls want to come in while you wait?"

Brittany and I hesitate, and then he puts both hands up. "Oh! Never mind. Stranger danger. I got you."

He looks behind him into this apartment and back at us. "In

fact, if your mom heard you weren't being careful, she'd probably be mad! Glad you two are safe, coming in numbers too.
Good on you."

Even though I'm disappointed that my mom's not home, I'm
still giddy that she's here in Oxnard. Not something I dreamed
up because I wanted it so bad. She's real. John proves it.

"Can I leave you my phone number so she can call me?" I
ask.

John nods. "Of course."

I tell him my number and watch him type it in his phone.

"So, you'll tell her Maria came by and have her call, right?"
Brittany asks John. He nods and she smiles at me reassuringly.

"Thank you." I look at John. "Please tell her I can't wait to
talk to her."

"You got it," John says. "Can't wait to see you again, this
time wrapped in your mother's arms!"

I smile as emotions whirl through me. Adrenaline. Excitement.

On the drive home, all Brittany and I can do is talk about
my mom.

"It bugs me that I don't know why she left," I say. I put my
arm outside the window and let it hang in the cool air.

"You could ask her."

"I could . . . and I will, but . . ."

Brittany tilts her head. "But?"

I pull my hand back inside the car. "I just don't want to mess
this up. I don't want to scare her away."

"You won't, Ri. She's your mom. She's been waiting for you for two years. Maybe even longer." Brittany shifts one hand over to the steering wheel and taps my knee with the other. "You saw how excited her boyfriend was that you came. She must have talked about you constantly. Why else would he react that way? Just imagine how happy your mom will be."

I look at my phone. She still hasn't called. But she will, soon. I hope.

I flick on my living room light and toss my backpack on the ground before I kick off my shoes into the middle of the floor. My eyes flutter closed a second too long to be a regular blink. Thinking about my mom so much is apparently not just emotionally tiring. Wrapping myself up in blankets in bed and shutting out the world sounds really good right about now.

I turn toward the hallway when I hear footsteps from Grandma's room. Quickly, I grab my backpack and shoes and set them neatly by the couch.

Grandma's door creaks open.

"Grandma," I say, noticing her droopy eyes and ruffled hair. "I thought you were at work."

"I was, and I will be." Grandma stifles a yawn before pushing her hands down, smoothing the wrinkles out of her blouse. "I needed a quick nap. I stayed late last night and was so tired. But I have to go by Riviera Country Club now to pick up food for Mrs. Reynolds. Because she must eat that same salad every week. Why she can't have me get takeout from a normal restaurant . . ." Grandma trails off to let another yawn out.

The second her hand reaches for my shoulder, I'm hit with a flash of anger. Grandma can act like everything is the same as it's always been, but it isn't. Not to me, anyway. It was so easy to find Mom. She's been within reach this entire time, but Grandma kept her from me.

I sidestep Grandma's touch, but she seems too tired or distracted to notice.

"You have homework to do?" She's not looking at me but instead gathering her keys and purse.

"Studying for Spanish," I say, but then I remember I have to do some serious brainstorming for my video assignment. "And I have to think about my Multimedia project, pick a topic. All the high-tech video cameras at school are checked out for weeks, and since they have lenses way better than my phone, I have to wait to get started."

Shooting video, editing, doing voice-over—so not in her wheelhouse. Though Grandma likes to have an opinion on everything, she doesn't know much more than how to use a computer and a cell phone.

Grandma stands straighter. "Well, I'm sure you'll do all you can ahead of time, whatever is necessary to make sure you are prepared when you're able to check the equipment out."

"Yep." I don't want to talk to my grandma any more than I have to. Not when looking at her makes me want to scream.

"I'm off to work. Dinner's in the fridge." Grandma moves forward like she's about to kiss my forehead but doesn't when

I take a step back. "I love you, Ri. I know you enjoy running with Brittany, but don't leave your homework until late at night. Rest is important; we all need it. I should know."

I narrow my eyes at her guilt trip. Grandma has no idea where I really was. Grandma doesn't know anything. "Better get going, then!"

Grandma sighs and tells me good night.

To spite her, even though I know it's silly, I'm not going to do homework *right* now. I check my phone again. Still nothing from my mom. So, I plop onto my bed and pull up my Instagram and search for Carlos. What's his last name again? I don't actually know it, I realize.

Nina García, I type instead. We still follow each other even after everything. There's a profile photo of her and Miguel. Miguel's arms are wrapped around her from behind. She's smirking, like she's too cool to smile.

Without having to worry about them catching my stare, I study Cassie's and Nina's pictures. Their bodies, more womanly than mine. The way shirts cling to Cassie's chest, hug her hips and thighs. Nina's smaller up top but has that big apple butt guys seem to love. Not like me, with a runner's body. Thin and small, in all the wrong places.

Carlos, I type in the list of her followers. Carlos Moreno pops up. I stare at his self-assured smile. He's surrounded by a couple of guys from the football team and their girlfriends.

I scan through the pictures, visible on Carlos's public settings, going back further on his timeline.

I find a picture of him and Cassie, with her leaning her chest into him. He's looking down at her, grinning. Dislike button, if there were one. There are a few shots of Carlos playing football with the team, and some photos Carlos must have taken of Edgar shooting pictures of kids at the skate park doing tricks.

I switch to Edgar's profile and my mouth falls open. Beautiful landscape photos of the mountains. Purple clouds hovering over an orange ocean sunset. A gap-toothed child smiling. An elderly man hunched over the engine of an old truck, twisting a piece of metal. The colors. There are so many.

The expressions of the child as she grins and the man as he works. Joy. I've never seen photos like this before. They should be hanging somewhere, in an art gallery or a museum. And then there's a picture someone else must have taken, because it's of Edgar holding that fancy camera. His curly hair ruffled, his fingers expertly attached to it.

I keep scrolling. There are pictures of Edgar and his brother, I'm guessing, given the strong family resemblance.

My phone buzzes. A number I don't recognize is calling. I practically jump out of bed to answer. A raspy voice I instantly recognize, even though it's been years, greets me.

"Maria?"

"Mom?" I choke out.

A whooshing sound of an exhalation cracks in my ear. Her voice trembles. "Oh, baby." Grandma calls me that sometimes. *Baby.* I hold my breath as my mom starts to cry.

"I'm so sorry I missed you." She laughs a watery laugh. "Oh,

I wish I would have checked my phone. I could have made it back in time."

I stumble over my words. "It—It's okay. But we could try again . . . to see each other, I mean."

"Yes!" she exclaims. "There's nothing I'd love more. I can drive up to meet you on Sunday, if that works for you."

I was supposed to do my first golf lesson with Brittany, but I'm sure she'll understand. "How about Leadbetter Beach? In the afternoon? After church?"

Mom laughs softly and the sound makes my stomach warm. "I love that beach. Yes, I'll be there."

"I can't wait," I tell her, and I mean it with every part of me.

"I have to get going, but I wish I could stay on the phone," Mom says. "I could talk to you for hours. I want to know everything. I want to hear everything about you. We've missed so much."

My shoulders slump. I have so many questions. So much bottled up, it feels like it could bust me open, if I let it.

I roll over onto my back and stare at the ceiling.

"I get it. I can call you back later?"

The words hang in the air for a moment. "I've got a lot going on, some things I need to take care of, plus it will all be better in person. Can we wait until Sunday?"

The smile slides off my face. I blink, surprised, but I try to copy her relaxed tone since I know I'm just excited. And I don't want to scare her off. "That would be great."

"I love you, baby," she says, and I hold my hand to my chest, almost unable to believe I'm hearing these words from my mom.

I don't say I love you back, although I do. I mean, she's my mom, of course I do. I've missed her so much. But I have so many questions. Why didn't she come for me, rather than just writing that letter? *Why did she leave?*

Despite those reservations, after we hang up, I imagine all the possibilities. Mom and me hanging out, her giving me advice, maybe helping me get ready for a date. I could tell her all the things I can't tell Grandma. I could ask her for advice about Brittany. I could tell her about my dreams of being a journalist. Traveling the world hearing and sharing other people's stories. Learning what makes them tick, what makes them who they are, and having adventures of my own in the process.

Maybe she'll see me. Or who I want to be, at least.

She won't tell me who to be like Grandma does.

I flip back over in my bed, tapping my feet together in excitement. I text Brittany, telling her what just happened. Things are going to change. I can feel it.

My mom is nothing like Grandma.

Chapter
SIX

I'm barely able to contain my excitement at church Sunday morning. After Brittany told her mom we'd have to reschedule our golf lesson, Tara made a big deal about how busy the instructor was, how it was a personal favor to her to get us in so quickly, and how it would be a while before our next lesson could be put on the books after this. Like that's my biggest problem, though. Or a problem at all.

Thoughts of Mom distract me, so I can't keep up with the worship music, which causes Grandma to give me a look. As always, she seems out of place among the congregation of hippies and college students, with her outfit that's more suited to mass: nylons under a long blue dress covering most of her slight body. I still don't understand why she switched us out of our Catholic church after Grandpa died. Not that I'm complaining—this place is a thousand times less stuffy. Though, as I look around at the sea of white people, I wonder if it was another way to whitewash us.

I watch Grandma, a walking contradiction.

I scan the room to see who is here. A few girls from the

swim team, looking pretty in boho dresses. I tug on my oversized sweater, look down at my black jeans. Grandma wishes I'd dress up, but a lot of people at this church wear jeans because it's so casual. Several kids from Westmont, the private Christian college in Montecito, are here and wearing jeans too. The guys are tall and lean and can talk about theology until they're blue in the face, or I am.

I can't focus on them, though, or anything really, when my stomach's in knots. Mom is probably getting ready to come see me now. At. This. Exact. Moment.

The music ends, and we bow our heads in prayer. Then Pastor Mark starts in on the sermon about chastity.

Carlos's face breaks into my thoughts.

His toothy grin, like we're sharing a secret.

His brooding eyes.

I can almost feel his hand on the small of my back, slipping down to my waist, confidently guiding me as we walk together. I can hear his laugh tickling my ear, his breath kissing my neck. His fingers softly pushing a wisp of my hair away from my face.

I wonder what it would feel like for him to kiss me.

I choke, suddenly aware of my thoughts in a church.

"You okay, baby?" Grandma looks at me with concern.

I cough and avert my eyes from her, without answering. Like I would ever, ever tell her about Carlos. She'd probably make up some stupid reason why I shouldn't hang around him.

After a few moments, I sneak a glance at Grandma and notice the lines on her face. The crow's-feet. The sagging underneath her eyes. She's strict, she's tough, and I'm so mad at her I could scream, but . . .

She sacrifices so much for me. I feel it in the way she watches me when she thinks I'm not looking. I taste it in the meals she cooks for me, after a minimum ten-hour workday, without fail. Without complaint. I sigh, watching Grandma mouthing the words to her silent prayer.

She loves me. And I love her, my abuela—though I can never call her that to her face. A tear trickles down her cheek as she prays silently.

My stomach squeezes. She's probably praying for me. Little does she know I'm plotting, hoping, *praying* to secretly meet her long-lost daughter in just a couple of hours. I dip my own head and cast my eyes down—don't close them in case anyone is watching.

God, I know we don't talk much, but if you could, please let Mom and me have a good reunion today. Please help her to see how much she misses me and wants to be around again. Forgive me for lying to Grandma, but she doesn't understand—you know how she is. She can't take my own mother away from me. She can't keep me from learning who I truly am, from becoming who I'm meant to be. Please help her to see that, God. I want to be a family again. Me, Mom, and Grandma. Please.

In Jesus's name, amen.

After church, I eat lunch with Grandma at home. We don't talk much. It's like I have a million things to say to her but not one will come out. While Grandma's clearing our plates, I stalk to the couch and fling the *Yale blue* blanket away from me. Grandma clears her throat as she stands at the edge of the living room. I hadn't realized she was watching me. I grab the blanket and set it on the arm of the couch sheepishly.

"So, what did you think of the sermon today?"

"It was fine," I mumble.

Grandma settles next to me on the couch. Out of the basket she keeps on the side of the couch, she grabs a needle, along with a ball of pink yarn as well as a purple one, and continues knitting a beanie she started last week. "It was more than fine, I think. Pastor Mark really knows what he's talking about," Grandma says, staring attentively at the hat as she switches from pink to purple. "Warning you against the wrong sort of boys."

I lift my eyes to her, feeling my blood pressure rise. "And what kind of boys are those, Grandma?" Grandma met my ex-boyfriend Eric last year and liked him okay. Even though he only had one thing on his mind and when I told him I wasn't ready, at least not with him, he dumped me. Not that I told her that, but still.

Grandma cocks her head. "Well, Eric was a nice young man, not quite motivated enough, but he came from a good family."

I grit my teeth. "What does that even mean, Grandma? You never met his parents."

"Oh, well. I know they work hard. They have that nice house on the Mesa."

I scoff. "So, what, since they have money, they must be a

nice family?" I don't doubt that if I told Grandma about Carlos right now, she would react exactly how I fear, even if he likely comes from a family with a "nice house" somewhere not here.

Thinking of how much Grandma pushed me to spend more time with Brittany instead of Nina, I add, "Or is it because they're white?"

Grandma heaves a heavy sigh. "Dios mío. Not this again. I am not talking about"—she waves a needle in front of herself—"whatever thing you have all confused in your mind. I am talking about the sermon. Pastor Mark telling young girls to keep their legs closed to honor God. Something your mom should have listened to."

My mouth falls open. Grandma, who can't be bothered to talk about my mother, who never tells me stories about her growing up or what it was like when she lived with us, decides *that* will be the thing she wants to talk about? I almost laugh at myself. Why should I expect different than slut-shaming from my judgmental grandma?

Despite my rage, my voice is cool and flat. "If she had *kept her legs closed to honor God*, I wouldn't have been born. Is that what you want?"

Grandma huffs but continues staring at the beanie she's working on, "Of course not, Ri. You know that's not what I mean. But the Bible says—"

I cut her off. "I know what the Bible says, Grandma." Heat floods my body, and I know I have to get out of here before I say something I'll regret. "I'm going for a run."

Before I get the chance to stand, Grandma sets her knitting down. She leans over and hugs me, and as soon as I remember to breathe, I smell the vanilla scent of her hair.

"Baby," she whispers, her voice soft and loving, not huffy like it was a moment before. "You know that's not what I meant."

She pulls away slightly, so she can see my face. "You don't see it, but you have so many options. So many more than I ever had. Even more than your mother did, before she got pregnant. A pregnancy, right now, would take that all away. It would ruin the future that *is* possible for you." Grandma tucks a piece of hair that's fallen out of my ponytail behind my ear. "I only want you to have the life you deserve, so I focus on preparing you to get into university *and* warning you about boys. You do not want a hard life like Grandpa and I had, working at all hours for low wages, not being treated with respect."

Grandma's eyes crinkle at the edges and down her cheeks as she watches me for a moment. I fidget under her stare.

"Don't get me confused. Your grandfather and I had a beautiful life. We were in love." Grandma's eyes get this faraway look.

Even though he was a strict, somber man, Grandpa had a soft side. I saw it when he put me to bed with his made-up bedtime stories every night. And the times I snuck out of my room, having heard the Spanish music playing in the living room, and saw the two of them slow-dancing, Grandma beaming.

I miss him, too, but I don't bring him up because Grandma

doesn't seem to like it. She says the past is the past, but I think it makes her miss him more when she talks about him.

"We were lucky he had his relatives show us the way to get into this country," Grandma tells me, "with the paperwork and everything. His uncle helped your grandfather get a job here. It wasn't the job he would have wanted. But it was good, honest work. Here, in America, we had a chance to start over. Away from our families."

I want to stay mad like I usually would be, but she's being so sincere and open. This is nearly the most she's ever said about their families. All I know is that there was some kind of falling out, that was all I could get out of her. But she has always said it didn't matter, because Grandpa was her family. All she needed. Until my mom came along. And then me.

Grandma continues, her voice taking on a harsher tone. "You know, my life isn't easy. People, when they think I can't speak well, they talk to me slowly, like they think I'm uneducated, stupid, and some think I don't belong here." Grandma takes a long, deep breath, and I hold mine, not wanting to say anything that would get her to stop. She never talks about stuff like this. Like, really talks about it.

"Some people hold their purses close to them when I walk by them in Mrs. Reynolds's side of town," Grandma continues, "like they think I'm a criminal. *Like I would steal from them.*"

My head whips back. I know people can be assholes, but we live in California. I didn't think that people here would be so . . . that they would treat Grandma so unfairly makes my blood boil.

"Grandma, that's so messed up. I didn't—"

"This is why you need to get an education," Grandma interrupts. "Get a good job that can give you security and a future."

There's not a ton of financial security for journalists, but it's a good career. One Grandma would be proud of me for, I'm sure, if I were to actually make it as one. I hadn't planned on telling her, but Grandma opening up to me makes me feel brave.

I turn completely toward Grandma on the couch and am so daring as to look her straight in the eye. "I *do* want to go to college and get a good job. It just might not be what you had in mind . . ." I trail off, steeling myself. "You know . . . well, you know how I always write in my journal . . . I want to be a writer."

Grandma's lips pucker in confusion but I don't give her the chance to interrupt. "Maybe I could be a journalist and write long-form stories, ones that take months to research from interviewing people and going to different places. I could go on adventures, travel all over, and write about people changing the world doing brave and important things."

Grandma blinks but says nothing. Her silence scares me, but I push on.

"It's what I love to do, Grandma, to write. I know it's not what you had in mind for me and I'm sorry but—"

Grandma starts knitting again, not looking at me. "Do you think Brittany would like this hat for when the weather cools? You haven't worn the one I made you last year"—Grandma tsks—"so I'd rather have it not go to waste."

My mouth drops open. Grandma is seriously going to dismiss everything I just said to her, without a word? I poured my heart out to her, and that's it? She wants to talk about a stupid beanie?

Grandma ignores my shock and keeps talking. "Well, if not Brittany, I can donate it through church. Our Bible study group is making blankets this year for the homeless. I'm sure I can add this hat to the pile."

"Grandma!"

She blanches at my raised voice.

"I told you my dream is to be a writer, and you've got nothing to say?" I shake my head in disbelief, unable to form the words for the hurt I feel.

"Well, getting into Yale or Harvard is very competitive, and I'm sure it would be even harder to get in as a writer. Better to try for an engineer or another program that is more practical, don't you agree?"

I grit my teeth and will myself not to cry. "No, I don't agree! And that's not how college works either!"

Grandma sets her knitting aside.

"I'm sure you love writing, and from what your English grades show me, you are good at it." Grandma pats my leg and I bristle. "But we have to think practically. I need you to have a better life. You can't make the choices your mother did, her head in the clouds not thinking of the future, getting pregnant when she was just a child." Grandma stops abruptly to gauge my reaction.

"*You*, my sweet baby, are not a mistake," she says softly. "You are a gift, and no matter the timing of when your mother had you, I will be grateful she did until the day I die. That is not what I'm talking about. Your mother made a lot of decisions for herself that had nothing to do with you. Decisions that I would never want for you. You will not ruin your future like she did when she—"

The shock on my face causes Grandma to stop.

"What do you mean by that, Grandma?"

Grandma shakes her head quickly and looks down at her wrinkly hands.

"Grandma, but Mom . . . what do you mean? What are you saying she did that was so bad? If you don't mean having me . . . ?"

Grandma keeps her eyes on her knitting. Her voice rises. "I am not talking about your mother. I am talking about you, Ri. I want you to work hard and take advantage of what you have, being born in this country, with skin like yours that allows you the opportunities that so many would kill for."

I . . . I don't know what to say. She started to say something about Mom, but I know my grandma and I can tell she won't give me anything else.

She bends her head and takes a deep breath. "I know I can

be hard on you, baby, but I love you so much, more than you'll ever know. More than *my life*. You're what I live for, what I wake up for in the morning each day."

I swallow the lump in my throat and nod. It's obvious she's trying to guilt trip me. And even though she's doing what she always does—hiding secrets and telling me to be who she wants me to be—I do feel guilty.

Grandma touches my cheek softly. "As I said before, I think you would do better to be in cross-country, to volunteer at the soup kitchen, because that will help you get into the best universities. You want to write, go ahead and write. But you must also be practical and choose a real career."

I blink several times, my eyes unfocused, disappointment washing over me.

"Just think about it." Grandma smiles. "Have a good run, baby. I'll see you later."

End of conversation. Masterful how she can do that. She found a way to make me feel bad for being angry but gets to have the last word about my future.

My future. Not hers.

I head for the door without another word. Ready to run off my hurt and anger. No matter how much Grandma says she loves me, would she still if I didn't do the things she wants? If I study writing at a school that isn't what she deems the best? If I speak Spanish? Or God forbid, hang out with kids who live in our neighborhood and look like us? Or *her*?

Phone in hand, I pop my earbuds in and shut the door behind

me. My feet propel me, taking me away from Grandma. I run toward the hope that Mom is better, that she'll actually want to know me. *The real me.*

I head for the harbor, like I've done since I was a kid. It started as something Nina and I did together, because she loved the Art Walk on East Beach. Every Sunday, for as long as I can remember, artisanal street vendors line the sidewalks, selling their creations to the tourists who walk by. Nina and I would linger around the booths, mostly because she loved staring at the paintings. She'd take extra care to study them and later try to re-create what she liked with a cheap watercolor set she got for Christmas.

I loved her paintings, all of them. They were so beautiful, so vivid and bright, even if she didn't have fancy tools. For years, Nina gave me a new painting for my birthday. Ten, it was of the sunset over the beach. Eleven, it was of the eucalyptus tree that stood tall in her backyard. Twelve, it was the back of me as I jogged on the running path near the wharf. Almost as a joke, since we thought we were too cool for kid stuff by then, when we were thirteen, she painted the Teenage Mutant Ninja Turtles for me, since we liked the movies so much when we were little. I kept every painting, hidden away in a box in the back of my closet, exactly where my friendship bracelet that matches hers ended up.

My feet hit the pavement harder, faster. Nina and I saved our birthday money and any loose change we could scrounge up to see if we could haggle the pricing down on the cheaper items—no ocean landscape paintings for several thousand dollars, thank you very much. I still remember how excited we were when the old woman with the long gray braid saw us counting our change as we eyed her multicolored, beaded friendship bracelets. She smiled big and told us to pick one for each of us, no charge.

I smile as I run, just remembering it. Until I flash to the time I ripped the bracelet off my wrist after crying myself to sleep over Nina ignoring me. That's when I tossed it to the bottom of the box of old memories.

Since then, I've run alone on Sundays, no Nina, no Brittany. It's just me.

Once I jog past the railroad tracks and cross the street onto Cabrillo Boulevard, it's like I'm in another world. Instead of broken-down cars, I run past palm trees lining the sidewalks, sand and ocean on my left and fancy hotels and restaurants on my right. My feet bring me to East Beach, like hundreds or maybe even thousands of times before. It's full of college bros playing volleyball and tourists lounging on the sand. The calm ocean breeze wafts the smell of salt into my nose.

I slow my pace. Walking past the ocean always calms me. My thoughts. My worries. My breathing, even. I relax and I'm able to just be. That's why I asked Mom to meet me at the harbor. It feels safe there. It feels like *me*.

At the edge of the boardwalk leading in is the sculpture of three life-sized dolphins that make up the famous fountain. Tourists pose for selfies in front of it as I pass by. Behind it, the boardwalk, full of souvenir shops and restaurants, is teeming with people. I hear a bark of a laugh and look beyond the walkway, where some kayakers are chuckling, as one of them almost fell overboard when he saw a sea lion ahead of them in the water.

Adjusting my earbuds, I turn up the volume of my music. I start jogging again once I pass the boardwalk and am back on the runner's path. I wonder if Mom ever came to the wharf to kayak or eat lunch, or to run like I do.

I take care to keep my breathing even. I don't want to work myself up before I even meet her. Soon, the ever-present fishy smell of the harbor infiltrates my nostrils. Boats that fishermen live in sit next to world-class yachts that cost more than I'll ever make in a lifetime. Families, seemingly so much happier and intact than mine, bustle in and out of the maritime museum. I walk to the slice of sand leading into Leadbetter Beach. It's my favorite spot because it's often empty—most people move along for Shoreline Park's benches and grass. Once I stop, I take a deep breath.

I wonder if my mom is nervous to meet me too, whether she might be here already. I whip around to scan the parking lot behind me. Several empty cars, some with the equipment to hold surfboards on them. No Mom. Not yet.

I stand toward the waves and watch them as the minutes tick by.

My thoughts race as I imagine what it will be like to see Mom. What will we talk about? Maybe she'll tell me why she left and never came back. I bet she didn't want to end up a glorified cleaning lady like Grandma.

I drop my head and pinch the inside of my hand with my fingers. That was mean. Grandma's job is honest work, and she does it without complaint. Liar or not, Grandma does all she does out of love *for me*. What's my mom's excuse?

In my darkest moments, I ask myself what I did wrong for her to not want me. But lately, I wonder more and more if I had nothing to do with it. Maybe she wasn't trying to get away from me so much as Grandma, with all her judgment and my-way-or-the-highway attitude.

I wipe a stupid tear from my eye and sit on the sand, settling in to wait.

The sun hides behind a cloud, and a car engine starts behind me as some people leave the beach.

I watch the waves as they come closer to me and then slink back to where they came.

I wait.

A family I watched walk into Shoreline Cafe comes out, having already been inside for probably at least an hour eating a meal. I check the time.

Mom's really, really late.

My stomach plummets. *What if she's not coming?*

I hadn't considered the possibility until now. Of course she'd come, right?

The laughter of a few small children as they dip their feet in the water yards away makes me wince. I watch as their parents lead them back to their car in the parking lot.

I text my mother. I'm here, let me know if you have a hard time finding me.

No answer.

More time passes. Still no Mom.

"Hey."

I didn't expect that voice. Not here, when I'm waiting for my mom. I whip around to face Nina.

The wind blows a black waterfall of Nina's hair around her face.

I stand. "What are you doing here?"

Instead of answering, Nina asks a question of her own. "Remember when we used to come here all the time?" She smiles. "Running, hanging out at the Art Walk?"

My eyes dart to Nina's right wrist, where she used to wear her friendship bracelet.

"That feels like a million years ago. I hardly remember it." I shrug.

"You here alone?" she asks me.

"Uh, yeah. I always come here alone."

"Me too, but usually not until later in the day"—she pauses—"when I think there are fewer people out and about."

Nina smooths her hair away from her eyes. They're lined with taupe and coral shadow. We both look at each other for a moment and then awkwardly look away.

"I'm glad to run into you today, actually." Nina's smile returns, but this time it's small. Tentative. "I've been wanting to tell you that I think it's cool that you transferred to Spanish. It's been so long since . . . and you know, maybe it would be fun to hang out."

I stare at her, dumbfounded. "But . . . but . . ." I don't finish the thought. I don't get it. Sure, she was fine to me in Spanish and invited me to play basketball. But now, reminiscing about the past?

Nina looks away, past me at the oncoming waves. "I've missed you," she says.

My eyes start to water. Oh my God, I can't do this, not here.

Because when Nina stopped hanging out with me, she broke my little kid-sized heart. Without warning. Without explanation. And now she's acting like nothing happened. But why? And what if I do whatever I did last time to make her not like me? Will she just ditch me again?

"That would be fun," I finally tell her. "Hanging out, like we did . . . before."

Nina's smile falters for a second. I'm such an idiot. Why did I say that? But then she looks at me and I look at her. It's awkward, yeah, but her grin returns. And all I want to do is rush over and hug her, but that would be weird.

"Want to sit? I was . . ." I look toward the parking lot. Mom's not here; she's not coming.

I swallow, trying to not let thoughts of Mom intrude. I can't think about her now when I have Nina standing right in front of me.

I take a deep breath. "I was just watching the waves. Enjoying the day." The dumbest thing I could have said, I know, but Nina walks toward me and we both sit in the sand.

"I'm surprised to not see Brittany with you." Nina looks at her gray Chucks, one of which is untied.

"Oh," I say. "Um, she doesn't come here with me, really. We mostly run around East Beach together."

Nina's quiet for a moment. "How's she doing?"

A seagull flies overhead and I watch it pass by before answering. "She's fine, same old. Her mom recently talked us into doing golf lessons with her."

Nina snorts. "Typical."

My chest tightens. "Yeah, Brittany's mom's kind of a lot. I mean, you remember?"

Nina nods. "Their house was so big. The first time we went over, it felt like being in a movie or something. Her nanny was nice, though. Miss Camila. Does she still work there?"

I shake my head. "She found another job a few years ago, when Tara cut her hours since Brittany didn't need a babysitter anymore. Brittany misses her, though, I think." Not that she's actually said that. "Or, well, she misses having someone around."

Nina's eyebrows shoot up. "You're kidding, right? Her mom was hovering all the time when we were over there! Remember, always telling us not to touch anything so we wouldn't break it? Or trying to hang out with us and get us to watch reality TV with her?"

I laugh. That was before Tara joined the country club and

didn't have many friends. Brittany was so embarrassed by her back then, but I bet she'd take back those days now that she can't get her mom to give her the time of day.

"You should hang out with Brittany and me again some-time." I turn toward Nina. "She'd love to hang out with you too, I bet."

Nina chokes on a laugh. "I doubt that."

I swallow. Before, I would have rushed to defend Brittany. I'd tell Nina that she was probably reading into something wrong. I'd say it was in her head. But I can't do that now that I've started to notice Brittany . . . I don't know what I've noticed, but it's something.

"Oh . . . well that's definitely her loss, then." I pause, not sure how much I should say. "And I'm not . . . she's not . . . *I* want to hang out with you."

The quiet lasts for a moment, and I look at my phone. Still nothing from Mom. I don't want this conversation to end. It's a needed distraction from the sinking thought that my mom's not coming. And it's *Nina*. Right now, hanging out with me.

"Carlos and Edgar are cool," I say, trying to get us back on track and away from the awkwardness that Brittany's name brought up. "We went to lunch together the other day."

"I've noticed you've been hanging out with Carlos." Nina flips her phone around in her hands. "He's okay and all, but I'd . . . I'd be careful with your heart."

Heat floods my cheeks. I look at the water ahead, rather than at her, as I try to work out what she just said. Finally, I respond.

"Are you saying that because of your friend Cassie? Didn't there use to be a thing with them or something?"

Nina laughs. "Guessing Carlos told you about them." She rolls her eyes. "Cassie isn't still into him, if that's what you're getting at. She's talking to some girl from San Marcos that she's all about now. But yeah, Cassie and Carlos were a thing for a while. And I told her to be careful, too, but you know, she didn't listen. Carlos is just . . ." Nina hesitates. "He's not someone I'd recommend any of my friends getting too serious about."

I purse my lips. *Now we're friends?* Now that Nina wants to give me dating advice. But where was she before? All these years when I really needed her. It sounds like Cassie and Carlos ended on bad terms and now Nina just wants to get in my business. But I don't say that. Instead, I mutter, "I'll keep that in mind."

Silence hangs awkwardly between us. "Well, I guess I should get going, then," Nina says. "My mom wants me to help with some chores."

I stand with her and freeze as she hugs me.

"See you at school, Ri."

I watch her walk away and my stomach drops. We'd been sitting here talking for a while, and it was confusing but still nice to be with her. But now it's over and I can't ignore the fact that I haven't heard a peep from my mother.

I call her and get voicemail. Her raspy voice, just hearing it, hearing her, almost breaks me. I hold back tears and hang up.

I flop facedown on my bed. I think about screaming into a pillow like I've seen in movies, but what would that get me? I flip over and put my feet on the bed, sneakers on and everything. Like Grandma hates. To spite her, as though this little action could hurt her at all, no less than the way she's hurt me. If Grandma hadn't kept Mom being in Oxnard a secret this whole time, I wouldn't even be in this situation of getting blown off. Because Mom asked to see me two years ago. She wanted me then.

I swallow the huge lump in my throat, my chin twitching like it sometimes does when I try not to cry. *I don't know what's changed.*

I jump as my phone buzzes. It's a text from Mom. Relief floods through me quickly, dramatically, and I let go of the pain in my chest with an exhale.

I'm so sorry I didn't meet you today, baby. We will make it work some other time, I promise.

She's not blowing me off. She wants to see me. She wants me.

I reread the message. The words start to sink in.

That's it? No explanation.

I stare at my phone as unease slowly creeps back in, dread filling my gut.

I wait to see if she's going to text more. Maybe she'll give a date and time for that rain check.

But she doesn't.

Instead of going back to being pissed at Grandma, I ask myself, is there more to why Mom left than what Grandma has said? What kind of *bad decisions* did Mom make that Grandma hints at but never tells me?

I didn't want to pay attention to Grandma's digs before. I thought maybe it was just her way of making me feel like I was better off without Mom or a way for her to ignore how she could be at fault for Mom leaving. But now, how could I not wonder?

Even though I'm hurt and sad and confused, I answer my mom. I hope so.

Chapter

SEVEN

It's early evening but it feels like the middle of the night, with the day I've had. I head outside my room to get a snack. Grandma's sitting at the dining room table, reading the newspaper.

Grandma turns and once she sees my face, she sits up straighter. "Is something wrong, Ri?"

Mom didn't show. She doesn't care. She doesn't want me.

I blink a few times. *I'm okay. I have to be.*

"No, I think I . . . uh . . . I think I'm just a little tired." I head toward the kitchen. "I ran harder than I meant to."

I fill a glass of water and gulp some down before grabbing a banana.

Grandma looks at the wooden clock on the wall. "Oh! I need to make us dinner."

Grandma pushes her seat back and stands, and since the kitchen is so small and she never wants my help cooking anyway, I walk around her to make space.

I consider taking the banana to my room but instead plop into a dining room chair. My stomach gurgles before I can take a bite. Is it possible to be so sad that it makes me sick?

I felt like everything was going to change once I saw that letter. But my mom has known where I've been this whole time and never came. And now I went and found her, and we're still no closer to being together. What if her reason for leaving was never about Grandma? What if *I'm* not enough?

In front of the open fridge, Grandma tsks. "Not much food in here. I better go to the mercado to pick up some things."

She looks at me and I shrug, putting my banana down.

Grandma's brow furrows as she stares at me. She hesitates but then asks, "Would you like to join me?"

My head jerks back, surprised. "Sure," I stammer. Grandma never brings me to the neighborhood market with her anymore. Usually, it seems like Grandma doesn't want me with her when she runs errands. Most of the time it's like our lives are completely separate. Mine is at school and hers is at work.

The drive to the market is short. Inside, there are aisles full of foods from Grandma's home country. As we walk, she piles tortillas, cilantro, jalapeños, tomatillos, and beef for carne asada, but shakes her head when I reach for a Jarritos fruit punch.

"Too much sugar," Grandma says, before pushing the cart on.

A young woman with long black hair in pigtail smiles as she passes us.

Grandma smiles curtly and then keeps walking. I wonder what it would be like to stop and chat in Spanish, like the woman does with someone else, as we walk away.

Once we're checking out, I load the conveyer belt with groceries behind a family of four ahead of us. The woman bounces a toddler in her arms as the father and young son load their items to be scanned.

"Hola," the man says to the smiling clerk, who, though I can't place her, looks familiar. "¿Cómo estás, Adriana?"

"Estoy bien. ¿Y tu familia?" she answers, grinning at the little boy and girl.

"¡Estamos bien!" the little boy answers happily. He bounces on the balls of his feet, eyeing the pack of Jarritos his dad is loading. *Figures.*

They finish their exchange and Adriana starts ringing up our groceries. A piece of her salt-and-pepper hair falls from her bun and she tucks it behind her ear. The gesture is what brings the memory back. I knew I recognized that messy bun— Adriana was always at mass when we used to go, years ago. One of the neighborhood boys who Nina hung out with, Diego, had a crush on Adriana's niece, Isabella, and talked about what big chichis she had. I'd forgotten about that until now.

I'm about to say something when Adriana greets Grandma with an awkward "hello." Her lips pull into what seems like a forced smile.

I blink, taken aback. Where did all the warmth go that she gave the family ahead of us?

Grandma replies, "Hello."

And that's it. No friendly "¿Cómo estás?"—no talk at all— as Grandma slides her credit card. As soon as Grandma looks away, Adriana's smile falls off her face. She makes quick work of bagging the groceries silently, without making eye contact with

Grandma. And though it's tense, I'm able to get her attention. She returns my small smile.

Grandma shops here every week, and this store is tiny. I bet she sees Adriana all the time. But their interactions are strange and I wonder what happened between Grandma and her. I grab the groceries in my arms as Grandma begins to push the cart to the side of the store where the others go, without so much as a goodbye. Unease fills my belly as I get a sense that this is how all of Grandma's visits to the mercado go.

I turn to Adriana and rack my brain for something nice to say in Spanish. "Mucho gusto," I offer. Even though we've already met and by the way she's looking at me, Adriana remembers. She grins. "Que bueno verte, bonita," she replies warmly. She hesitates and then adds, "Maria."

I wave until I see that Grandma is already leaving. I rush to catch up with her, and after unloading the bags, I ask. "Grandma, that was Adriana from mass, right?"

Grandma starts the car. "I'm surprised you remember. It was so long ago, but yes, that was her."

"Why . . . ?" I pause, trying to think of how I want to ask this. "You both got along fine back then. Why didn't you talk to her now?"

Grandma reverses the car out of the parking spot, replying all nonchalant. "We said hello. What more is there to say?"

A lot, I think. Sure, Grandma doesn't have to be best friends with the people who work at or shop at the mercado. But, coming from Grandma, this chilly interaction seems deliberate.

Like she wants it that way. It wasn't that they didn't exchange pleasantries like the family Adriana saw before us—that's not abnormal in and of itself. But Adriana knows us and it's like Grandma went out of her way not to talk to her. And it seemed that Adriana was used to it.

"You don't really hang out with anyone from our old church, though. Mrs. Sánchez is always asking how you are. She used to come by the house and invite us over." *But stopped after you said no every time.*

"I have plenty of friends," Grandma replies quickly. "From our *current* church. I go to Bible study and we make things together."

Grandma drives through the parking lot as I turn her words over in my head. She's dismissing everything I say, like it's not significant. But it is. I look at Grandma's face; her cheeks wrinkle as her lips purse under my stare.

"Is there a reason why we're completely separated from our—" I stop myself short. I don't want to say *people*; that would draw some serious side-eye. "Community," I finish weakly.

Grandma scoffs. "Don't be ridiculous, Ri. We *have* a church, and I am busy with work, and you are too, with school."

I swallow. Her wall is up, and once again, I'm on the other side of it.

Grandma and I spend the rest of the car ride home in silence.

The next morning, I'm still bothered by that weird trip to the mercado with Grandma and the fact that my mom hasn't given me a date or time for meeting up. Both things just make me determined as ever to learn Spanish, though. Even if Mom wants nothing to do with me, and Grandma wants to have nothing to do with our heritage—I'm still going to class. I still want to learn, to find some way, *any* way to connect with my culture. I don't need either of them for that—I'm doing this for me.

I head out the door just in time as Brittany pulls up. The fall air dampens my hair, flattening it, I'm sure. The car's door handle is cold on my fingertips as I open it and hop in.

As soon as I'm in the car, I realize Brittany turned the ignition off. She turns to face me.

"What happened with your mom yesterday? I tried to call you last night, but your phone went straight to voicemail."

I close my eyes. I was so disappointed, and I didn't want to have to relive that by explaining everything to Brittany.

"Nothing. She didn't show."

My words are monotone, and I shrug like I don't care. But the way Brittany's face falls almost breaks me. I turn away, look out the window.

She reaches out to my shoulder. "I'm so sorry, Ri."

I shake my head, fight back tears.

On the other side of me, I hear Brittany inhale deeply. "Maybe . . . she was just busy."

Brittany doesn't sound like she even believes the words she just said, but I know she only wants to comfort me.

My thoughts turn to Nina, how the day wasn't a complete waste.

"But something interesting did happen at the beach." I compose myself and look at Brittany. "I ran into Nina. We hung out."

Brittany's eyebrows shoot up. "Really? Okay, well . . . that's good." Brittany's statement sounds like a question.

"Yeah," I say. "It was. I've really missed her. Remember when we all used to be friends? We had so much fun."

Brittany licks her lip before biting it. "I remember how close you two were when we met. She came over to my house a few times."

I think back to the questions I've been asking myself about our past and how Nina seemed to think Brittany wouldn't want to hang out with her.

"We were all friends, the three of us," I reply tentatively, now unsure if this was ever actually true.

Brittany's exhale sounds breathy. "I don't know—I never got the feeling she liked me that much."

My neck snaps back at the irony. "That's not true."

Brittany shrugs. "She just wasn't all that nice to me. She wasn't mean or anything," Brittany adds quickly at the look I give her. "I just feel like we didn't have anything in common."

Brittany's words echo what she said about Carlos and Edgar. I think of the way Brittany's house seemed to me and Nina, like a big, fancy mansion that we didn't belong in. How her mom told us not to touch anything. How Brittany went around showing me all her toys, while Nina often hung back and chatted with

Miss Camila and helped her prepare snacks for us.

I remind myself that Brittany apologized about being a jerk to Carlos and Edgar. I'll say something to Brittany when it's needed now, but I can't react to something in the past when I'm still trying to figure out if I'm remembering things correctly. "I'm glad that maybe Nina and I can hang out again. She was my best friend."

I know I picked the wrong words—*best friend*—the second I say them because Brittany's arms shoot to the steering wheel and in the blink of an eye, she turns the car back on and pulls onto the street.

I search for something to say but Brittany beats me to it. "It'll be cool to hang out with her again, I guess," Brittany says, "if you don't mind that she ghosted you back then. I remember how sad you were. Did she ever say why she did that?"

I look out the window, not wanting Brittany to see how hurt I am by the memory. "No," I mutter. "She didn't."

We pass a cluster of middle schoolers heading for the nearby bus pickup. I decide to change the subject, be *normal*. Or at least try to. "So, what do you think?" I wave a hand over my outfit, a navy blue dress with a low scooped neck. "Trying to look good for Spanish class. Key word *trying*."

Brittany raises an eyebrow at me. "That reminds me, how'd the walk go with Carlos?"

Brittany's tone is measured. I can tell she's not excited about Carlos, because her voice isn't gushy like it is when she talks about Finn or even back when Eric and I were a thing.

I give her the side-eye. "It was good. A little awkward, but good."

We got into an argument about *her*, but it's not like I'm telling Brittany that.

"Hmm." At the green light, Brittany hits the gas faster than I expect. She changes the subject to French class. No more talk about Carlos, apparently, which shouldn't be a complete surprise. She clearly has some issue with him, and that bugs me. I listen to her talk about whatever she wants, whenever she wants. And it's not like I think Finn or any other guy Brittany has ever been interested in is the most awesome person ever. My jaw is clenched for the rest of the car ride and as we walk into school.

Brittany sees Finn across the hall and grins at me. I think about rolling my eyes or doing something to show her that I'm annoyed but decide against it as the conversation plays out in my head.

Brittany didn't do anything wrong, per se. She did ask about Carlos, even. Maybe I'm making too much out of nothing.

So, instead of calling attention to my annoyance, I wiggle my eyebrows at Brittany, eyeing Finn. She smiles as she leaves me to go talk to him.

Down the hall, Edgar is walking toward our lockers, so I wave. He smiles as soon as he catches sight of me, his curly hair bouncing slightly atop his head as he makes his way over.

"We have to stop meeting like this." Immediately I flush

at my attempt to be funny. Edgar gives me an awkward smile. "You look nice today," he says.

I look down at my dress and back up, not meeting Edgar's eye. "Thanks. Thought I'd dress up." *Because I'm trying to impress Carlos.*

I grab my stuff and close the locker. I feel someone behind me, and I turn to see Nina.

"Hey!" My eyes widen at my exuberance, arm flailing in a wave and voice an octave higher than usual. Nina and Edgar share a look, and then when it's clear they're both trying not to smile, I laugh. "Okay, hi, yeah. Ri Fernández, most awkward person ever, *apparently*. Nice to see you."

"I like your awkward," Nina says. "It's good to see you're still the same Ri who used to play Ninja Turtles with me."

Edgar raises an eyebrow, and I nod. "It's true. Except instead of the obvious, I always pretended to be Splinter because—"

I stop talking mid-sentence as I see Brittany looking our way, her nose crinkled as though she smells something bad. She starts walking toward us.

"Party started without me, it looks like," Brittany says. She's smiling, but it's not a real one. Her lips are upturned but her eyes remain flat, reminding me of what her mom looks like when she's talking to Brittany and me about something she's pretending to be interested in but really isn't.

I clear my throat. "You know Edgar, and of course Nina." I move an arm in between everyone by way of unnecessary introduction.

Nina looks at me quickly and then, as though she senses my distress, she grins at Brittany. Like Brittany's, Nina's smile doesn't meet her eyes.

"It's been a while, Brittany. How've you been?"

Brittany shrugs. "Oh, you know. Busy. Ri and I are about to start golf lessons at the club my mom goes to. It's, like, really stuffy and boring, most of the time. You'd think for how much my parents pay to be members, there would be more to do. But, like, golf should be fun, I guess, and at least Ri will be with me, like always."

Well, that was obnoxious.

Nina and Edgar look at each other and then back to Brittany. Silence.

"I've taken pictures of the school golf team before for an assignment," Edgar finally says, in his usual genuine way. "I'm gonna be honest and say I don't get the appeal. But I bet it's only because I don't understand the game. Maybe once you get good at it you can explain it to me."

Edgar smiles and I exhale.

"Right, golf's not for everyone." Brittany doesn't drop whatever show she's putting on. She grins at me and it's super over the top and forced. I know Brittany well enough to be able to tell when she's being fake. I don't return her smile.

"Golfing can be slow," Brittany admits, not taking the hint. "But my dad says it's like the best game to play if you want to be a professional, so you can network and make deals."

When none of us say anything, Brittany looks at Nina and

Edgar and adds, "You two should try it sometime, you know, get some lessons."

My face and chest are on fire, and I'm completely stunned speechless. Brittany knows I can't afford golf lessons, and the only reason I'm even taking them is as a favor to her. Neither of us know Edgar's financial situation, but from how things were with Nina's family back when we used to all hang out, it's safe to say they wouldn't waste money on golf lessons either.

Nina's response is slow and seemingly measured. "Oh, um, I think there are a bunch of other things I'd rather do."

I give Brittany the most powerful glare I've probably ever given, before I nod at Nina. "I don't blame you."

My subtext is clear. I don't want to go to these stupid lessons either. And if Brittany keeps this shit up, I probably won't.

Brittany blinks several times, her eyes round and her mouth puckered. Like she's surprised at my response. Which is shocking because what normal person would respond any other way to her bullshit right now?

Edgar clears his throat and shifts his weight. We are all silent for an uncomfortable amount of time.

"Well, we better get to class," Edgar eventually says.

I turn to Nina and Edgar, and we start to walk away, without a word to Brittany.

"See you at lunch," I hear her say from behind me.

Inside the Spanish classroom, Nina sits behind my desk in her usual spot beside her boyfriend. "You know what I just realized?" she says, looking from Miguel to me. "You two haven't officially met, right? Miguel, this is Ri. We used to hang out all the time when we were kids."

I swallow, still not used to Nina talking to me, *publicly*. First in the hall, and now this. "Hey, Miguel."

"Hey, Ri Ri!" Miguel answers. "Can I call you Ri Ri? Like *You can stand under my umbrella, ella, ella, eh, eh, eh?*"

Nina laughs and playfully shoves Miguel's shoulder as he continues to sing Rihanna's "Umbrella" off-key.

"Don't listen to this fool singing that old-ass song." She laughs and shakes her head. "Embarrassing."

"Classics have no age!" Miguel exclaims.

I'm trying to think of something cool to say but all I can do is laugh. And then Carlos walks in, just before Señora Almanza. He leans toward my ear as he passes and whispers, "You look good today." I can't keep my smile from spreading, my body tingly and light.

"Buenos días, clase," Señora Alamanza says.

She heads to the board and starts the lesson. Quickly, I find myself lost in the fast-moving lecture. I was supposed to study extra hard yesterday, but I didn't even open the textbook. I couldn't face homework when my head was swirling with thoughts of Mom and Grandma.

Señora Almanza goes silent. She asked a question, I think. No one raises a hand.

"¿Y tú, Miguel?"

Miguel answers, in Spanish I mostly don't understand. I

picked up what was said in line at the mercado, but this isn't like that. I hear one sentence and try to decipher the meaning only to get lost in the next and the next. My throat tightens, sadness turning into panic.

"Muy bien." Señora Almanza steps back from the front of the room and consults her teacher's textbook. She continues to call on people, asking questions in Spanish that she expects them to answer. In Spanish. Then she looks at me.

"¿Y tú, Maria?"

My throat starts to close, my face burns, and it feels like a weight is crushing my chest all at once.

"¿Y tú, Maria?" Señora Almanza repeats, staring at me. Like the rest of the class.

"What?" I mutter, squeezing my sweaty palms tightly on my lap. "I'm sorry. Can you repeat the question?

Señora Almanza clicks her tongue. "En español, por favor."

I bite my lip, blink rapidly.

"¿Puedes repetir?" I finally mumble, not using the correct conjugation for speaking to a person you respect, like a teacher. But I don't know how to say it that way off the top of my head.

I hear a few guys snicker behind me. I sink into my seat. I want to disappear.

Señora Almanza gives me a small smile before slowly repeating, "¿Cómo tomas tu café?"

I lick my chapped lips. I love chocolate mochas, but I don't know how to say that. Everyone's staring at me. "Negro," I blurt.

A few snickers behind me again. I close my eyes and force myself to ignore everyone around me and think. "Me gusta el café solo," I say.

Señora Almanza watches me quietly for a moment and I plead with my eyes. *Please move on, please, please, please.*

"Muy bien," she finally says. And then she picks her next victim. I try to deepen my quick and shallow breaths.

"You feeling okay?" Carlos whispers. "You look like you're going to puke."

On his other side, Edgar glances from Señora Almanza to me and back quickly.

"Yeah," I croak. "Just . . . I hate talking in class is all."

Carlos nods, and then shifts away from me when Señora Almanza glares in our direction for not paying attention.

I bet I spoke better Spanish when I was five. I understood more of it then—I was around it so much. Even though Grandpa insisted we speak English at home, Mom and Grandma didn't always listen to him, especially when he was at work and didn't know. But Grandpa scolded me whenever I tried to speak Spanish, and now here I am, struggling.

I close my eyes and rub my temples, my thoughts racing. I don't know how I'm going to do this.

By the end of Multimedia later in the day—during which I tried and failed to forget about the horror that was Spanish earlier—my eyes hurt from staring at a screen for so long. I close my eyes and rub them. I should talk to Grandma about getting glasses, but it's not covered on our insurance.

"Are you okay, Ri?" Brittany's eyebrows furrow as she looks at me. I'm pretty sure, based on the careful way she greeted me after Spanish and ever since, that she knows she messed up earlier with Nina and Edgar.

I roll my chair back from the large computer screen—the class is full of the highest tech, paid for by the boosters and rich PTA parents, and my family can't even afford basic health care.

"I think I need to see an eye doctor, but . . . it's expensive."

Brittany's eyes linger on me for a moment before she focuses back on her own screen. "Have you told your grandma?" she asks slowly. "I mean, I know money is tight, but I'm sure she'd want to prioritize your vision over—"

I cut her off, unable to stop the anger from coming out of my voice. "Over what, food?"

Brittany's mouth falls open. I was pissed earlier about her golf comments but didn't expect to get heated so fast right now.

Eyes wide, Brittany looks away and stammers, "I didn't mean . . . You don't have to get so mad."

I don't have to get so mad? It's not like *she*, Brittany, didn't just put her foot in her mouth again. Earlier, she went out of her way to throw her family's money in Nina and Edgar's faces. But it wasn't just theirs.

I can't pay for golf lessons. So, by her separating herself from them by talking about something so out there, that's what she was doing to me too. Even if she didn't mean to. Even if she doesn't know she did.

Even though I want to yell at Brittany for telling me not to get mad, I don't. Because I can't keep expecting her to be better if I don't tell her.

"Brittany." I look at her and wait for her to meet my eye. "I know you know . . ." Uggh, why is this so embarrassing? I pinch the bridge of my nose. "You know my grandma and I don't have that much money. It feels shitty when you say stuff like that, when you forget. Because, like, of course she would want to get me in to see an eye doctor and to buy me glasses if I need them, but we just can't afford stuff like that a lot of the time."

Brittany's quick to respond. "Totally, you're right, you're right."

"And with the golf lessons, you know they're expensive. You know that I couldn't afford them on my own."

"Of course," Brittany cuts in, her voice reassuring, like this is what she can comprehend, "and you're doing it for me, so you'd never have to! Don't even worry about it!"

It takes a herculean effort not to glare at Brittany.

"I know," I say through clenched teeth. "But when you said, like it was no big deal, that Edgar and Nina should get lessons too, it's like you don't even think about how that would come off to them either."

Brittany's eyes pop. "I didn't mean it that way, I swear."

I blink. I want to believe Brittany, with the way she's looking at me, like she's embarrassed and guilty and sorry. I don't say anything as I let unease fill the air.

"I get it," Brittany finally says.

"Cool. Good."

"Good." Brittany repeats and nods.

As we walk out of the lab, an awkward tension between us, I see Carlos and Edgar at his locker. Behind them, Finn is strolling down the hall.

"Hey," Finn says, nodding to Carlos and Edgar as he stops next to Brittany.

"Hey, surfer boy." Carlos answers Finn before I can. He slides his arm around my shoulders. "I was just going to walk my girl Ri home again."

Brittany raises an eyebrow. "*My girl?*"

"Not *my* girl. Damn, Britt. I don't own her." Carlos grins at Brittany's discomfort. "I meant my girl, like my homegirl, Ri."

I lock eyes with Brittany for a tense moment.

She hesitates before looking at Edgar and then Carlos. "Riiight," she laughs awkwardly. "So, how's it going?"

Edgar perks up next to me. "Good. We've got a Spanish test coming up on Wednesday, but other than that, same old, same old."

The test.

With everything else going on, I completely forgot about it! Normally, I'd be afraid to study with people in class, because they'd be likely to discover how truly terrible at Spanish I am, but my fear of Grandma's wrath at a bad grade supersedes that fear.

"Actually . . ." I look up at Carlos. "I was hoping we could study together for it. Are you free after school today or tomorrow?"

"I got something today," Carlos says. He doesn't offer anything else.

"Don't you guys all speak Spanish already?" Finn asks.

I hold my breath. *Do they?* Maybe I'm not the only one who doesn't—

Edgar answers, "Carlos and I do. But learning it in class is kind of like learning it for white people." He wiggles his eyebrows at Brittany and her face flushes. "We speak it a little differently, but we're graded the way you would learn it, Finn. So, brushing up on what we've learned helps."

Finn nods. "Makes sense. Plus, it doesn't hurt that the Spanish teacher looks like she does, am I right?"

Carlos whistles. "Don't I know it!"

"That's why *I'm* there," I deadpan.

Edgar catches my eye. "Never feel bad for wanting to study, Ri." He smiles, but his expression is so sincere, I'm taken aback.

Carlos pats Edgar's shoulder. "This guy's got a four-point-oh GPA. Making the rest of us look bad."

I look at Carlos, his broad shoulders, toned chest, and muscled arms. I guess there's nothing wrong with appreciating someone for their physical attributes, although I wish Carlos would be appreciating *mine* rather than Señora Almanza's. "You ready to go?"

Carlos nods. "Later," he says to Edgar, Brittany, and Finn.

"Bye, Carlos! Good talking to you!" Brittany calls after us.

I try not to roll my eyes at her, but I'm smiling despite myself. She may have totally botched it with Nina and Edgar earlier, but she's trying.

I wave at Edgar. He continues talking with Brittany and Finn as Carlos and I head out. Carlos slides his hand into mine as we walk out of the school parking lot.

"So, what does a girl like you do when not at school?"

"What do you mean a girl like me?"

"Pretty, smart, amazing—a girl like you."

I laugh softly, relieved, but my voice comes out higher than I mean it to. "What do *you* do for fun?"

"Oh, you know, the usual. Nothing that special—watch sports on TV with my dad, try to keep him and my mom happy with my grades, hang with the guys after school." Carlos runs his thumb over mine. "Although I've got to say things are looking up—way more exciting, now that you're around."

I smile big, my whole body warm, especially my hand in Carlos's.

"So, don't dodge the question. What are you into? Other than me."

I blush but don't argue. Damn, this boy has game. I'll give him that.

We turn onto my street, and I lead him toward my house. "I like running," I say, ignoring his comment about me being into him. "I sometimes go alone just to think."

Carlos looks into my eyes. "Maybe I could join you sometime."

I nod enthusiastically. I imagine Carlos's body moving next to mine, him getting sweaty. I've got no chill just thinking about it.

Once outside my front door, Carlos tucks a piece of hair out of my face. We lock eyes. He leans in. Slowly.

I can't believe this is happening right now, but I don't have time to think as his warm, soft lips graze mine. I breathe him in, my body seemingly melting in his arms.

His kiss deepens. And then his lips move to my neck. Each spot his lips graze tingles, waking up nerves I didn't know were there. I want more.

"Want to come in?" I surprise myself by saying the words aloud.

Carlos keeps kissing my neck, and then moves back to my mouth as if he hasn't heard me.

"My grandma's not going to be home for hours," I mumble against his soft, full lips.

His hands slip down to my waist and then move to my butt.

I step away from him quickly and look around. No one's outside, thank God.

"Hmmm." Carlos smiles. "Sorry. I'd love to come inside, but I'm meeting a friend."

"Oh?"

"Yeah, I promised I'd come over after school. Sorry, girl." He takes in my expression and laughs softly. "I'd love to come in and pick this up. Another time."

I adjust my dress, make sure it's covering the right places.

"Um, yeah. Of course. That'd be great. I'll see you at school tomorrow?"

"Looking forward to it." He leans in and kisses me again, sending shivers down my spine. I laugh a little as he pulls away slowly.

"This must be a really important friend."

Carlos grins at me, walking away backward a few steps, before he turns around.

Inside, I skip the kitchen and head straight for my laptop in my bedroom. I flop onto my bed, wondering what it would be like if Carlos had come inside. Images race in my head. I bite my lip, grinning. I've never felt that way before, tingling at someone's touch, lost in someone's hands.

Breathless, I grab my journal. Write what I'm thinking and feeling until my wrist cramps. If I had Mom around rather than my strict-ass grandma, I'd be able to tell her about Carlos kissing me. I could tell her how I feel giddy when he looks at me, how I almost don't want to wash my hand after he holds it.

But who am I kidding? Mom doesn't want to see me. She hasn't messaged me with a time to reschedule seeing each other. She hasn't called.

I make myself get started on the practice exam and worksheets in my Spanish textbook until my phone buzzes. I practically jump with surprise when I realize it's my mom. Finally.

I want to tell you why I didn't meet you when I said I would.

Can we meet at Leadbetter this afternoon?

My heart hammers. My mom didn't just blow me off for no

reason? She wants to tell me why. She wants to see me. Today.

Though Grandma's not here, I still need a cover for where I'll be and why. Just in case. So I put on my running clothes and text Mom that I can make it before heading out. My feet hit the pavement loudly to the beat of the music on my running playlist as I pass each house on my street and the next, bringing me closer to my mom.

After she left that last time, Grandpa never talked about Mom. But I could hear him and Grandma fighting about her late at night. Back then, Grandma wanted to talk about Marisol. Grandma sometimes told me I reminded her of my mom when she was a little girl, because we were both so sweet and loving. Grandpa was the one who wouldn't have it. Once he died, I thought the silence around the topic of my mother would change.

It didn't.

I reach the beach sooner than I normally would have, given how fast I ran. I bend over and try to catch my breath. The ocean breeze feels cool on my sweaty, sticky skin as I stare at the ocean, seemingly endless.

"Maria?" Her voice says my name tentatively.

My skin prickles and my breath catches in my throat.

I turn around slowly. My hands and shoulders start to shake.

I know her because she looks like Grandma, only younger, with longer hair.

I know her because I have seen her, although I can barely remember.

I know her from the pictures I've committed to memory, the face I see in my dreams.

"Maria, it's me." The woman says, her deep brown eyes welling with tears. The lines around her mouth curve as she smiles.

I know her because she's my mom.

Chapter

EIGHT

I stare at her for a moment. As though I'm taking a photo in my mind, I try to capture everything. Her large eyes that are locked on me. Her eyebrows that look as though they are tattooed on. Her tight curls that make her hair look like wires. Her brown skin that is lighter than Grandma's but darker than mine.

My mother is watching me, her smile fading, her arms slightly outstretched, like she wants to reach for me but won't.

She clears her throat, and out comes her deep, raspy voice again.

"Maria, it's me." She hesitates and then adds, "Your mom."

She takes a step closer to me, and then another, until I'm in her arms, the force of her pull knocking the breath out of me, the smell of her—a combination of stale cigarettes and vanilla, like Grandma's shampoo—filling my nostrils.

I stare at her, this woman I've imagined, hoped for, cried for. In the flesh. I've dreamed about this moment for years, prayed for it, and now it's here and I don't know what to do.

She stares at me, her eyes drinking in my face in like I might disappear. We're quiet again for a moment, until she breaks the silence. "I remembered you loved the beach as a baby, this beach." She holds an arm out in front of us to the sand at our feet. "You probably don't know this, but I love this beach too. I came here all the time when I was pregnant with you."

I look away from her, feeling a strong emotion I can't place as my chest tingles. The sea ripples in the wind, calm and steady. I swallow and steal a glance back at my . . . *mom*.

A tear falls down her face as she smiles weakly at me. "I know. I know."

She gestures for me to sit with her on the sand. I look around. The beach is empty and quiet, the only noise around us the waves lapping the shore rhythmically and a band of seagulls flying overhead.

I sink into the ground, kicking my feet out in front of me. My fingers dig into the sand and pull, releasing fistfuls, and then again slower, grain by grain.

"Tell me about yourself—tell me about everything," she says, her eyes alight.

I don't ask her why she blew me off the other day. Not yet. I want my mom to want to be here, with me. I want her to want me.

"I . . . uh . . . well, I was on the cross-country team, but I quit this year," I start.

My mom smiles at me, encouraging.

I take a deep breath. "I hang out with Brittany. My best

friend; she came with me to your place when we met John. She and I do everything together. She's not a huge fan of some of my new friends, but—"

"Oh?" Mom lifts her eyebrows. "Why not?"

I sigh. Why did I have to go there right away? I choose my words carefully. "I don't know if that's true exactly. It just seems like . . . there's this guy—"

"Aah," Mom says.

I hurriedly add, "And he's great and I think he likes me, but Brittany, I don't know, I think she would rather keep the status quo."

"And what's the status quo?"

"Just us two, I guess. I mean, I dated another guy, Eric, a while back. He hangs out with some of the girls we used to be on the cross-country team with. He was . . ." I don't say white. "Expected. Like the kind of guy Brittany and I would normally hang out with."

My mom furrows her eyebrows.

"But this other guy is special," I continue. "He's funny and charming and really, really good-looking. I get along with his friends pretty well too, which Brittany doesn't seem too thrilled about either. I met them in Spanish class." I bite my lip.

Mom cocks her head. "You're taking Spanish?"

"I started just recently," I say quickly. "I'm learning so I really know how to speak it and not just understand bits and pieces."

Mom's quiet for a while, and my chest tightens. Her face is

scrunched up, her brows furrowed. Maybe she's disappointed in me, that I waited this long to learn.

"What is it?" My voice is high. *I shouldn't have told her.* "Did I say something?"

Mom shakes her head. "No, it's not you. I wish I would have started speaking it to you when you were learning to talk. Your grandparents were so dead set on you being just like everyone else. They thought you would be better off, the more you looked and acted like, like . . ." She shakes her head.

"Like I was white?" I ask, looking right at her. "Is that what you mean?"

Mom's jaw sets. She nods. "They thought, your grandfather especially, that since you have a light complexion, you'd be better off than they were. People wouldn't be racist sons of bitches to you because you look like them. I remember when they first started telling me those kinds of things when I was a kid. It confused me . . . made me feel ashamed of who we were. I didn't want that for you. But, that's just how your grandfather was." She sighs.

"Well, he was a crazy old man, wasn't he? And he's gone now, so what does it matter?"

I bite my lip and look away. She has no idea how Grandma is just as bad as Grandpa now, how she and I argue about this all the time. She hardly knows anything about me.

And I don't know anything about her.

"You said you were going to tell me why you didn't come

before," I begin. "And I want to know that, but you've lived so close by. And it's been two years . . ." I let the rest of the sentence hang in the air unsaid. I can't bear to look at her, so I stare down at my hands.

I hear Mom inhale deeply. "I didn't come because I was afraid. I was afraid of my mother."

My mouth drops open and I jerk my head to look at her. That I wasn't expecting.

My mom reaches out as though she wants to touch my face but I tense, and she drops her hand.

"It's why I didn't come over the years, and even why I didn't come after I called. I was afraid of what my mother would do if she found out." Mom's lower lip quivers as my thoughts whirl at what she's saying.

"Years ago, after I'd moved out, I tried. Oh, baby, I tried over and over to reach you. Calling and dropping by uninvited, but she never let me in," Mom says. "She threatened that she would pick up and move away if I came and saw you against her will. I thought not being in your life was unbearable, but not nearly as bad as having you gone entirely. At least this way, I knew where you were."

I stutter. "That doesn't make . . . Grandma said . . ." I can't form a sentence. None of this makes sense.

Mom pushes her flip-flops into the sand, and then she turns to face me. "They sent me away, your grandpa and grandma. Both of my parents didn't want me around you." She pulls her eyes from me to stare out at the waves. "I didn't want to leave, but"—her voice breaks—"they made me."

I gasp. "No. No, Grandma said . . ." I sputter the same thing I said before. Mom's eyes narrow, and she shakes her head fast.

I swallow, hard. Clench my teeth. "She said you left me. That you weren't ready or able to be a mom."

"Not true," she whispers before closing her eyes, as if she's in pain.

I keep my mouth shut because I don't trust the words that could come out. Grandma has always said that Mom left because she couldn't take care of me, not that she forced her to go.

I release the last bit of sand I'd been clutching and stare at my mother's weathered hand, so close, close enough for me to grab and hold. The tension in my chest hardens and drops, like a rock in my gut.

A couple of tears fall down my mom's cheeks. "I couldn't come, I couldn't. Papá"—she pauses—"your grandpa would never allow it, not after he forced me to sign my parental rights away to them. My father tricked me. He told me it would only be for a little while and then once I got back on my feet, once I paid off the money I owed from being in jail—" She stops suddenly. And I can tell by the way she's looking at me that I haven't covered up my shock very well.

My mom flushes, embarrassed. "I was young and in love. I got in trouble with a boyfriend and got caught up in a barfight. It seems so stupid now."

Mom takes a deep breath. "Your grandparents acted like I was such a horrible person, like I had a drinking problem, but

I was just a rebellious kid. I was having fun, being reckless, but nothing that other kids didn't do. You have to understand, my parents were so strict." Her voice strengthens. "And even though I knew I wasn't an alcoholic, I stopped drinking altogether. I promised your grandfather and he lied to me, he said I could have you back, once I had a job and a safe place to live. I haven't touched a drop of alcohol since I signed those papers. But it was never enough."

I pull my knees up to my chest. Grandma hinted that Mom got into trouble, that she wasn't a *good* girl, whatever the hell that means. But that's not what really matters.

I want to believe my mom wanted me. But part of me still can't help but feel abandoned, even if it was my grandparents' fault.

"I haven't been far," she says, mirroring me by pulling her knees closer to her body and sitting up straighter. "I lived in Las Vegas for a couple of years, and then in Los Angeles for a while, but mostly, I've been staying in Oxnard. She meets my eyes. "So many times, Maria, so many times over the last few years, I found myself on the highway driving here, driving to Santa Barbara. Sometimes I even made it as near as a few streets away. But I always turned around." She takes a deep breath and closes her eyes for a moment.

I clutch my phone in my hand. "You could have called."

Mom looks at me. "I did, baby. I called so many times. First, your grandpa said I couldn't talk to you yet. I needed to save money, find a better place. Then he said he didn't want to disrupt your schooling, and I couldn't call or come visit yet because you were starting to get used to your routine." My mom takes my hand, and I let her. It's cold and clammy, smaller than mine, and bony, like Grandma's. I force the thought of *her* away.

Mom runs a finger over my palm. "He said that it was so important for you, and he didn't want to disrupt the good changes in your behavior. As if you were some troubled child before I left."

"So, you just stopped trying then?" My hand falls to the ground.

Mom watches my hand as a tear trickles down to her lips. "Your grandfather told me I had to stop calling or he wouldn't let me see you. It was like he was holding you over my head."

My mother lowers her voice. "That was the original deal, when I first signed my rights away. If I wanted them to help me with you, I couldn't be around until I got better. I wasn't right to do it, baby." She pauses to look at me seriously, as if she can convince me with her eyes. "I shouldn't have agreed, but I was in a bad way. I was young and I couldn't take care of you myself. Your father wasn't in the picture and—"

My head snaps up at that. *My father.* I know nothing about him, except that he's white.

My mother inhales sharply and looks away. "To be honest, I'm ashamed to say I'm not even sure who he is."

My shoulders slump. So much for finding out about him. Mom looks back at me and in her eyes, I can see that she senses my disappointment. "But it doesn't matter, because whoever he was, he gave me the greatest gift, he gave me the best thing I've ever had in my life. You."

Her voice is filled with emotion. Pleading. "I just needed to get my life together, and I didn't think it would be forever. But when I didn't act perfectly for them, fit their timeline for my progress, they started to use you against me to control me. When your grandpa died, I thought things would be different. But they weren't," The wind picks up, blowing my mom's wiry curls into her face, and she brushes them off, along with a few more tears. "She wouldn't let me come to my own father's funeral."

My mother doesn't say who she is, but I know right away. *How could Grandma do that to her own daughter?* How could she be so cruel?

I turn away, unable to look at the pain on my mother's face, unable to imagine how it must have felt to be her. I barely remember Grandpa's funeral—just snippets come to mind. Grandma dressing me in a long-sleeved velvet dress. People hugging her and then me, saying how sorry they were. Looking up through tears in my eyes at Grandma's strong, stoic face from the front row at the church. Mom wasn't there. I could have had her there with me, holding me.

She moves her hand closer to mine. I could take it. I could reach out and take it, like she took mine. But my hand lies flat on the sand, as if a magnet holds it down.

She's stopped crying, but her voice is low and guttural. "I'm so, so sorry. For everything. For not sending that letter sooner, for giving up—I should have kept trying. It just hurt so badly to be turned away by my own family. And, truly, baby, I was afraid that if I kept fighting your grandmother, she'd move you away, somewhere I'd never be able to find you. I shouldn't have left in the first place. I missed *so much*."

She raises her chin and looks at me. "That's why I was afraid to come after I told you I would, but ultimately I couldn't lose the chance to see you. So, I'm here. I'm sorry it took me so long, but I'm here." Her voice breaks. "Now."

My mother is here, and she's sorry. I don't want to see Mom sad like this, not when I can fix it. Not when I can try to, at least.

So I grab my mother and hold her in my arms. She lets out a huge exhale, like she'd been holding her breath until I finally let my walls down, and she cries into my shoulder, shaking softly.

Or maybe that's me. I'm the one shaking.

This is real. I'm with my mom. She's *real*.

I pull away slowly. "Did John tell you that Grandma doesn't know I found the letter?"

She nods.

"Grandma wouldn't want me to come. I knew before, and I really know now, after everything you've said." Because everything Grandma kept me from knowing wasn't to protect me; it was to protect herself.

"You can't tell her that I came here and saw you," my mom

pleads. "She can't stop you if she doesn't know."

I swallow. *Like I'm telling that woman anything.* I don't even know how I'll be able to look at Grandma at home, much less talk to her. "Of course, Mom." I stutter over the word, so foreign on my lips. And my mom beams. I softly touch her hair, move it out from in between us. "She won't know."

After a moment, Mom pulls away from me. She straightens her shirt and composes herself.

I look at my phone again. "It's getting late," I say without thinking.

Her face falls. "You have to get going, don't you?"

"I have to study for Spanish later. I don't want to leave you—"

Mom puts a hand on each of my shoulders. "I'll tell you what, you get going and study and we can meet back here, same time next week or whenever works better for you. And you know what else? Bring your Spanish book." Her eyes twinkle with delight. "I can help you study next time."

Mom's face swims before mine as I blink my watery eyes. I hug her. She's my mom and I can see her again. This isn't the end.

I don't see the waves or the sand as I walk away. I don't even see the bicyclist heading in my direction—I'm on the wrong side of the path—until I feel the air whoosh by me.

It's her face, the love in her eyes, that I see in my mind. The pain, when she talks about what Grandma and Grandpa took from her.

What they took from me.

That was real. That was all real. Mom is real.

And Grandma is a liar.

Next thing I know, I'm waking up from a nap to the sound of Grandma coming home from work. I hear her rustling around, before something clatters in the kitchen.

I passed out after seeing Mom, exhausted from all the emotions. I look at my phone, noting the time. It's late.

Everything Mom said about Grandma comes back in a rush. I call from my bedroom. "Don't worry about cooking anything for me."

The sounds of dishes clanging continue, so I walk out there. Do my best to keep my searing anger in check to protect my and Mom's secret. I sit in the dining room and nod at the pile of Grandma's sewing stuff on it. I lift a black shawl off the table. "What's this?"

Grandma, standing in front of the open fridge, looks to see what I'm talking about. "Oh, my boss needs that shawl mended before a party tomorrow. She said it was very important, but it's hard to find the time when I'm doing all my normal work at the house."

I look at the shawl rather than at my grandma. Focus on the conversation we're in rather than all that I know now and risk screaming at her. My brow furrows as I slide my fingers down the soft fabric, noticing a small tear. "Cashmere?"

"Mmm-hmmm," Grandma confirms as she pulls some meat

out of the fridge and sets it on the counter.

"She couldn't take this to a tailor or dry cleaner or something? Pay someone to do it?"

Grandma cuts a lemon in half. "She does pay someone to fix that," Grandma says. "Me. And anyway, she just decided she wanted it mended today, so there wouldn't have been time."

I grunt because despite how furious I am with Grandma, I'm annoyed that this woman takes up all my grandma's time not only when she's at work, but even when she's at home with me.

Grandma covers a yawn with her hand, her eyes drooping. "Don't worry about it, mija. I'll finish it after dinner."

"Mija?" I repeat.

"Lo siento, I mean sorry, baby." She answers quickly and then starts humming to herself a song from church. She begins warming some tortillas on the stove and pulls some shredded cheese out of the fridge. Hearing her revert to Spanish when she's tired, it just makes it more apparent how natural it is for her. I wonder if she thinks in Spanish and still has to translate everything in her head. Why does she force her language, her past, away like that? Questions bubble up in my throat.

"I remember, you know. When you and Mom use to talk in Spanish when Grandpa wasn't around, even though he didn't want anyone to speak it."

That's not how I thought I'd broach the subject of Mom with Grandma, but here we are: Grandma speaking in Spanish, me having so many questions that only lead to more.

Grandma sighs. "I loved your grandfather so much. I still do," she adds. "I knew it was important to obey my husband."

I roll my eyes at Grandma. But I remind myself she grew up in another time.

Grandma smirks at me. "Yes, yes, I know you don't see the importance. But Grandpa worked so hard to learn English, we both did, and since the people he worked with in the fields mostly spoke Spanish, he needed all the practice he could get. Once he learned English, he hoped he could get a better job. And he did, working as a janitor at that office building, but that wasn't the life he wanted for you."

I can almost feel Grandpa, with his slicked black hair and serious expression, next to me. I remember him coming home bone-tired from long hours working the night shift cleaning conference rooms before he got sick. I hadn't realized he only got that job after years of learning English. It didn't come up in my conversation with Mom, I guess.

"You probably didn't realize this, but your grandfather tried so hard to be taken seriously. Not as an immigrant but as a man."

My eyebrows shoot up when Grandma continues of her own volition. I quickly rearrange my face.

"He would practice his voice so that it didn't sound like him at all. And it worked, if he was on the phone." Grandma nods at me solemnly. "Once, when we were overcharged on our phone bill, he called to try to make it right, sounding as himself, and the customer service person did nothing to help us. The next day, he called again and did his best to disguise his accent, and you know what?"

Grandma's eyes lock with mine and I hold my breath, knowing without being told what must have come next.

Grandma nods. "They gave us our full refund."

I remember once asking Grandpa why he wouldn't let me speak Spanish with him. He scolded me, telling me if I were to make anything of myself, I better speak perfect English, I better dress just right, and I better make the right kind of friends, like the good girl he knew I wanted to be.

I was no more than five years old, and I didn't understand why he got so upset all of a sudden. I started to cry. My grandpa looked sorry for a moment, but instead of scooping me into his arms, like I'd hoped, he leaned down and kissed my forehead before walking to his bedroom.

I remember that conversation more than I remember the movie dates he took me on, just him and me. I remember that conversation more than the times he told me stories about knights and princesses he imagined for me at bedtime, before tucking me in and kissing me good night.

"I . . . I didn't know that," I say quietly, not meeting my grandma's eye.

Grandma adds a crispy tortilla to a plate. "When your mom was young," Grandma says, keeping her eyes on the pan, "we hadn't learned yet, so we spoke in Spanish. It was her first language. But we got better, and your mom learned English in school, in one of those ESL programs. But she liked speaking

Spanish at home. It was what she was used to."

I hold still. Like if I were to move, it might break a spell. Listening. Maybe, just maybe, we can talk about Mom. Maybe I can get Grandma to tell me the truth. I remain still and keep listening.

"When your mom tried to speak Spanish at home, after she learned English, your grandfather would stop her. *We live in America and we speak English*, he would say."

Huh. I have Grandpa to thank for Grandma's favorite saying. Still, I hold my tongue. Grandma continues, "Your mom would become so angry with him. And when he wasn't around, she spoke Spanish with me."

Grandma flips another tortilla. "I was easier on your mom, back then. I wanted to obey my husband—we had the same dreams for her as I do you, a good education and a good job, and that meant sacrifice. But I wanted to make my daughter happy, too, so I gave in a little." She trails off.

My throat tightens. This might be my chance. Now or never. "I know you've always thought it was best to keep everything about Mom a secret," I say. "But I'm not a kid anymore. I want to know what happened with her. I want to know why she left."

Grandma shakes her head as she uses tongs to remove the tortillas from the pan. "We've discussed this, Ri, and you know all there is that you need to." She looks away, busying herself putting the carnitas together.

"It's not enough, Grandma. I know there's more to it than that." I say it with conviction. Because I do know.

Grandma's back goes still. She abandons the food and rests her hands on either side of the counter. A moment passes before she speaks. "You might not like how I do things, Maria, but I am the adult here, and I make the rules. And one of them is that you stop asking about your mother. She wasn't ready to be a parent, so she left. But that was her mistake, her loss. I've worked so hard to give you everything you need, Ri, to give you the future you deserve. We have built a life without her, and we are doing just fine."

My mouth falls open. Grandma has been vague, she's dodged my questions, but now she's flat out *refusing* to talk to me about my mom. And I know now that she's lying. She's lying to my face, not leaving things out, but flat out lying.

Grandma sets a plate of carnitas in front of me.

"Whether you like it or not, Grandma, I am still her daughter. And that—"

The plate shakes as Grandma slams her hand on the counter next to it. "That's enough, Ri!"

"You can't just—"

Grandma cuts me off with a shout and I flinch. "End of discussion!"

I blink back tears. Grandma has never screamed at me like that before. I leave the plate of carnitas and walk to my room without a word.

Chapter

NINE

I spend the night tossing and turning. I'm awake before my alarm goes off but still not early enough to see Grandma before she leaves for work.

As I head to the kitchen for breakfast, my eyes land on the couch. The shawl is there. Grandma must have forgotten it. I pick up the soft fabric and look it over. She probably stayed up late finishing this, because there's no longer a tear in it.

I call Grandma but it goes straight to voicemail. By the time she realizes the shawl is here, it might be too late to come get it without her boss noticing.

I look up the address for Grandma's work in my phone. Grandma gave it to me in case of emergencies. I've never been there, but the last thing I want, even if we've been fighting, is for Grandma to get in trouble with her boss.

I call Brittany and ask if she'll give me a ride there. Of course she agrees and is here in under half an hour.

"Thanks for doing this, Brittany." I buckle in. "Grandma's boss will be pissed if she doesn't get this on time."

"That lady sounds like a real bitch," Brittany says. She puts the address in the GPS and we're off, climbing the hill toward Montecito. I don't tell Brittany about meeting my mom at the beach. I'd rather wait until after we drop this shawl off, so I don't work myself up right before I have to see Grandma.

When the directions tell us we've arrived, we head up a long, winding driveway until we reach a tall metal gate. I hit the intercom and a woman with a heavy Spanish accent answers.

"I'm Ri Fernández," I call over Brittany through her open window. "I'm Carmen's granddaughter. There's something important I need to give to her right away."

There's a pause. "Carmen's granddaughter?"

"Yes, and I know she really needs this shawl. It's for Mrs. Reynolds's party tonight."

I hear a sigh. "Okay, well, since you *are* Carmen's granddaughter. Just this once."

"Thank you!"

A loud beep sounds and the gate opens.

"Wow." Brittany whistles as she takes in the Mediterranean-style mansion that expands almost as far as the eye can see. There's a tennis court and pool to the left, and something that looks like a fancy barn, maybe a horse stable, beyond that.

"Yeah," I manage. I try calling my grandma again, but there's no answer.

We keep driving until we see a tucked-away lot where several cars are parked, including Grandma's. "This must be it," I tell Brittany. She pulls over and our feet crunch on the gravel as we make our way toward the nearest door.

"I feel like we shouldn't be here," Brittany says quietly.

And looking around, I agree, but we've come this far. I clutch the cashmere to my chest. I keep walking, and Brittany opens the door for us. "At least it's not locked," she says.

"Why would it be with that big-ass gate out there?"

Brittany nods. We walk inside and there's marble everywhere. A huge, rounded ceiling way above. A tall metal structure with some kind of appendages shooting out of it on either side, which I can't distinguish as art or a table, sits in the middle of the room. And there's an imposing, winding staircase to the left.

Footsteps clap on the marble floor at the end of the atrium. A middle-aged man wearing a uniform similar to what Grandma wears—black slacks and a white button-down and comfortable-looking black shoes—stops in his tracks. This man does not look happy to see us. "Who are you?"

"My grandma, Carmen Fernández, works here." I lift the shawl. "I need to give her this."

The man doesn't budge as he seemingly appraises us.

"My grandma forgot it at home, and Mrs. Reynolds needs it tonight," I plead.

The man's expression softens, and he beckons for us to follow him. Brittany exhales louder then she probably means to, and we walk down a long hallway with family portraits decorating the walls. The people in it, a man and woman and a younger man, probably the son Grandma complains about sometimes, look so serious, dressed up, not a hair out of place. None of them smiling.

He leads us to a small kitchen, not the kind of kitchen that I've seen before in other homes, but more like a . . . a . . . my mind struggles to find the word. A workers' kitchen?

As soon as Brittany and I step in, the man retreats. It's not hard to see or *feel* why when we notice how hot it is. Smoldering. There are no windows in the small room and the oven glows; something's cooking in there and making the room feel like a sauna. Grandma is hunched over a large sink, dishes piled high. Fans blow at her from all sides, but she still pauses to use a gloved hand to wipe the sweat off her brow. She's turning to load a plate in the open dishwasher beside her when she catches sight of us.

"¡Dios mío! ¿Qué pasa?" Grandma drops the plate in the dishwasher with a clang and steps toward us, fear lining her face. "Girls, are you okay?"

My voice cracks as I rush to answer. "Grandma, I called but you didn't answer." I lift the shawl. "You forgot this at home."

Grandma's mouth falls open in a silent O. She shakes her head, slowly, taking a moment before finally speaking. "You . . . you didn't have to bring it to me."

"I know how important it is for Mrs. Reynolds to have this tonight," I say, tamping down my annoyance because I doubt it's actually important at all. "You probably stayed up half the night working on it."

I look to Brittany and she smiles awkwardly, her eyes darting around the room. She looks like she can't wait to get out of here. I wipe off the sweat that's started to pool on the back of my neck.

The double doors we came in from flip open as the man from before walks in, sheets and pillowcases piled so high in his arms we can barely see his face.

"Carmen, toma esto. Necesitas—"

"Ya sé," Grandma replies quickly. She moves around us to take the load out of the man's hands. She sets it on the countertop beside her just as a timer dings. "¡Aaay!" Grandma rushes to the oven, turning it off. She grabs the mitts off the handle and opens it, inspecting the large ham inside before waving her hand in front, letting some of the heat out.

My mouth dries as I watch my grandma struggle trying to do everything at once. In this heat. At her age.

"Gracias, I mean, thank you, Julio." Grandma nods at Julio and he leaves.

Grandma keeps her eyes on the ham as she closes the oven.

Brittany pulls her hair off her neck and fans herself, before wrinkling her nose at the oven. "What are you making ham for this early in the morning?"

"Mrs. Reynolds wants ham sandwiches for lunch. Her friends are coming over for their weekly game of—" Grandma stops abruptly. "It doesn't matter. Ri, put the shawl right there." She points to the countertop. "Thank you for bringing it. As you see, I'm very busy. You have to leave. Now."

Brittany takes a step backward and when I don't move, she grabs my arm. "So sorry to bother you, Mrs. Fernández. We know the way out."

"Grandma, I . . ." I don't know what to say. Grandma spends her days like this? Working so hard, moving so fast, from early in the morning and sometimes late into the night? Grandma finally meets my eye. Her forehead is sweating. I'm sweating too. It's so hot in here.

"I will see you at home, Ri."

I follow Brittany out and it's several moments into the drive to school before Brittany or I say anything.

"Well, that was weird," Brittany offers.

I flinch. *Weird*. That's what Brittany would call it. But for me, seeing Grandma—a little old lady—work so hard like that, like she must every day . . . I don't have words for it. So I just repeat Brittany's.

"Yeah. Weird."

We make it to school just before the bell rings, and I plop down into my seat next to Carlos without a word.

"What's got your panties in a twist this morning?"

"Got in a fight with my grandma," I lie.

Carlos nods. "Aah, well. I'm sure it'll blow over."

That's it. He doesn't ask me what happened or say anything else before he resumes scrolling on his phone. And I'm not going to tell him about how I just saw my grandma sweating and rushed and stressed, and the way seeing her like that has me feeling guilty. How all I can think about is Grandma hunched over an oven, knowing that work is why her back hurts so much.

Every time I thought about Grandma before, I saw red. But how can I hate her now that I've seen what most of her days are like?

Because that life of hard work is what she *sacrifices* for me. And all I can do is argue with her about everything.

Class, the one I tell my grandma how well I'm doing in, goes by in a whirl, plenty of fast talking and *r*-rolling that just makes me feel even more like an idiot. A fake. I can't roll a stupid *r* to save my life. I'm going to bomb that test tomorrow.

The classroom starts to empty around us after the bell rings. I bristle when Carlos puts his arm around me, and Edgar seems to notice, watching from his seat. Quickly, I explain myself. "Uggh, sorry, just anxious about that test. I've barely cracked the book open outside of class."

"Don't worry so much," Carlos says. "Haven't we all been speaking it our whole lives? What's the big deal about writing down a few sentences the way Señora Almanza wants us to? This test will be easy, but if you want to study so bad, I got you next time."

"I can study tonight," Edgar says. "I can meet you about an hour after school ends, if that's cool with you."

Carlos clears his throat. "Nah, güey. I *need* you for this thing. I was hoping we could hang out after school."

Edgar looks at his friend for a second, then shakes his head slightly, before taking in Carlos's expression—I'm guessing. I can't see Carlos's face because he's turned his back toward me.

"Okaaaaaay," Edgar says slowly, as if he's still not sure what Carlos is talking about. "Sorry, Ri. Listen, you'll be fine tomorrow. I can send you my notes if you—"

But I don't hear the rest of what Edgar says because my ears are pounding. Confused. Embarrassed. Annoyed. Carlos can't ever make the time to hang out with me but is seemingly jealous enough to want to be the *only* guy I spend time with one on one. It's like he's into me one second but then acts like I barely exist the next.

And that's just the half of it. This test isn't a big deal to anyone but me, and I don't need to make myself look even more pathetic than I am by worrying about it in front of them.

"I'm good," I say much more brightly than I'm feeling. "Thanks, though!"

The end of the day can't come fast enough. At my locker, after the final bell with Brittany, I tell her for the third time that I don't want to talk about what's bothering me.

"I know it was awkward with your grandma earlier, but I'm sure she's not going to be that mad at you for dropping in on her like that. You were trying to help." Brittany rests her hand on my open locker door. "She was just busy."

That's what she thinks is bothering me?

I shove my books in my locker. "That's not even the point. It was just . . ." I nod for Brittany to move her hand so I can shut the door. I hold the locker for a second, paralyzed because I don't know what I want to say. It's more that if it weren't for me, Grandma probably wouldn't have to work half as hard. But would Brittany even be able to understand that?

"I'm walking home."

Brittany looks as if she's going to argue but then I give her a look. *Not today.*

Her shoulders sink in. "If you're sure."

"I'm sure. See you tomorrow."

Chapter
TEN

Today is test day in Spanish class and I'm staring at my exam, as though the harder I look the more likely it will make sense. The words start to blur and blend together the longer I look. I scrub out my poorly written answer.

Carlos looks in my direction and smiles. I've felt uneasy around him since yesterday. It's not that I can't study on my own, but it feels like he should want to spend time with me—if he actually likes me, that is. I snap my eyes back to my paper, filling in the last of the question-and-answer section and moving to the multiple choice. I know some of this stuff, maybe even more than I thought I would, but at times it's like the information is on the tip of my tongue—words I know but can't remember.

When the bell rings and Señora Almanza tells us to hand in our tests, I quickly fill in the last bubble on mine and march it up to her, like it was easy, like I could do this stuff in my sleep. When I turn back to my desk, Nina catches my eye and grins. I flush. I still don't know how to be around her.

I'm walking out of the classroom, hoisting my backpack up

as I go, when I hear someone's footsteps thudding on the floor behind me.

"Ri, what's the hurry? Wait up!" Carlos claps his hand on my shoulder. I slow my pace but don't say anything. I'm not feeling the cool-girl vibes I usually try to throw Carlos's way.

I stop once I reach Brittany at her locker. "Hey."

Brittany smiles at me. I told her about my meeting with my mom earlier—what I learned about my grandma—and she was supportive, promising she'd do anything she could to help, like giving me a ride or covering for me with Grandma, if ever needed.

"Hey, Ri, Carlos!" Brittany greets us, her voice an octave higher than normal. Carlos nods at her before he turns to me.

"Can we talk?"

Around us, people shut their lockers and head to class.

I nod at Brittany. "Go ahead. I'll see you later."

Although I haven't said anything to Brittany about how I'm feeling, she gives Carlos a *Don't do anything I'll make you regret* kind of look. Once she walks away, my heart starts to pound. I let Carlos take my hand when he reaches for it.

I follow him through the hallway and out a set of double doors that lead outside behind the school. Our feet crunch the gravel beneath them until we hit a patch of grass. Carlos takes me to the edge of the lawn, and we stop under a great eucalyptus tree, its thick branches providing shade as the leaves rustle in the wind.

He takes his sweater off and sets it on the ground, gesturing for me to sit. He joins me. "What's up with you?"

"Nothing."

He looks at me with those deep brown eyes skeptically. He's not buying it.

I stare at his muscled arms, his smooth skin that I want to touch. "I just . . . it's stupid. But I thought things were going good. I thought . . . ," I stammer, "the other day, when you walked me home . . ." I trail off and push my lips together.

Carlos's fingertips stroke my cheek and I shiver. "That's what this is about?" His full lips turn up. "It *is* going good. I had to go. I told you I had to meet someone. I'm just not trying to rush into—"

I try to pull away, but he holds me still, gentle but firm. So instead I look down at my hands. "Me either! I'm all about seeing how things go, but sometimes it feels like you want to hang out, and other times it's like . . ." I stop myself because there is no way I can finish that sentence without sounding like a needy psycho. We're not even together.

Carlos leans in, pushing his lips against mine. His hand moves from my face to my back and pulls me closer into his chest. His warm lips are soft. And I'm light and dizzy, lost in all the feeling.

Like before, Carlos's lips travel to my neck, and his hand wraps itself in my hair. I lose all thoughts other than this moment. I go deeper into the kiss, find myself in his lap, my jeans rubbing against his.

He pulls away suddenly. Gently but quickly lifts me off

his lap and sets me back on the ground beside him. He laughs softly.

Carlos's voice is husky. "This is good"—he clears his throat—"but not here."

I wet my lips, chapped and raw from kissing him.

"If there was any question that I like you before, I hope that clears it up." Carlos's eyes sparkle at me.

And I smile.

"Carlos kissed me," I tell Brittany as she drives me home later. She stops the car at the red light and turns to gawk at me. Brittany pushes my shoulder softly and laughs. "What? When?"

I lean back into the tan leather seat. "Once when he walked me home the other day, and again at school when we were outside," I say. "He's a really, really good kisser," I add wistfully.

Brittany coughs out a laugh as the light turns green. "I'm sure he is." She doesn't say anything as she pulls onto my street.

I look out the window, at our little home, the dying grass out front and the cracked sidewalk. I turn back to Brittany. She's quiet, as though she's waiting for me to say more.

"When I'm with Carlos, everything's more fun and exciting."

"So, you're serious about him?"

I pause for a second, weighing my thoughts. "I really like how I feel when I'm with him. So, yeah. I think I'm ready to go all the way. I want to know what it's like, with him."

Brittany's eyes widen so much it's almost comical. "He's the one you want to lose your virginity to?"

I laugh. "When you put it like that, it sounds like I'm giving him my virtue or something." *Although that's probably how Grandma would see it.* I am definitely not taking cues on what to do about my sex life from her.

Brittany chuckles, but it sounds forced.

"I don't feel like my virginity is something I have to hold on to or protect or anything. I just didn't want to do it before. Things were okay with Eric, but every time he tried to go there with me, I just kind of closed up." I glance at Brittany—she's leaning forward, hanging on to my every word. "I couldn't shut my brain off. I worried about a million things . . ." *Like getting pregnant, becoming a teen mom like my mother.*

"But with Carlos, when he's kissing me, my head isn't in a bunch of other places. It's there, in the moment with him. And I like that." I shrug. "I'm ready."

Brittany leans back. She smooths an already perfect sheet of her light brown hair out of her face, seemingly taking her time with a response. "Well, I'm not one to discourage a good time, but . . ."

My jaw tenses.

"It just seems like Carlos is . . ."

"Like Carlos is *what* exactly?" My face is hot, my fists clenched. "I told you I like him, Brittany. You don't have to, but I do."

Brittany's face blanches. "Right, right," she hurries. "I get it, I mean I get that you like him, just sex for the first time . . .

I just feel like the person should be—"

I scoff. Brittany lost her v-card in the back seat of Troy Danton's car freshman year.

"*Special?* Don't tell me you're going to say special, because—"

"No, I mean, yes. I *did* really like Troy, but I wish—"

"I *really* like Carlos."

"Right. I know that, but what I mean is, I really wanted him to like me so I . . ." Brittany trails off.

"You think I'm considering having sex with Carlos to get him to like me?" I scowl. "That's a great vote of confidence from my best friend."

Brittany shakes her head quickly. "No, that's not what I'm saying. What I'm trying to say is—" She stops talking when she gets another look at me. Brittany nods. "Right, it's your choice. What do I know? My first was in a smelly car with a guy who wasn't over his ex. Who would want to take my advice? Look, I'm sorry. I shouldn't have said anything."

I take in Brittany's pained expression. She overstepped, but I don't want to fight with her.

I clear my throat. "So, ready to go in? You have your running stuff, right?"

Brittany grabs her bag from the back seat.

In my room, as I wait for Brittany to finish changing into her running clothes, I check my phone. There's a text from Mom.

Can I see you again this Friday? I haven't stopped thinking about you, not ever.

But now especially.

Without a moment's thought, I text back, I can't wait.

In Spanish class the next day, Carlos drapes his arm around my shoulder when we walk in together. Miguel nods at me, while Nina's eyes focus on Carlos with what looks like annoyance. Cassie's staring too. No surprise there, since she's Carlos's ex-*something*.

Edgar walks in after we sit. His eyes linger on Carlos's arm, which is still around me. "Ri, how'd the test go?"

"It was a test." Like I'm going to tell him that I probably bombed the thing.

He waits to see if I say anything else, and when I don't, he turns to sit.

I realize I'm being kind of a jerk, so I smile. "Thanks for asking, though. Hopefully we can study together next time." I nod at his camera, hanging off his shoulder. "How'd the pictures go at your cousin's basketball game, by the way? You mentioned you were going to be at the middle school a while back. I never thought to ask."

Edgar grins. "Good memory. It was great." He puts his camera on his desk. "I've been editing the pictures after school and should have them ready to post online soon, if you want to check them out."

"Will do." I nod enthusiastically. "I was looking at some of the pictures on your feed the other day. You're really talented."

Edgar beams. "Thanks! I definitely could use more practice,

though, to get to the level of skill I want to be at."

From behind me, I feel someone leaning forward, so I turn. It's Nina, looking at me. "Do you want to sit with us at lunch tomorrow?" she asks.

"Hey, yeah," Edgar says to me. "You should."

I feel Carlos's arm twitch for a second, but he doesn't say anything, like how I should sit with them.

I flush. "Sure."

Before anyone can respond, Señora Almanza walks in. Carlos takes his arm back. I feel the absence of it as Señora Almanza starts reading sentences from the page we're on in the book.

"Ella lo quiso."

The class erupts in laughter, particularly Miguel and Jorge behind me.

Señora Almanza raises an eyebrow, gives the class a look that says, *Real mature.*

Not that she can blame everyone. *She wanted it.* I mean, *really?* At least it's not as bad as last week, when Señora Almanza had Carlos read, "Sus labios húmedos," and the guys behind us busted up laughing. Carlos winked at me. *Her lips are wet.* Yes, *I get it, Carlos,* I thought, half annoyed at his immaturity. But I couldn't pay attention to what Señora Almanza was saying for the rest of the class period.

"Maria," Señora Almanza says to me, role-playing the situation out of the textbook, that she is a waiter and is asking me, a diner at a restaurant, if I'm ready to order. "Buenos días. ¿Qué le gustaría ordenar?"

I read back the response, quickly and quietly, "Buenos días. ¿Me puede mostrar el menú primero, por favor?

Out of the corner of my eye I think I see Carlos snicker under his breath. I thought my pronunciation was okay, but it seems like he's laughing at me. I keep my eyes glued to my book for the rest of the hour.

When the bells rings, I nearly run to my locker. I try to make myself forget about Carlos laughing. Maybe I was imagining things, letting my insecurity get to me. The way to fix that is to just act normal. And things are looking up. Nina invited me to lunch, after all. She didn't need to do that.

Brittany approaches and I start talking immediately. "Nina asked me to sit with her and Carlos and them at lunch tomorrow." I watch my best friend for a response, feeling uneasy.

Brittany doesn't look at me right away. Instead, she fixes a piece of her hair in the mirror inside her locker.

As an afterthought, I add, "You should come too."

Brittany visibly swallows before closing her locker and smiling. "Um, you know, I think I'll just sit with Finn and the guys tomorrow. He gave me a standing lunch invitation a while back."

"Okay," I say, mulling that over. Brittany never told me Finn said that. Normally she'd be gushing over that kind of thing for days.

Neither of us say anything as we head out to the parking lot together, our silence stretching between us.

I bring a sandwich to school for lunch the next day and sit at a picnic table on campus with Nina, Carlos, and Cassie. Miguel and Edgar sit on the grass next to the bench, leaning against their backpacks.

Carlos has his eyes glued to his phone, texting nonstop, and Cassie's giving him some serious side-eye. He stands and says, "I'll see you guys later," before walking away. My turkey sandwich suddenly tastes like cardboard.

After taking a bite of the tamale she brought from home, Cassie says, "So, Ri, I have a really important question for you."

I force my eyes away from Carlos as he walks away and steel myself.

"Are you on *Animal Crossing*? Edgar acts like he's too good for it so we're clearly looking for someone to replace him." Cassie smiles.

I exhale out a laugh. "Oh, um, I guess I don't play video games much."

Cassie looks at Nina and then back at me. "We're going to have to change that."

Nina nods faux solemnly. "For real."

Edgar laughs from the grass across from me. "Whatever, you guys are such dorks."

Miguel pipes in. "You know you love getting in on some *Call of Duty* action whenever you come over to my place!"

I dig into my sandwich, feeling much more at ease. Cassie takes a sip from her water bottle before looking at me. "Ri, have I told you I'm going to have a party? It's going to be on Halloween, but no costumes or decorations or anything, because who's got the time for all that? You should come."

My stomach feels warm and tingly. At first, I figured Cassie wouldn't like me because of whatever history she had with Carlos. But she's been nothing but nice to me. I smile big as I answer her. "Yeah, I would love to."

When Friday comes, I head to the library after school. Mom suggested we meet there, rather than at the beach. She chose the branch that's not closest to my house to make it more likely that no one Grandma knows will see us. This library is just off of State, the main street of Santa Barbara that bustles with tourists spending too much money at fancy boutiques and restaurants. Walking past, I imagine Mom and me shopping together like Brittany and her mom do. But then again, Mom being in my life or not, I doubt we'd have that kind of money very often.

Inside, I walk around a bit. I'm here early, so I might as well. The computer banks are occupied by a couple of homeless men, one who oddly looks like a pirate with his eye patch and mane full of red, unruly hair. I smile at the librarian and continue forward, my shoes sinking into the worn carpet as I head toward some tables in the back.

I sit with my bag next to me and peer down at the worn wood's inscription. *Theresa was here*, it says. Stupid as it is, I consider taking out a pen and writing my name.

I look around again, at all the strangers around me. I don't know any of them, and they don't know me. No one would know I was here, unless I wrote my name on the wood too. Slowly my stomach sinks as anxiety starts to pulse through me. Mom is little more than a stranger to me, even though it's not her fault. She wanted to be in my life, to really know me. But Grandma wouldn't let her.

And now that I know the truth, it's like I don't know Grandma. And Grandma doesn't know me either. She only sees what she wants to see. She and Grandpa both had dreams of their daughter going to college and being successful, like becoming a doctor or an engineer. But Mom let them down, and now Grandma wants the same kind of thing for me. It's like I have to make everything she's done worth it, no matter what I want.

Surrounded by strangers. I feel so alone.

At least I have Brittany, I remind myself. She's like family. She's not perfect, but she tries.

My stomach wiggles, and the feeling is getting all too familiar. Does Brittany try, like *really* try? Because she didn't sit with me and Nina and all of them at lunch. Not that I particularly wanted her to, because that probably would have been awkward. But she could have at least pretended to consider the idea.

It's obvious Brittany doesn't like Carlos. But does that extend to Nina, Edgar, and the rest of them too? I remember what Carlos said about Brittany when we walked home together the first time: Brittany wants to put me in a box. But then there's Carlos, who seems to want this down-for-whatever, fun girl, and even though I really want to be her, that's not *me* either.

Edgar's face flashes to mind, unbidden, unexpected. How he looks at me when I talk. His watchful eye when Carlos says something that makes me question myself. How he tries to get along with Brittany and even Finn when he's there too.

My chest tightens as I remember that Edgar has been my locker neighbor for a while, but I never thought of him as a friend. I never tried to be his. After Nina and I stopped talking, I stopped paying attention to most people at school except the ones that Brittany was friends with and that meant, inadvertently, never being around anyone who shared my culture.

I went along with Brittany for everything. Who knows what offensive shit she's said in the past that completely went over my head until recently. I've probably laughed at jokes people made that I wouldn't deny were just plain racist now. They were talking about me, too; I just refused to see it. And they did too, because I'm white-passing.

A wave of nausea washes over me.

It's not just Brittany who's the problem. So am I.

I glance at my phone. Mom's still not here and won't be for maybe another twenty minutes. I take out my journal and write a few of the things I'm thinking. Not all of it, not when I'm here at the public library. But I feel like I have to put some of this on paper, so I'm not tempted to ignore it later. I can't hide the truth about how I've been acting anymore. By the time I'm done, my wrist aches. I have to not only face how I've been complicit but, more importantly, I also have to do better. I have to *be* better.

That's all I can do for now. Resolve to change.

I take a deep breath and pull out my Spanish book, workbook, and a couple of pencils. One for me, one for Mom.

Out of the corner of my eye, I see her walking toward me, her curly hair swinging around her face as she hurries. Mom's jeans sag off her hips, and her shirt is short and loose enough that I can see part of her stomach and hip bone. She doesn't seem to notice the way the librarian's eyes watch her warily as she approaches. I swallow, but then Mom's smile makes my unease fade as she leans in and embraces me. I cough a bit at the smell of cigarettes.

Mom pulls away and scurries over to the other side of the table to sit. "I'm so glad to see you, Maria."

"Me too, Mom."

She beams.

"I go by Ri now, by the way," I add. "I have for a long time." Since sometime after she left, that's been my nickname. Nina is the one who gave it to me, actually.

Mom nods. "Got it. Reeeee"—she draws the sound out with a grin—"it is."

I smile tentatively, trying to forget about the thoughts of being a stranger to everyone in my life, because I have a chance here, with Mom, to change that.

I pass her a pencil. Open the Spanish book to the section we're studying in class, and then my workbook to the homework assignment. I push the book toward her and tilt it so she can see. "These are some of the vocabulary words we're working on. Quise, toqué, hablé, comí, dormí, vi, dije." I watch Mom's expression as I pronounce the words badly. I know I don't sound like Señora Almanza or Grandma would. But Mom's face remains blank.

She grabs the book and pulls it closer. "I'll read them, and you translate. I'll tell you if it's right or wrong, or help you get the answer, and you write it down. Sound good?" She reads, "¿Qué viste en las noticias?"

I close my eyes. "What did you see on the news?"

Mom grins as I peek at her. "Very good, mija!" She pushes my workbook toward me. "Write."

I smile at the word *mija* and write the translation. We move on to the next question. "Yo toqué el gato," she reads, her voice making the words sound so fluid, so natural.

"I touch the cat," I say.

Mom tilts her head at me.

"I mean, I *touched* the cat. That was past tense, right?"

Mom nods. She flips the page to another section. "Okay, now how about you read one?"

I hesitate.

Mom's deep brown eyes hold my gaze, unfaltering. "It's okay, I'm here to help," she says.

I pull the book closer and read the words in my head. I know how they *should* sound. And sometimes, when I'm practicing alone, I can almost speak like Grandma or our neighbors. But when I'm around other people, I get nervous and I choke. It feels like I'm terrible at something that should come naturally, like

I'm an imposter and it's only a matter of time before everyone in class and—it's hard to admit this part—even Mom realizes it and laughs at me. Feeling frustrated and like we've covered enough of this part anyway, I flip to another section of the book.

"¿Tienes familia?" I ask.

Mom nods for me to read the answer from the book.

"Tengo una familia grande," I say.

"Very good!" she exclaims. "What does it mean?"

"It asked if I have a family." I point to the question box that has the words and an illustration. "And I answered 'I have a big family' like it says over here." I point to the answer box.

Mom smiles at me and nods.

I look down. I don't have a big family. For years, all I've had is Grandma. And now, in this moment with my mom, all I can think about is the time we've lost.

Mom must read my expression. She tilts my chin up. "What's wrong, baby?"

I stare at the book in front of me, but don't read a word. "I've really missed you is all."

Mom lets my chin go and leans toward me. "I've missed you so much, you have no idea. So, so much."

And here, with Mom, feeling emotional and out of sorts, I blurt out the words I've been afraid to say, to even think.

"Not like I've missed you, because if you had, you would have come. Whether you were afraid of Grandma or not, you would have come."

Mom inhales audibly. I brave a glance up to see my mother's lip quivering. "Baby, I know. You can't help but feel abandoned."

Mom looks at me straight in the eye and without blinking she says, "I will do whatever I can to prove to you how much, to show you how much I love you."

I take a deep breath and exhale slowly. I smile at my mom. "I love you too."

I laugh softly and look around to make sure no one is paying attention to us. The other library visitors go about their business, typing and reading as though everything is normal. For them, it might be, but here at this table, I'm with my mom. Something I've wished for and dreamed of for years. I don't want to waste our time together mourning the past. I close the book. "I think that's enough studying for today. But, um, we can do something else . . . if you want to?"

Mom perks up in her seat. "Do you want some ice cream? You used to love rocky road. Do you still?" Mom's eyes are wide and hopeful.

"My favorite." I don't even remember liking rocky road, but I must have been a toddler, if my mom is remembering it. Chocolate is my favorite now.

"I have some money." She grins. "We can go to Rite Aid and get a double scoop!"

"That would be great, Mom."

I pack up my bag, and we walk out of the library together.

As we stroll down State Street, I think about how normal

this could feel. How normal I *wish* this felt. Walking around with Mom after studying, about to get ice cream, no one around giving us a second glance. We're just a mother and daughter hanging out after school. This could have been my life. I shake my head. I don't want to go down that rabbit hole again, at least not today. Now I'm with my mom, and we're having fun.

Mom pushes the door to Rite Aid open and the bell tings, letting the clerk inside know he has customers. We head for the ice cream counter.

"Hello, lovely ladies!" the elderly man says. "What can I get for you?"

"Two double scoop rocky roads, please." Mom claps her hands together with excitement.

"Cone or cup?"

"Cone! Cone for sure, right, mija?" Mom looks down at me hopefully.

"I love cones."

The man scoops up the first cone and hands it to Mom, who quickly gives it to me. And then he serves her the second. We follow the man to the register and Mom opens her wallet and pays.

Seeing her grin as she watches me eat my ice cream, I feel a pang in my chest. Maybe with time, this won't feel so strange. We'll be a normal, regular, happy family.

Mom and me.

Chapter

ELEVEN

Señora Almanza tells us that we have an oral presentation next Wednesday. Things have been going better in class because I've been seeing Mom once a week at the library to study for Spanish, but most of it is written stuff with the occasional rehearsed answer.

An oral presentation means that Señora Almanza is going to ask each of us different questions from the unit we're studying, like usual, and she'll call on us at random, in Spanish, like usual. And we're to answer in Spanish, like usual. Except this time, we're supposed to stand in front of the entire class and hold a conversation. We'll be graded for accuracy and delivery. And with all eyes on me, everyone will really see how bad I am at this.

Finally, the bell rings and the panic in my chest starts to creep down into my stomach, a cold, slimy kind of fear. I look at Carlos to get his attention. Since we've been *seeing each other*—which is how I decide to categorize what we're doing in my head, anyway—Carlos hasn't asked me on a date or shown interest in defining our relationship. And I won't drop any hints about it—wouldn't want to scare him off.

I don't want to seem needy either, so when he doesn't look up from his phone, I turn to Edgar. "Study buddies?"

"Sounds good to me."

On my other side, Carlos perks up. "I could do Saturday afternoon."

"Awesome," I say. "Want to do it at my place?"

Edgar stands and reaches for his backpack. "That works. Can you text me your address?" He takes his phone out of his pocket.

Carlos stands. "You can just come with me. I know where she lives." Carlos grins with bravado, his meaning crystal clear.

Edgar reaches for my hand. I jump before realizing that he's grabbing for my phone. I swallow. Edgar quickly saves his number and hands it back to me. "Just in case." He nods at Carlos. "See you later."

Carlos puts his arm around me as Edgar walks out the door. "What's his hurry?" I ask.

Carlos shrugs and leans in to whisper into my ear. "After he leaves Saturday, I don't have to." His lips graze my earlobe, his warm breath tickling it.

I'm light-headed, high with excitement, and giggle like an idiot. "That would be great."

Friday after school, Carlos walks me home like he usually does now. Outside my doorstep, I lean into him and kiss him deeply. Then, before he can get any ideas, I pull away and watch his eyes go dazed as I quickly twist my key into the lock and open the door behind me. "See you tomorrow!" I call cheerfully. Leaving him outside.

I lean my back against the closed door and smile. It feels good to be the one to make him wait.

Grandma is working late again. About a half hour after the door clangs shut, announcing her return, she calls me from my room to join her in the kitchen.

The smell of warm chocolate fills my nostrils once I'm in the hallway. Grandma's been baking.

She sets the pan of chocolate brownies on the counter to cool. "For your girlfriends tomorrow, when you're studying."

Making these is probably her way of sucking up since I've been giving her the cold shoulder. Seeing Mom in secret, getting to know her, has made me feel closer to my past, but more distant from Grandma at home . . . but that's Grandma's fault. It's not like I can forget what she did to Mom.

Her offering softens me, though, so I'll make a stab at conversation. "Thanks, Grandma." I shuffle from foot to foot. I didn't tell her I'd be studying with girls, but I'm not going to correct her. "How was work today?"

"Work is work," Grandma replies, smoothing her hands over her apron before she takes it off. Neither of us have brought up when I dropped off the shawl, and it feels like Grandma prefers it that way.

Guilt slinks down in my belly. Seeing her sweat in a hot

kitchen, cooking and cleaning and working nonstop, for us. For me.

"Grandma," I begin, "I know your job is hard."

Grandma looks at me, her lips pursed.

I blink several times. "I . . . I know you work long hours."

Grandma appraises me with a stern look. "Yes, I do. So I expect you to work hard too." She sits at the table. "How was school?"

"School is school."

Grandma gives me an annoyed look.

"I like being in Spanish class," I offer as I sit across from her. "I'm making some new friends."

"That is a positive."

"Well, not all of them are new. You remember Nina? She's in Spanish, and it's been great getting to hang out with her again."

Grandma's eyebrows shoot up. "Oh? I thought . . ."

I stare at her. "What is it?"

Grandma shrugs, averting her eyes. "I thought you two found other friends." She looks back at me. "I hope Nina is staying out of trouble."

My eyes narrow. Nina was never *trouble* when we hung out. We rode our bikes, braided each other's hair while we watched movies, strolled around the Art Walk, and hung out at the park with some other neighborhood kids. Those are the kinds of things we did together.

My words come out cool and menacing. "Nina's great. She always has been. I'm really happy we're friends again."

Grandma stands and makes her way to the kitchen. She pours a glass of orange juice and sets it in front of me, though I didn't ask for it, before busying herself in the kitchen making decaf coffee.

"Well, as long as these new friends don't keep you from paying attention in Spanish class. You promised to keep your grades up, remember?"

I lift my eyes to the ceiling in frustration. "Yes, Grandma, I remember."

The coffee maker beeps, and Grandma grabs a mug from the cupboard. "You need excellent grades so that when you apply to Yale, Harvard, and Stanford, along with the other good universities, they will accept you."

Not this again.

"I am not going to get into Yale or Harvard or Stanford, even if I wanted to, which I don't! I want to go to UCSB, where they have a good writing program and in-state tuition." I pause and lower my voice. "I can even live at home and save money."

Grandma's eyebrows furrow into a deep V. "But UCSB—"

"Is a good school, Grandma! And I don't want to be a doctor or an engineer or follow whatever grand life plan for me you have. Why can't you give me a chance?"

Grandma's face falls as she watches me struggle to catch my breath.

My eyes prickle but I don't want to cry, so instead I glare in the other direction.

"You know, I had dreams once. I didn't always think I'd be an assistant."

I blink several times, tear my gaze from the wall and bring it back to Grandma.

She walks toward her knitting basket in the living room and slowly lifts a needle. "I love crafting. Not just knitting and crocheting, but other activities. Sometimes we make stained glass in Bible study—have I told you that?"

I shake my head. "You've never brought anything like that home."

Grandma waves the hand not holding the needle. "Oh, you know, I just donate it to the church thrift store, because they can sell it and use the money for the needy. I don't need to display everything I make. It's more about the act of creating."

I stare at Grandma. She likes making things. I knew about the knitting and the occasional crocheting, but I thought those were just old lady hobbies. I take a long drink of my orange juice and set the cup down before heading for the living room, Grandma's words drawing me in.

"When I was a couple of years younger than you, I learned how to weave from my grandmother. I loved it, and eventually I was able to make my own textiles. After we moved here, my dream was to own my own hobby store. One where other women like me could meet and work together, while also buying and selling our crafts. I used to visit the fabric store downtown and dream. I thought maybe I could get a job there. I wanted to learn what I could and save money to start my own shop one day . . ."

Grandma trails off and sighs, running a finger along the needle. I watch her, transfixed. She's never mentioned *her* grandma to me before.

"But God intervened, giving me a much better opportunity for me and our family. I met Mrs. Reynolds's old assistant at mass. She was looking for someone to replace her and introduced me to Mrs. Reynolds. Your grandfather and I couldn't believe our luck. The pay was so good, much better than what he made as a janitor and taking the odd furniture assembly side job. I couldn't turn it down."

Grandma sets her needle back in the basket. "So, I did the responsible thing, pushed childish dreams away for a more practical career. It isn't a fun choice to make, Ri, but the right one. When you are financially stable in a good career, then maybe you can write."

Grandma rests a hand over the yarn in her knitting basket before turning to me. "We all make sacrifices. My job is hard, you've seen that for yourself now, and I will never love it, but the work is well worth it because it allows me to take care of you."

The lump in my throat bobs as I swallow.

Grandma yawns before leaning in to kiss me on the forehead. "I love you, baby. It's late. Get some rest for tomorrow."

She pats my shoulder and walks around me, heading to her room.

Just like that, our conversation is over, and I'm alone.

Grandma's already gone to work by the time I wake up on Saturday morning, per usual. I shower and rummage through my closet, settling on a gray sweater dress and black booties, even though I'll be in my own house and there's no need to wear shoes. They make my legs look good, though.

I'm curling my hair into soft waves, applying more makeup than strictly necessary for a study session, when my phone dings. A text from Carlos.

Sorry, but something came up. I can't make it today.

I slap the phone down on the bathroom counter.

Carlos is blowing me off. Even after what he said about staying over when Edgar left. Even after the way I kissed him yesterday.

I grab my phone, considering canceling on Edgar, but my fingers don't move. I really do need the help studying. And I like Edgar. I'm comfortable around him. No need for me to bail on him like Carlos bailed on me. I stab a quick message, my address, and hit send. Edgar quickly replies. See you soon.

I pull my dress down—it has the tendency to ride up—and stomp to the kitchen, pulling out the brownies Grandma made. I set them on the table, kick off my booties, and the doorbell rings.

I open the door to see a bespectacled Edgar looking annoyed as he quickly types a message in his phone. I've never seen him wear glasses before now—they're cute. He looks sophisticated and artistic all at once.

"Thanks for coming."

I shut the door behind Edgar. He notices a few pairs of Grandma's shoes at the doorway and my socked feet. "Should I take off my shoes?"

"Only if you want. Whatever makes you comfortable."

He slips off his shoes and sets them aside, next to Grandma's on the wall. I glance at my booties, kicked off haphazardly in the middle of the living room. I grab them and set them neatly beside Edgar's.

Edgar follows me to the kitchen table. I gesture for him to sit, pushing the plate of brownies toward him. "Want some milk to go with these?"

The light from the window catches Edgar's skin, making it look bronze as he chuckles. "You didn't need to do all of this."

I widen my eyes a little impatiently, telling him to answer my question.

He nods quickly. "Milk would be great. Thanks."

He unzips his backpack as I get the milk. "How's your Multimedia project going?"

"Oh, um." I'm surprised he remembered. "It's fine, I guess. I figured out how to use the school's fancy video camera, finally."

Edgar pulls his Nikon out of his backpack and lifts it up for me to see. "You can borrow mine," he says with a smile. "I should have offered before—this baby, it's a DSLR and I have a few really good lenses, like a telephoto one, and it shoots great video—but I didn't think of it. I can show you how to use it." He pushes the camera over the wooden table to me.

I pop the lens cap off and run my finger across the rim. Shake my head. "I already took the video, actually. I'm just doing the editing now during class."

Edgar's face falls slightly. Truth is, when I shot the video, I did think about him—how talented he is. But I never thought to invite him or ask for help. Not when I was capturing a place so personal to me. The beach where I've run to think ever since Nina and I stopped being friends years ago. When I needed space from Grandma and Brittany. The place where I reunited with my mom. I won't say those words on the voice-over for my project, but I will say how important the space is for me. It's the only physical place I can truly be myself. Free of judgment. Alone.

"But if I need editing tips, you'll be the first person I ask," I add as Edgar takes a gulp of milk, and then a bite of brownie. "This looks really cool. I mean, the camera. It's nice. So are the pictures you've posted." I pause, feeling myself start to blush. "But I've already told you that."

Edgar swallows. "Thanks. Which is your favorite? Or which one were you talking about specifically?"

"All of them." My words come out in a rush. "The sunsets, the mountains, the ocean. You're super talented."

Edgar smiles wistfully at the camera. "I learned in a summer program after third grade. I've been back every year since to practice." He reaches a finger out and twists the strap around it.

"This camera seems really fancy," I say awkwardly, wanting to be nice, to get to know him better. I'm always with Carlos when Edgar's around—I never really get the chance to talk to him one on one.

"I saved my birthday money for three years for this and it still wasn't even close to being enough." Edgar chuckles and looks at his camera. "When my brother José gave me a ride to the camera store and I realized I was short, he covered the rest. He said I could pay him back when I'm a famous photographer someday."

Edgar looks down, his expression turning somber. If it's because he thinks he won't make it as a photographer, he couldn't be more wrong.

"What is it that you like about taking pictures?"

Edgar reaches his hand for the camera and rests it on the top. I don't move my hand from the lens. We lock eyes. My chest warms and I laugh softly before looking away.

Edgar looks at the camera, chewing his lip for a second. "I like the way pictures can tell a story," he finally says. "How someone who doesn't even know the photographer or the subject can see truth in a photo."

He looks up at me. "You can see something real in an instant, sometimes something you'd never be able to describe with words, you know?"

Before I get the chance to respond, Edgar brings the camera

to his face and snaps a picture of me. It happens so quickly that I don't smile or react. I wonder why he did that, why he'd want a picture of me. He turns the camera around, looks at the screen, and smiles.

"What do you see?" I ask.

Edgar's eyes flick to me and then back at the picture. "Someone who's searching for something."

My breath catches, stuck in my throat.

Edgar fumbles the camera back to the table.

I stare into Edgar's eyes for a second before lifting the camera myself and snapping a picture. I turn it around to look at his image on the screen. See Edgar with his glasses and his curly hair getting longer. The way his lips turn up and his eyes brighten when I look at him.

And now he's looking at me and I'm looking at him, and I realize it's really hot in here. I close my eyes and nod quickly. "I, uh, here. Now you have one of you." I slide the camera back toward him.

Edgar picks it up and looks at the picture briefly. "I like the one of you better." He laughs softly and looks down at the table.

I swallow, my cheeks flushed. Neither of us say anything for a moment.

"So, Spanish." I finally pull my book from the other side of the table.

"Spanish." Edgar slides his camera out of the way.

I flip through my textbook to the opening of the section we're working on in class.

"All right," Edgar says. "How about I ask some of the practice questions here, after the end of the first section we studied a few weeks ago, and you answer them."

My throat tightens. I nod.

"Oh, wait." Edgar pulls his book and a stack of notecards out of his backpack. "I made these for you." He pushes them to me.

I reach for the cards, revealing some of the words we've been working on. Salió, empezó, pidió, recibió, decidió.

"You don't need them to study? I thought you said before that . . ." I trail off, not wanting to give too much away about my lack of Spanish-speaking ability. I'd rather seem like I have test-taking anxiety. "Don't you study too? To learn it the way white people speak it?"

Edgar's hand rests on the table, about a foot from mine. He looks into my eyes, his warm and without pretense. "I don't need them. I do the worksheets and pay attention in class. My mom and aunt tutor Spanish as side jobs. They were careful that we learned the way it's taught in school, not just how we all speak it. They say it might be valuable to be able to tutor people since so many are trying to learn to be bilingual nowadays."

I blanch. I had hoped I might be able to get away with hiding my ineptitude, but that seems unlikely now if Edgar could theoretically tutor people.

Edgar's thick black eyebrows furrow. "What's wrong?" His hand twitches slightly closer to mine. "Did I say something?"

I shake my head. "You didn't. And thank you, this is nice,

since I've been so nervous. It's really nice." I nod my head again, vigorously, and stand. "I'm just going to get some water. Want some?"

Edgar grabs his milk. "I'm good here, thanks."

I hold my hand on the water pitcher in the fridge before pouring some into my glass. I take a long drink, the cold water sliding down my throat slowly, juxtaposed against my warm, embarrassed body.

I wipe my hands off on my dress and walk back to the kitchen table.

"¿Quién decidió esto?" Edgar reads from his textbook, his voice deep and fluid, his words natural.

In my mind I translate the words, "Who decided this?" I look at the pictures in the book, indicating a woman under a thought balloon in the box showing this happened in the past. I swallow, close my eyes, and blurt. "Ella lo decidió." I have this idea that if I say the words quickly, it will sound more natural, because a lot of Spanish is spoken fast. I watch Edgar, and his expression doesn't change.

"Muy bien," he says. "Nunca habíamos vivido en la ciudad. ¿Y tú?"

Quickly, I reply, "Nunca había vivido en la ciudad," the syllables blurring on their way out of my mouth.

Edgar smiles. "Relax. It's just me here."

Who was I kidding? It only took Edgar a couple of minutes to notice.

"I'm really not good at speaking Spanish," I finally admit. My eyes are glued to my hands, sweating in my lap. "My grandparents didn't teach me. They always focused so much on fitting in." Shame floods through my body. I've never said these words out loud—not like this, to someone with my heritage, anyway.

"We know a lot of people who don't speak Spanish," Edgar says. "Especially people who are older than us, since it's kind of a generational thing for immigrants' kids. They were trying to assimilate. And you know, for families who have been here forever too. Not everyone learns it and that's totally normal."

I raise my eyes to his. I want to believe him so badly. Even if some people I know don't speak Spanish either, I assume it's likely that their families don't push them towards whiteness the way Grandma does with me. They know they're part of our community. Unlike me.

He shrugs. "You're learning Spanish now."

I exhale, long and heavy. I'm afraid that if the others in class found out all about me and how I was raised, would they agree with Grandma? That I'm not Mexican. Not like her or them. Or Mom.

Edgar's still looking at me, with a reassuring smile, his face void of judgment.

"I can understand some," I tell him, "especially now that I'm hearing it spoken regularly again. It's just speaking it's hard. Especially in front of people our age, who are fluent. Like in class."

Edgar looks down at the book. "Like Carlos?" His glasses slip down his long nose, and he pushes them back up with his index finger.

I blink. Not liking the way Edgar won't meet my eye all of a sudden. "Everyone. Carlos, Miguel, Nina . . ."

Edgar looks back at me. "You must have never watched any of them give a speech in class. You'll see that everyone has a different relationship with Spanish and it's okay."

I sigh. He's right. I *am* learning now, but even if I weren't, wouldn't that be okay too? If Edgar didn't speak Spanish, I wouldn't think any less of him. So why can't I give that same treatment to myself? I want to. I really do.

He grabs the textbook in front of him and pulls it onto his lap. "And even if people speak Spanish, they can still get nervous giving speeches in front of everyone. That's pretty much a universal fear. So, if your accent or delivery or whatever isn't perfect, no one is going to pay that much attention to it. It'll probably just seem like you're nervous being in front of a bunch of people."

Relief floods through me as Edgar flips to another page in the book. With not so much as a pause, he reads the next question—"¿Que quieres beber durante la fiesta?" in Spanish and I answer in Spanish "Quiero beber muchas cervezas," and we both laugh and go on like it's no big deal.

Chapter

TWELVE

The morning of oral presentations, the knot in my stomach twists and eventually starts to gurgle.

As if reading my thoughts, Edgar leans close so only I can hear him whisper. "You got this."

Carlos smiles at me and looks surprised at the glare I give him. I never responded to his text about not coming to study and haven't talked to him since. He faces forward, his legs splayed wide, taking up his space and some of mine.

Señora Almanza calls on Nina first. Nina drags her feet to the front of the room, and her eyes dart around until they land on mine.

Nina keeps looking at me and I can't look away. Does she get nervous speaking in front of the class? When I hung out with Nina at her house years ago, everyone in her family spoke Spanglish, so I thought this would be easy for her. But when Nina answers Señora Almanza's questions, she fumbles on a couple of words.

I keep eye contact with her and smile. Like I'm encouraging

her. Like it's just us in the classroom. She finishes her answers quickly.

"Muy bien," Señora Almanza says. Nina shoots me a grateful look before returning to her seat. "Good job," I whisper, and she smiles at me.

Carlos goes next, his speaking fluid and assured, and then Señora Almanza calls on me.

I stand and face the class, grasping my sweaty hands together in front of me to keep them from shaking. Jorge whispers something to Miguel and laughs. Miguel doesn't. My whole body tenses.

Nina looks right at me and nods reassuringly.

I hear Edgar's words echo in my head. *You got this.*

Señora Almanza repeats the same question she asked Nina and Carlos. "¿Qué te gustaría hacer este fin de semana?"

The answer tumbles out of my mouth fast. Señora Almanza gestures for me to try again. "Habla despacio, por favor."

I take a deep breath, glance at Edgar and then back to Nina, before repeating my answer slowly. "Este fin de semana, si es posible, quiero ir al cine." I don't actually go to the movies that often, but it's the first thing that pops into my head. I know I don't sound natural like Nina and Carlos. Señora Almanza asks me another question, and I answer as slowly and calmly as I can, praying my voice isn't shaking. I feel sweat pooling at my hairline, but I don't want to draw attention to it by wiping my face. I keep my eyes trained on Nina as I'm asked a couple more questions, and I answer.

And then it's over; Señora Almanza says, "Muy bien," mercifully.

I lunge toward my desk, practically falling back into my seat. "You did good, Ri," Edgar says.

I wipe my slick hands on my jeans. "Thanks," I breathe. In and out. It's over.

The bell rings and Edgar and Carlos walk with me out of class. Carlos wraps his arm around my waist. "I didn't know you don't speak Spanish. Now I see why you wanted to study so much."

I look down at my feet as my cheeks burn, despite myself.

Edgar keeps pace with us. "I bet she did better than you did, since she spoke it by the book. And no one asked you, Carlos."

Carlos laughs. "Touchy, touchy." He pulls me in closer to him, and though I'm angry, I let him.

Edgar looks at me for a second but then seems to ease up. He shakes his head and chuckles at Carlos, who is still grinning.

Don Abrams and Nate Sanders walk toward us. Carlos takes his arm off me, and I try not to visibly react.

"Hey, Carlos, now that you're not on the team, you too busy for us?" Don asks with a smile.

"Nah, man. I was too busy for you *then*. I just couldn't admit it, otherwise you'd never hand off the ball!" Carlos chuckles as he mimes catching a football and running away with it.

Nate laughs and pats Carlos's back. "So, we'll see you later, at—?"

Carlos cuts him off. "Yeah, I'll be there."

Carlos grabs my hand and pulls me in the direction of my locker. Edgar, who looks annoyed, mumbles he'll see us later, before he walks away.

Stung from Carlos not acknowledging me, I start to ask, "What was that ab—"

Carlos interrupts me. "So, there's a party coming up at Cassie's house next weekend. Wanna come?"

I open my locker and switch out my Spanish stuff for what I need for my next class. "I know. She already invited me."

Carlos gives a half smile. "Well, look at that, you're already Miss Popular."

He looks me up and down with exaggeration, before leaning in close, whispering into my ear. "Wear something sexy for me."

I watch him walk away, flustered by my boomerang emotions. Passing by him, Nina strides toward me. "Thank God that presentation is over," Nina says. "I hate having to stand in front of the whole class and have everyone watching me."

I nod vigorously. "Me too. And . . ." I hesitate, but since Nina already knows, I might as well. "Well, it's hard for me especially. You remember how my grandma is? Never wanting me to learn Spanish."

Nina's expression darkens. "I remember your grandma."

Something about the way Nina says *grandma* makes me pause. Her not teaching me Spanish is ridiculous, but not enough to warrant such a strong response. But then again, Grandma is Grandma and there are a number of things she could have done to piss Nina off way back when.

I sigh. "She's tough, my grandma, now as much as ever. Lately, it's like we can't be in the same room for more than five minutes without going at it."

Nina puts her hands in her pockets. "That sucks." She rocks back on her feet for a second, uncharacteristically quiet. A moment passes and she brightens again.

"So, Cassie's party. I'm really glad you're going to come." She pauses as though thinking. "You could even invite Brittany . . . if you want."

"Invite me to what?" I flinch as Brittany's voice rings out behind me.

Nina turns to Brittany. "To Cassie's party next weekend. Her parents are going to be out of town. There'll be food, drinks, music, everything. It'll be fun."

Brittany looks from Nina to me, her lips pursed. "Uh, well, that's when Brody's having his Halloween party. I figured Ri and I would go to that one. His parties are always epic. He usually gets a few kegs, and his house has a massive yard with a firepit and a hot tub. Partying there is, like, the best."

Nina's smile fades, but I quickly jump in. "Brody's parties are tired, and anyway I'd rather try something new."

Brittany tenses beside me. "I guess we could go to Cassie's, then."

I roll my eyes and honestly, I don't even care that Brittany sees as long as Nina does. Because I don't want her to think I'm like Brittany.

"Why don't you go to Brody's?" I plaster on a fake smile. "You obviously want to, and we don't have to do everything together."

Nina chuckles, but quickly rearranges her features when Brittany's eyes dart to her, wide.

Brittany's voice comes out small. "It just . . ." She looks at Nina, visibly uncomfortable. Brittany gives a little throaty laugh and then clears her throat. "We haven't, um, spent much time together lately and Brody's parties are great, but I'd rather hang out with you."

I swallow, my chest tightening at the guilt I feel. Slightly embarrassed by Brittany's earnestness in front of Nina, I nod. "Yeah, definitely. We'll go to Cassie's together, then."

The next day, Señora Almanza hands us each printouts detailing how she graded our oral presentations, but before I can read her reasoning, my eyes focus on the grade on the top. B. I got a B!

It's not the A I would hope for, but for an oral presentation, where pronunciation is taken into account, I'll take it! I scan through Señora Almanza's notes, commenting on a few places my delivery faltered or when I messed up a word, but overall, what she wrote is complimentary.

When the bell rings, Carlos leaves after a quick goodbye, and I feel slightly rejected for a moment before I remind myself to not be clingy. I turn toward Edgar as he puts his Spanish book and workbook in his backpack. I flash him my graded paper and smile. "I don't think I would have been able to get up there and talk in front of everyone without barfing yesterday if it weren't for you."

Edgar raises his head to look at me, his curls bouncing slightly as he does. His eyes rest on mine a full second before he speaks. "You had it in you the whole time. You just needed to be reminded." But his usual smile is absent. He looks like he has something on his mind. He stands, but holds his footing, waiting for me. I quickly finish packing up.

We walk together through the regular in-between-classes rush in the hallway, silent. When we reach my locker, I turn my back to it, so I'm completely facing Edgar. I have no idea what to say, other than something stupid like *thanks for following me to our lockers?* But my palms are sweaty, and I wipe them off on my jeans before I meet his eye. Edgar's brow furrows, like he's about to say something, but then he quickly looks away.

"What is it?" Without thinking, I reach out and touch his forearm.

Edgar leans closer to me and my stomach flips. For one intense instant I think he's going to kiss me. Instead, under his breath, he says, "Carlos . . . he's my boy, but he's not exactly . . ."

Edgar's face is pinched, his tone unsure.

Heat rushes to my face. "What? He's not exactly what?"

Edgar doesn't make a move to speak. He twists the strap to his camera over his shoulder.

Okay, yeah, Brittany's never been a fan of Carlos, but Nina also warned me about him, and now Edgar too. But whatever it is Nina and Edgar know that I don't, they could at least have the decency to tell me. I manhandle my locker open, shoving my backpack in and clawing through the locker's contents.

"Are you going to tell me whatever it is you came here to or just be all weird and cryptic?"

Edgar sighs and looks toward his locker. "Look, just forget I said anything. Okay? See you later."

I stare into my locker rather than watch him walk away. Stand still and check my anger. Nope. Not going to let *whatever that was* ruin today. The worse thing I can think of—even though we're still unofficial—is that Carlos's dating other people, but he *can't* be. If he were, why would he have bothered to ask me if I wanted to come to Cassie's? I need to stop worrying about that and instead figure out what to wear. Something Carlos would like. Something he couldn't help but notice. I won't want him even thinking about taking his eyes off me.

I rack my brain. Nothing I own feels right, not sexy enough.

Borrowing something of Brittany's seems wrong somehow, but a thought crosses my mind.

Maybe Mom can help.

I text her, and seconds later, my phone dings.

I'm smiling as I close my locker and head down the hallway. I always dreamed of having a mom I could go to with this kind of stuff and now, it seems, I do.

From our regular library table, I watch Mom smiling as she approaches. "Here it is!" She plops into the seat across from me, sliding her large handbag to my side of the table.

I unzip her purse and feel some soft fabric with my fingertips. Out comes a very slinky, very sexy little black dress.

"It's my favorite dress from when I was around your age. I wore it all the time, and even still do sometimes." She grins at me proudly. "Anyway, I brought some makeup too, for you to borrow. Look."

I lean closer and Mom opens the bag wider to show me. "Here's eyeliner, mascara, and even fake eyelashes I bought from Rite Aid. What do you think?"

"You didn't have to do all of this." I smile sheepishly.

Mom shakes her head quickly and puts her hand on top of mine. "I wanted to, I really wanted to." Her eyes start to well, and she grabs the bag and pulls it to her, fumbling awkwardly. "That's only if you like the dress. If you don't, it's fine. I don't want to be one of *those* moms. You can tell me; I won't be mad."

I pull the bag back to me. "Don't even think about changing your mind. It's for me. So hands off."

Mom laughs, I laugh, and everything feels good. Right. Like it should be.

Before I know it, it's the night of the party.

Brittany comes over to help me get ready. She's already got her makeup looking like it was done by a professional. Sexy, smoky eyes, perfectly puckered pink lips. Brittany's had her makeup done enough times that she can do it almost as good as any of the girls at the MAC store.

I lay the black dress, fake eyelashes, and my mom's makeup on my bed for Brittany to peruse, next to all the stuff she brought from home. Brittany holds the dress up by one of its slim straps. "Where did you get this?" she marvels.

"My mom lent it to me. It's great, right? Vintage!" Mom's smile when she passed me the dress flashes in my mind.

"Yes!" Brittany grins and hands the dress to me. "Put it on already!"

I slide off my jeans and toss my T-shirt aside. Brittany starts laughing. "Nice bra!"

My face burns. I throw the dress on over my faded beige bra. The dress is way more low-cut than I realized before. Revealing.

"So what?" I quickly retort. "It's not like anyone is going to see—" And then I stop, because one, isn't that what I've wanted all along, for Carlos to get me out of my clothes? Although I wouldn't want it to happen at a party—no, not like that. I'd rather be here. In my own bed, since Grandma's never around. The nagging thought of Carlos hooking up with other girls crosses my mind, but I quickly stomp it down. I'm overthinking this.

But Brittany's right about my bra. The thick beige straps will totally show.

She leans forward from her perch on my bed. "Take it off, Ri. Live a little!"

I stare at her in confusion for a second until I realize she means go braless. I take the bra off from underneath my dress before turning to look into the mirror on my closet door.

"Ah-may-zing!" Brittany squeals. "Nice rack, Ri! You can for sure pull this off."

I blush. That was the easy part. "Okay, so now makeup? That's where you come in." I do my own makeup every day, but for tonight I'm pulling out the big guns.

Brittany gets to work on me—smoky eye like hers, fake eyelashes, bright red lips.

When Brittany finishes my makeup, she goes noticeably quiet.

I look at her reflection in the mirror. "What is it?"

"The party . . . None of our friends will be there."

I grab my Diet Coke from atop the dresser. "Not true." I swallow a big gulp, the bubbles burning my throat as they go down. "Nina will be and Carlos and Edgar too."

Brittany leaves it unsaid that they aren't exactly her friends. Her mouth puckers at the sound of Nina's name. "Nina's been . . . nice. But, I mean, she's the one who ditched us when we were all friends, remember?"

"I know. But things change. People do." Like me, though Brittany can't seem to accept that fact.

Brittany's hand holding the eyeliner drops to her side. "You're right." She looks up at me. "It was really cool of Nina to invite me. And I meant what I said; it feels like we haven't gotten to spend as much time together lately and I want to fix that. Tonight will be great."

My lips purse. I appreciate Brittany's effort, but there's something else that needs to be said. "Brittany, about tonight." I hesitate, and she stares at me, waiting.

I pick at my nails. "Please just don't . . . just don't be . . . I don't know . . . Remember what I said about the way you brought up our upcoming golf lessons and *how* you talked about it? You need to be more mindful about how you talk to Nina and everyone else . . . including me."

Brittany shrugs, keeping her eyes turned down. "I get it."

She lifts her chin and her face brightens, but something feels off, like it's an act. "Well, *since I can't mention it at the party,* I might as well tell you now that my mom finally got our first golf lesson rescheduled."

I muster up all the enthusiasm for this that I can. "That's good."

Brittany grabs a mascara off my desk and pretends to inspect it for a moment. "I guess we should get going, right? Are you ready?"

As I'll ever be.

I can hear the rap music pounding as soon as we reach Cassie's street, even over the pop playing inside Brittany's Mercedes. A bunch of kids I recognize from school—and many I don't—hang out on the sides of Cassie's front door. Others spill onto the sidewalk, smoking cigarettes and talking.

Brittany's hands clutch the steering wheel while she parks the car, but she doesn't say anything.

I grab my phone out of my black handbag. "I'm just going to text Carlos and tell him we're here."

Someone's knuckles rap on the window, and I jump up from the heated car seat in surprise.

Edgar.

I hit the button to roll down the window.

"Hey!" he says. "Good timing, right? I just got here."

Brittany visibly loosens up. "Yes! Perfect!"

As the three of us walk toward the door together, no Carlos in sight, Edgar trails behind me, putting his hand on my back as we walk through the group of guys smoking out front.

"¿Qué onda, little homie?" one says after he takes a drag of a cigarette.

Edgar nods. "No mucho, Javier. Cassie didn't mention you were visiting from college. How's it going?"

"Just hanging. Good to be back—I almost forget mi primita preferida throws this party every year."

Brittany eyes Javier and the guys he's standing with warily as we walk past. So what if they were a little older and outside smoking? Apparently, Cassie can't have her cousin and his friends over, according to Brittany. We walk into the foyer inside, where the beige tile is already sticky with spilled beer.

Music pulses, beating against my eardrums. In the hallway, a couple folds into each other, the girl sitting on the guy's lap on a chair outside the bathroom. Going to town, seemingly not caring that people are standing behind them on the stairs and the upstairs overlook, laughing. A guy tosses a nickel, trying to get it inside the girl's low-cut shirt. With a thud, the nickel bounces off her head, and she looks up to scowl before the guy she's with pulls her face back to him.

Edgar looks at me, but before he says anything, Brittany laughs in the direction of the kissing couple. "Classy."

I roll my eyes. Brittany's comment bugs me, even if the couple is being gross.

We walk on, to the living room. The music's louder in here, but the lights are dimmer. Smoke fills the air, lingering in a cloud above the people on the couch, who are passing a joint back and forth. I pick up the pace, knowing Brittany can't stand it when people get high, and not wanting to give her anything to complain about. Edgar's gaze shifts to the kitchen, where a group of girls raise their shot glasses, Nina among them. Cassie catches his eye and waves us over.

"Go!" Nina calls, and each of them throw back their heads and gulp down the liquor. She slams her glass down as we approach. Nina's eyes meet mine and she grins, her maroon lipstick making her teeth look extra white.

"Thanks again for the invite, Cassie." I smile and look around awkwardly. "You know Brittany, right?"

Cassie nods. "I've seen you around, not that we've ever

officially met." She gives Brittany a small wave. "I'm Cassie."

Brittany smiles politely, "It's nice to meet you too."

That was super formal, but it could be going worse, I guess.

One of the girls fills a shot glass up and hands it to Cassie. She shakes her head. "I don't drink, girl. That one's all yours." Her smile fades when she looks behind me. "It looks like Carlos made it too."

I turn to follow her gaze. Carlos has just walked in with a group of people, including his old football friends, Don Abrams and Nate Sanders.

Don calls, "Hey, man!" to Santiago Esparza in the living room. He and Nate break off from Carlos and walk over to the other group.

Everything is fine until Amy Thomas, one of Brittany's mom's friends' daughters, emerges from behind Carlos. Panic floods my chest. Did he *actually* bring another girl to the party?

I take a breath, no need to lose my head. I knew from Insta that Amy and Carlos were friends. When I turn back, Brittany's face is buried in her phone and she's got a ridiculous Cheshire-cat smile on her face.

"Who are you texting?" I ask.

Brittany's eyes stay glued to her phone. "It's Finn, telling me how much better the party would be if I were there. . . ."

I am not spending this whole party babysitting Brittany while she sends Finn flirty messages. Not when Carlos hasn't even bothered to text me to see if I'm here. I search for him in the crowd and legit gasp like an idiot when I see Amy leading Carlos up the stairs.

Brittany starts to ask if I'm okay, but I wave her off.

Edgar appears beside me with two red cups in his hands. He offers one to Brittany, who shakes her head because she's driving. I don't think twice before accepting mine and chugging the beer inside it, then slamming the empty cup down on the counter, next to Nina's glass.

I keep staring toward the stairs, thinking of Carlos. *What the hell?*

Nina catches my eye. "Did Carlos just go upstairs with *Amy*? I thought he was all about—" She stops herself and takes a drink instead. "What an ass. I hope you see now what I've been trying to say about Carlos."

Brittany glances at her phone before turning to Nina. "Me too. *I've* been telling her all along that your friend—"

I cut her short. "Brittany, shut up about that already."

I don't hear how Brittany responds because I'm too focused on the alcohol making my stomach warm and my thoughts a little foggy.

Brittany, apparently already done with our conversation, squeals. "Oh my God, Finn's calling me. What do I do?"

"Answer it," I snap.

Cassie sucks in a breath at my outburst. Brittany looks at me incredulously before Cassie softly touches Brittany's elbow, steering her to the left. "There's a laundry room behind the kitchen. It'll be quiet in there if you want to call."

Brittany hesitates, looking at me and then toward where Cassie pointed.

"Just go. I'll be fine," I say.

Brittany turns toward the laundry room and says, all breathy, "Hi, Finn," before disappearing through the kitchen.

"Have Carlos and Amy been hooking up?" I ask no one in particular. "Was that what you were all being so cagey about?"

Before anyone answers, I spot an unopened beer nearby on the counter, and I grab it and pound it down like I did the first one.

A pretty girl with bright red lips and black curly hair approaches our group. She touches Cassie's shoulder and Cassie's face lights up. They hug and, my outburst apparently forgotten, Cassie introduces her as Mia, from San Marcos.

I manage saying hi to Mia but that's about it. Still stuck on Carlos and made brave by the drink warming my belly, I text him. Three little dots appear and then disappear. If he's checking his phone, he's not hooking up with Amy, at least not yet.

"I'm going up there." I start walking.

I hear Edgar call something behind me, but I wave him off. I push through the stoner circle in the living room, past the couple eating each other's faces, and up the stairs. At the top, more people are drinking and laughing, yelling at each other over the music. The upstairs hallway leads to the right, where three closed doors await me. I pause, my heart thumping wildly in my chest. I don't know what I'm expecting to find, but I can't just stand here.

I stop at the first door on the right and knock on it.

"Occupied," some guy's voice calls from inside. A girl giggles. I walk to the next door, rap on it, and wait. A moment later the door opens, and Amy pops out. "Heeeeey!" She shouts over the music, her long blonde wavy hair hitting me in the face as she throws herself at me, pulling me in for a hug.

Stunned, I freeze until she steps back.

"I know you!" Amy grins wildly. "You're Brittany's friend! Ri! Hi, Ri!"

She grabs my hand and pulls me deeper into the room, where I see her friend Stephanie Bennet sitting on the neatly made bed.

Stephanie's normally pale, round face seems flushed. She pulls a strand of her curly red hair and twists it around her finger relatively hard.

Something feels off.

Amy plops herself down, her back facing us, in the chair in front of Cassie's desk—at least I'm guessing it's Cassie's based on the photos of her and Nina over the years covering the walls. Amy bends and makes a long sniffing sound, her head hanging over a mirror I just noticed in front of her.

She looks up, and I see she's inhaling through a rolled-up dollar bill. She sniffs deeply again and pulls her head back, using her legs to turn the rolling chair toward us.

Oh.

That's what they're doing in here. Amy and Stephanie, though, *alone.*

"I was just looking for Carlos," I say. "I'll . . . uh . . . check another room."

Stephanie snorts. "I wouldn't if I were you. He was looking for Tasha. If he found her," Stephanie narrows her eyes and grins at Amy, "I'd say give him a good *five* minutes."

Amy shrieks, laughing. "Damn, savage, Steph!"

My face falls. "W-what?" I stammer.

Amy blinks several times and her perfectly glossed lips pucker. "Wait a minute. You're not seeing Carlos, are you? He's been hooking up with our friend Tasha for months."

It's like the air is sucked out of my lungs, out of this whole room. He's been hooking up with someone else this whole time? When I've been obsessing over him. Planning to sleep with him even. A part of me worried he could have been seeing other girls, but hearing it confirmed like this is much worse than I imagined.

I'm such an idiot.

"I . . . um . . . well, not officially." I can't meet either of their eyes. My mind is foggy from the beer. This is so humiliating. "I should go."

Stephanie stands and puts a hand on my shoulder. "Don't let it get to you." Stephanie's words come out fast, extra noticeable because usually she has a particularly slow cadence. "Carlos is great, and to be fair, he's not a cheater. He, like, never promises anyone anything. He's just not the type to have a girlfriend. Tasha's not looking for anything serious either, so they just get on pretty well."

Amy sniffs and wipes at her nose. She rolls her chair closer to me and says, "If you want, I can totally kick him in the balls for you. Like, as a public service."

My laugh comes out nervous and high pitched. Amy and Stephanie are not my friends—Brittany can't stand either of them, despite their moms all being close. Still, they're being really nice.

"That's not necessary, but thanks. He and I never defined anything. He's free to see other people. I guess I was just hoping he wouldn't want to."

Amy looks down at her phone. "It's Tash," she says. "Oh, I guess she's not with Carlos. She's at Brody's. So that's good for you, right?"

I shrug. "Doesn't change that they've been hooking up this whole time."

"So, no need to go find him then," Stephanie says, resuming twirling a piece of her curly hair around her fingers. "Hang with us. We've just been in here killing time waiting for Don and Nate to finish catching up with their friends so that we can finally get to Brody's."

Amy gestures at the mirror and my chest tightens. The coke, I almost forgot with my thoughts spinning out about Carlos.

"This shit is the best," Amy says. "From now on, I'm only ever going to my guy at UCSB for this stuff!"

My heart beats, faster and faster, crawling up my throat, as she leans her head down over a thin white line of powder.

I've seen people do coke at a few of Brody's parties. But

whenever that happens is usually around the time Brittany and I get out of there. I mean, weed, yeah, I've tried it a few times. It didn't really do anything spectacular, just made me silly and hungry. But Brittany has always been dead set on not being around coke, and I never had the desire either. I feel the instinct to make for the door, as fast as I can.

But instead, I stare at Amy. She looks so happy, so excited. She doesn't have a reputation at school. She makes good grades, as far as I know. She's on the school basketball team and in the leadership club. Though I haven't actually seen Stephanie do any coke tonight, I'm pretty sure she has too. And she also has always seemed pretty put together. Most people at school like them. Except Brittany, that is.

Stephanie walks to Amy and pushes some of the white powder on the mirror into a line before leaning over and sniffing. Her phone dings and she looks at it. "Tasha, telling us to hurry up."

Tasha. Uggh. Carlos. *Double uggh.*

Amy's light brown eyebrows furrow. "Don't be upset." She pushes the mirror to the edge of the desk. "Here, this might make you feel better."

Stephanie returns to sit on the bed, her big green eyes wide and glassy.

Amy's shirt hangs low on her chest after leaning down to sniff the remnants of a line.

Then she looks up at me. "Ri, seriously, you've got to try this stuff. You'll love it!"

"Oh, uhhh . . . I don't know."

Stephanie and Amy share a look, like they think I'm not fun or something, and my chest flares hot.

"I got you. This stuff isn't for everyone," Amy says. "It's cool."

My mind goes to Brittany, what she thinks is and isn't me. But has she ever asked me? She just assumes that what she wants is what's best. That I'll go along with it, no matter what. It reminds me of my grandma. I'm not going to let the disappointment of Carlos ruin this night for me. I can be spontaneous. *Fun*.

I walk toward Amy. "I'll try it."

Amy passes me the dollar bill. I lean my head down like she did, and don't even think another thought as I inhale the powder straight into my nostrils. It burns coming in, and I can feel it in the tiny hairs I have in my nose.

Amy claps her hands together. She pushes a little white mound of powder from the side of the mirror to make two more. Stephanie waves her off. "I'm good, thanks. She passes the mirror to me so I can sniff the line off it. I can feel electricity pulsing through me as I wipe my nose.

I inhale, it burns, and my heart beats faster, time moves quicker, everything illuminates in the room. The pumping music from downstairs. I want to jump and dance.

I want to do another line, and I reach for it, before Stephanie pulls me back. "Maybe go easy for your first time. That's probably enough for now."

Amy looks at her for a moment, like she's confused, before her eyes land on me. "Actually, Ri, do me a favor and don't tell anyone about this, okay? Carlos is chill and all, but he hates this stuff. He made us promise to never to bring it around here and his friends are pretty straight edge too. They definitely won't let us come to any of their parties again if they find out."

I blink several times. *Huh.* I better not go around broadcasting what I've been up to. The last thing I need is to give Cassie or Nina a reason not to like me. "No problem."

"We should probably get going to Brody's. See if sober Nate's ready to drive us. You wanna come? This place is getting lame, anyway."

I snap my head back. Amy talking shit about this party shocks me alert. I'm here to hang out with Nina and my new friends. Not *Amy* and *Stephanie*, of all people.

"I'll pass," I say. Neither of them seem to pick up on my coldness. Amy sweeps the pile of powder into a little baggie on the desk and puts it in her purse. "Soooo great to hang out with you, Ri! See you at school!" Stephanie leans in for a hug and kisses my cheek. "Love you!"

Just as sudden as my anger came on, it evaporates, and I laugh, uncontrolled, and hug her back.

Amy practically skips to the door with Stephanie behind her. In the hallway, I catch a peek of Carlos walking with Nate. He sees me staring and widens his eyes.

"Ri," he says, before coming into the room, shutting the

door behind him. "What were you doing in here with Amy and Stephanie?"

I narrow my eyes at Carlos acting all concerned. "Hanging out. Why do *you* care?"

Carlos cocks his head and looks at Cassie's desk where there are a couple dots of white powder left behind. "Ri, seriously? You didn't do coke with them, did you?" He groans. "I'm never letting those two near here again."

Before I can think of a response, maybe even lie to him and tell him I didn't do anything, Carlos pulls his phone out of his pocket and types something very quickly.

While he's distracted, I'm overcome with the music downstairs. A Cardi B song is playing that begs to be danced to, so I head for the door.

Carlos puts a hand on my shoulder to stop me, and I can't help but think of Tasha. I all but jump out of my skin and yank my shoulder away.

His face falls. "Are you okay, Ri?"

"Never better! See you around, Carlos! Have fun at Brody's!"

I try to move past Carlos, but he blocks my path. "I don't think you should be on your own. Why don't we go find Nina?"

I was about to go find Nina anyway, but I still don't want Carlos telling me what to do. "Don't you have people waiting for you to go to Brody's?" I snap.

He looks at his phone again and I lean over to see that he's already sent Nina a text asking her to come find me.

Uggh. I unleash the best death glare I can muster, and he backs away.

"Okay, got it. See you later, Ri. Text me if you need me."

If I need him? When he's going to have his hands all over Tasha? Hard pass.

Now that he's gone, I feel lighter. Better. I hear the song change downstairs and remember how much I want to dance.

At the foot of the stairs, I see Nina and Brittany. Nina looks up from her phone, "Ri! Party's downstairs, in case you've forgotten." Her brow furrows as I jump the final two stairs.

Brittany gives me a look. "Well, someone's excited to see us."

My heart pounds in my ears, my senses alert, seeing the hall around me, the pictures on the walls, the people laughing, their faces—*really* seeing them this time, not like before. *Before.* I sniff and wipe my nose. Make sure no powder is left over.

Nina's look of worry catches my eye again. She leans in for a hug and whispers, "Carlos texted me to keep an eye on you. I let him know you're with me. You good?" I don't answer, racking my mind for what to say, as she leans back and speaks louder so Brittany can hear.

"Why didn't you tell me Carlos was hooking up with Tasha? You tried to hint at it, but you could have just told me."

"I wasn't sure. I had my suspicions, but Carlos doesn't really talk about who he's seeing. I was hoping maybe things were different this time," Nina says. "Forget him! I know Brittany agrees with me." She smiles at Brittany, who has the decency to look sheepish for talking about me with Nina while I was gone, at least.

"It's whatever," I say. "Carlos is hooking up with other girls. I don't own him, but I don't have to like it."

Brittany lets out an exasperated sigh. "Fiiiiiinally," she says. "Please tell me you're done with Carlos."

I nod. "So done, like a well-cooked steak."

Brittany makes a face at my ridiculously corny joke, and I start laughing really hard. Tears stream down my face. She looks at Nina. "Apparently, Ri is becoming a lightweight." Brittany smiles and looks at me. "Maybe no more beer for you."

I watch Nina for any clue that Carlos told her what I was up to but see none. Nina laughs, seemingly believing Brittany that I'm a lightweight and drunk. "Wild little Ri," she yells so we can hear her over the music, her words slurring. Her knees wobble as we push through the crowd. An old hip-hop song bangs in my ears, one that I haven't heard since middle school.

"I love this song!" Nina shouts as she tugs Brittany behind her.

Brittany's smile is contagious, and I want to jump, to bounce, to *move*.

I feel the music pounding within me, in my ears, in my chest, in my fingers. Nina's hand reaches for mine, her smile warming every part of me that used to feel cold and alone. I whoop and laugh, and Brittany and I follow her through the sweaty crowd.

Nina leads us to the middle of the living room. The couches

are now pushed back out of the way and people are dancing.

She takes my hands, moves me with her. Music pulses, through my body, through the air, through the whole world.

Brittany looks at me jumping to the beat. For a second, it's like she can tell something's not quite right, but then Nina pushes her softly and yells, "I know you can dance, Brittany. Let's see it!"

Brittany gives Nina an appreciative look, and Nina hoots as Brittany starts moving her body to the music.

We're dancing and Cassie approaches, holding Mia's hand.

"You okay?" Cassie shouts in my ear. I nod, appreciating that she cares.

"Hey!" Mia yells to me over the music before she and Cassie start dancing. I'm lost in the feeling of my body moving and music bumping and my heart banging wildly in my chest as Edgar comes into sight.

He starts to back away slowly to watch, but I grab his hand and he's dancing, his hips and feet moving slightly in time with the music and we're close and I can feel his breath on my forehead and it smells like bubble gum and the music is bumping and Cassie and Mia are laughing and Miguel appears and weaves in between us throwing up his hands and Nina's hands are in the air and she's rapping along with the words and Brittany is joining in and I'm here with them and I'm singing and laughing too and I finally feel like I'm me. I'm Ri.

I'm Ri.

After a few songs, sweating and dancing like I've never danced before, Brittany's smile fades and I am not going to listen to whatever shit she's planning to nag me about, so I keep dancing. But I know something is really bothering her when she takes my hand and pulls me to the side, away from the group.

"Ri," she yells into my ear. "What's up with you? You seem . . . different."

I wipe the sweat off my neck with the back of my hand. "I'm having fun!" I shout. "You are too. Let's get back—"

Brittany grabs my arm as I start to make my way toward Nina and the others. She wheels me around and brings her face uncomfortably close to mine. Her eyes widen as she stares into my eyes.

"You're not drunk," she whisper shouts. "You're high! What the hell, Ri? What are you on?"

When I don't answer, Brittany keeps barking at me. "I thought you and Carlos were making out up there, or arguing once you found out about him seeing other girls, not—"

I yank my arm free of Brittany. "Stop being such a buzzkill. It's fiiiiiine."

Brittany looks as though she's never seen me before. "It's not fine," she snaps. "Since when do you do drugs, Ri? What were you thinking?"

I jerk away from Brittany as someone walking by gives us a look.

"I'm taking you home."

I bark out a laugh. "That's a no; I'm going to go dance now and you can't stop me."

Brittany doesn't follow me. Instead, she walks up to Nina and shouts something in her ear that I can't hear over the music. Nina says something and keeps dancing. I bounce toward Edgar and he smiles as he dances with me, until Brittany starts to close in on us. Before she tells him whatever she thinks she's going to, I grab her arm and drag her away.

"Brittany, way to cause a scene!" I hiss in her ear, loud enough that she can hear over the music but hopefully Edgar can't. "Fine, let's go. I'd rather leave than stay and let you embarrass me."

People are starting to clear out anyway. Cassie and Mia are walking around with a garbage bag throwing away plastic cups and empty bottles. I'm sad the party is ending. Before tonight, I'd never been so alive.

I tell Edgar and Nina goodbye and hug each of them. Edgar gives a wary look to Brittany—I'm pretty sure he didn't miss our little spat while we were dancing. I think Carlos left earlier without saying so much as a word to me, but I don't really care.

"See you in class, wild girl." Nina grins at me.

I wrap my arms around her again, and she laughs and squeezes me back. Though Nina doesn't notice, Brittany glares at her. It seems like Nina is on her shit list, too, apparently.

Brittany is murderously silent as we walk to her car.

Brittany stomps past the guys who are congregating outside. We walk quickly and silently down the street lined with cars until we stop outside her Mercedes.

Brittany's luxury car looks ridiculous next to all the others on the street, so I laugh, maniacally. Once Brittany's in her seat, she slams her door.

"What the hell is wrong with you?"

I stare at the scowl on her perfectly glossed lips. Brittany being mad is stupid. So stupid. She clearly had an amazing time dancing with all of us.

I sneeze uncontrollably several times and wipe my nose quickly.

"Nothing is *wrong* with me! So I tried coke! I'm a big girl, I can do what I want. It's not, like, the end of the world."

Brittany's face contorts. "Ri, slow down. I can barely understand anything you're saying." She looks at my legs—I'm trembling. Hadn't noticed.

A bottle breaks somewhere in the distance and Brittany jumps in her seat. She starts the car and turns the heat up, but we stay parked.

I sniff, and the inside of my nose burns. Brittany's overreacting. She's always trying to control me. Tonight was perfect. Until she ruined it.

"We had a great time, all of us did, even you. So why are you so mad?"

Brittany's voice turns icy. "Even me? What the hell is that supposed to mean?"

I chew on my lip until I bite too hard. It's wet and I taste copper. *Shit.* Quickly, I wipe my face with the back of my hand.

I know I've hurt Brittany's feelings and normal Ri would try to dial it back. "You weren't . . ." I make an effort to stop my shaking hands. "I don't know, so uptight."

Brittany shakes her head, glaring at me. "So that's what I'm being now, uptight? Since I don't think it's a good thing you did drugs? Wow, Ri. Just wow."

"Look, I know you hate that stuff and that's why I haven't tried it before, but really, it wasn't a big deal. Actually, it was fun."

Brittany scoffs.

Heat rises in my chest. "You don't seem to have a problem with it when it's happening at Brody's parties! When Finn is there!" I'm yelling now, and a few people walking by the car are gaping at us. I give zero shits. "Finn smokes weed every weekend. What about that?"

Brittany looks at me incredulously. "I *do* have a problem with it at Brody's parties—that's why we leave when anyone starts doing it. And you know Finn doesn't do coke, otherwise there's no way I'd be into him. It's not his fault if some of his friends do."

"Why are you being so judgey, Brittany? You haven't even tried it. You don't even know what you're talking about. Maybe you'd even like—"

"You think I want to be like one of those bored, depressed

housewives at the club? Partying and sleeping constantly? Wasting their money and time and *lives* on drugs?"

I wince. My eyelids feel heavy and suddenly it's an effort to keep them open. I'm coming down from the high, I guess. "Can we just go? Tired now." I swallow and look outside the window, see a few stragglers stumbling out of Cassie's.

Brittany nods, jaw as tight as ever, and puts the car in reverse. In the side mirror, I see Cassie's place get smaller and smaller until we turn off the street. We pass houses that I've seen before. They're the same, but I'm not. I close my eyes and lean my head back. Notice the sensations in my body. My head aches. My throat is sore and there's a nasty taste in the back of my mouth, and it feels like it's dripping down my throat.

But Brittany's not done. "You know I don't love that Finn smokes weed, but you can't tell me you think weed and coke are the same kind of bad," she says. "People overdose and die from doing coke. It's addictive. It's *illegal*."

"It's illegal for Finn to smoke weed too. He's underage." My words come out sharp.

I open my eyes, lean up, and glare at Brittany. "You don't like coke. You don't like that I did some, but I frankly don't care."

A tear falls from Brittany's eye and that makes me even more annoyed. She's being so dramatic.

"This is exactly what I was afraid of, Ri!" Her fingernails dig into the steering wheel. "Those people aren't good for you."

My head whips back. "*Those people?*"

Brittany hits her hand on the steering wheel, and I flinch. "Damnit, Ri, that's not what—"

"Hmm," I snap, "so, it's whatever if Amy and her friends do drugs at Brody's, but when it happens at Cassie's party, it's because of *those people*?"

"This isn't a race thing, so stop trying to make it one! Can you just trust me on this?"

I laugh coldly, loud, and I don't stop for several moments. I get it now. Finally, I see what's really happening. It shouldn't have taken doing coke to see Brittany clearly, but now that I have, I can't keep lying to myself. She thinks I was doing drugs with Carlos. She thinks he gave me the coke, not the white girls who hang out at Brody's. Not Amy and Stephanie who asked me not to tell my friends—*those* people—about the coke because they wouldn't approve.

Brittany gives me a confused look before parking outside my house. She turns the car off and breathes deeply a few times, as though she's trying to calm herself.

When I finally meet her eye, Brittany recoils at the way I look at her.

"I didn't do coke with Carlos," I say through gritted teeth. "Amy and Stephanie gave it to me. They asked me not to tell anyone because they knew Cassie would never let them come to her house again."

Brittany's mouth falls open. She stammers, "Oh, I didn't mean—"

"You never *mean* anything by the racist shit you say, do you,

Brittany?" I interrupt. "Because let's be real; you immediately assumed that the people who brought coke to the party and shared it with me were brown."

Brittany's eyes widen. "I'm not . . ." She huffs. "I'm the *least* racist—"

I bark out a laugh. "Very believable. Typical."

Brittany opens her mouth to argue but I talk over her.

"You say passive-aggressive shit, and you separate yourself from Nina and all of them every time you get the chance. Is that how you would treat me if I didn't look like this?" I wave a hand in front of myself. "Because I'm Latina too. My grandma is Mexican! And what, you aren't okay with it all of a sudden? Because being around people who don't look like you makes you uncomfortable?"

"Ri, stop. You don't mean what you're saying." Brittany's shaking her head like she knows what she's talking about. But she doesn't.

"It's because you're—"

"Don't you fucking dare blame it on that," I roar. "I know how I feel. I've known it for a while. How many times have I asked you to think about how you treat Nina and Edgar and Carlos? But it didn't change anything. If you had it your way, I wouldn't talk to anyone but you. Or your other friends who are—guess what—also white. And I let you get away with it until now!"

I grab the handle and throw the car door open. "People change. You should too."

I slam the door and start walking, the heels of my boots clicking on the sidewalk as I go.

Brittany doesn't follow.

I turn back and see her watching me, still turned in the front seat. As I reach my front door and open it, I look back.

She's still there.

I lock the door behind me, before sneaking a look through the window blinds.

Brittany finally starts the car and drives away.

Chapter

THIRTEEN

By Monday morning, Brittany and I still haven't talked. She can blame the drugs all she wants for me yelling at her. But I'm sober now, and I'd do it again. I'm ashamed it took me so long to confront Brittany for her bullshit. So instead of our normal ride, I walk to school wondering what it will be like when we have to face each other.

Brittany's nowhere to be seen near our lockers. I wave Cassie and Nina over from across the hall. "Hey, girl!" Cassie says, leaning in to hug me. "Great party, right?"

Nina chuckles. "Way to toot your own horn, Cass."

Edgar appears at his locker next to us. He eyes me carefully for a moment and then smiles at us all. "The new three musketeers?" he asks. "I like it."

My chest warms, but outwardly I play it off. "You're such a dork, Edgar."

Cassie ruffles his curly hair. "In the best way," she says.

My phone buzzes and Brittany's name pops up. I tap on the text.

Ri, you're my best friend, which is exactly why I have to

tell you the truth. You're not being yourself. I'm sorry, but
I can't just sit by and watch you throw your life away. I
hope you come around and see that I'm right.

I shove my phone back in my bag. *Throw my life away?* It
isn't anything like that. That night, I was still me, only better.
My senses were alert, my energy skyrocketed, the world felt
open with possibilities. Everything was great. Until Brittany
ruined it.

Self-righteous, ridiculous Brittany who of course wants to
make this about me doing drugs and not her backwards, racist
thinking. I don't respond to her text.

At lunch, Brittany's nowhere in sight. She must have gone
off campus to eat, with Finn and his friends probably. I spot
Nina, Cassie, and Edgar—Carlos hasn't shown his face at school
today—at a nearby table. I ask if the seat's taken across from
Cassie and Edgar, next to Nina. Cassie smiles, lips closed over a
mouthful of food, and extends her arm for me to take it.

Nina glances behind me. "No Brittany today?"

I shake my head. "What about Miguel?" I look around, not
seeing him. I don't mention Carlos not being at school today
because I prefer it that way.

"He's got some make-up work to do in geometry," Nina
says. She gives me a knowing smile. "But don't change the subject. Are you guys in a fight?"

Edgar's eyebrows furrow as he looks at me. I squirm at all
three of them staring, waiting for my reply.

"Something like that."

Nina grabs my arm and pulls me from my seat. "Leave your backpack," she says, and then picks up my sack lunch in her other hand. "Let's go talk."

I wave at Cassie and Edgar, resigned, as Nina pulls me to an empty spot on the grass.

She sits, sprawling her legs out in front of her, as I plop down on the grass.

"So." Nina lifts an eyebrow. "What's up with you and Brittany? I kind of sensed some tension between you both a while ago, but I figured you worked it out. You both seemed happy at Cassie's party. I actually kind of got why you and Brittany were still friends—she seemed really different from when we were kids."

I sigh and kick my feet out, so they're sprawled out like Nina's.

"Brittany's mad at me because I've been trying new things, or at least that's how she sees it." I glare at my feet. "But I . . ." I don't know what to say, or how to say it.

I watch Cassie chat with a few girls who came by the patio table. Edgar sits at the edge, talking to Miguel, who has now joined them.

Nina's eyes follow mine, and she holds Miguel's gaze for a second before she gives a little wave.

I suck in a breath. I need to do this. "But I can tell it's more than that, which is why *I'm* mad at her. Brittany's trying to control who I hang out with. She doesn't like my new friends."

"I can't say that I disagree."

It feels like I've been punched in the gut. After being so nice to me, after the party, after all the times in Spanish class, Nina doesn't want to be friends with me?

"Wait, what? I thought . . ." I swallow. "I thought we were having fun together. I thought . . ." I look away and take a breath to try to compose myself. Even still, my voice comes out tragically small. "I thought you wanted to be friends with me again."

Nina squints at me in confusion. "Girl, I meant that Stephanie and Amy are basic. Carlos mentioned you were hanging out with them for a minute at the party."

I feel the heat of embarrassment wash over me—I can't believe I just unloaded all that on Nina—but force my tone to be light. "Oh, um, my bad."

Nina looks at me for a long moment, and I think she's going to say something about my pathetic outburst. Instead she says, "But I guess that's not *exactly* what you and Brittany are fighting about?"

I hesitate. "No, not really. I think I'm seeing Brittany for who she really is for the first time and it's not someone I can be friends with if she doesn't change. I've been oblivious to so many things with her."

Nina pulls her legs up and wraps her arms around them. She looks at me, and I press on, knowing that it's the right thing to do, even if it makes me uncomfortable.

"A while ago Brittany told me that she thought you didn't like her when we used to hang out together. At the time, it surprised me, but now I realize that I probably don't remember things the same way as she does—and maybe you. Is she . . . is she part of the reason we stopped being friends?"

Nina's eyes widen. "Well, yeah. Brittany used to say microaggressive crap about our neighborhood, my family. Whenever she did, she'd look at you and laugh. Like you were both in on some joke." Nina shrugs. "It got old fast."

My stomach clenches. Because I know Nina must be telling the truth; even though I don't remember laughing, I'm sure I must have.

"That was shitty of me," I say, forcing myself to look at Nina. "I . . . I'm really sorry. I think . . ." I close my eyes and try to concentrate on what I want to say. "I know it doesn't make it okay, but I think I've been starting to understand how messed up the way I've acted has been, the way I saw things." *The way I saw myself, even.*

I tuck my hair behind my ear—my straight black hair, just like Nina's. Our features are similar too. My eyes are big and round like hers.

Nina nods. "It was a long time ago. How you let Brittany treat me didn't help the situation, I'll give you that, but there is a lot more to the reason why we stopped being friends. Your grandma told me I had to stay away from you."

I choke on air and start coughing. "What?" I sputter, thinking about how weird Grandma was when I told her I was hanging out with Nina again.

"She said I was a bad influence, and that I should let you

hang out with good girls like Brittany. I told her she was nuts, but your grandma, she doesn't mess around." Nina slides her hands in her pockets, shakes her head at Miguel, who's trying to wave her—or us?—over.

"I don't . . . I don't understand."

My thoughts jumble. I can't even think that. . . . Not Nina too. Is there anyone Grandma won't try to take away from me?

The wind has picked up and a few fallen leaves from the trees nearby flutter and blow by our feet. I'm shaking. But I'm not cold.

"Part of me felt blindsided, but you know what? I shouldn't have been all that surprised," Nina says. "I could *feel* her preferring Brittany, not wanting me around as much, being cold, and then she goes—and this is pretty much a direct quote—" Nina deepens her voice to be an impression of my grandma. "'My granddaughter doesn't need any trouble, Nina, and that seems to be where you're set on heading, blowing off church to hang out with older boys. I think you should probably find some *new* friends who have interests like yours.'"

I gasp. "How could she do that to you?"

How could she do that to me too? There were so many nights I spent crying because Nina was ignoring me, wondering what I did wrong, missing her, feeling like it was my fault. Grandma held me and said it would be okay, that friends come and go. She brushed my hair and cooked my favorite foods. She encouraged me to hang out with Brittany more and to forget about Nina.

"I didn't want to listen, but your abuela is a pretty persuasive lady when she wants to be." Nina shakes her head. "She said she'd tell my mom about the older guys I'd been hanging out with—which, by the way, was only the one, Mario, remember? We *dated* for months after that and he never so much as kissed me on the cheek because we were babies. Anyway, Carmen said she'd make sure my mom kept a better eye on me if I didn't stay away from you."

Nina and I were so close back then, like sisters. For no reason other than I feel like I have to *do* something, I stand and Nina does too, so we're face-to-face.

"I should have told you." The wind blows Nina's long black hair into her face. "But I don't know, you and Brittany were starting to leave me out of stuff already, and I just thought it would happen eventually. Like you didn't really belong with me and my friends, because you were this good little girl who always listened to your grandma. I didn't want you to turn on me, too, like she did."

Nina pauses, looking far off, like she's somewhere else and not here with me. "I'd been hanging out with you at your house for years. *Years.* And I saw your grandma as like a second grandma to me." Her voice rises. "She was always looking out for me, I thought, sending me home with leftovers and knitting me and my little brother sweaters. She was this nice church lady and my mom respected her."

I blink quickly. "I . . . I know, I mean, I remember."

There's real hurt in Nina's eyes. "So just for a second imagine how it felt when I could feel her pushing me out, even before she said that stuff." She crosses her arms in front of her chest and glances at Miguel and the others before looking back at me. "Imagine how that would make me feel. You think I wanted to be around that, be around you? Feeling like crap knowing your grandma didn't want me around and that soon you probably wouldn't either? That you'd rather hang out with Brittany because she was rich? Or worse, because she was white?"

A tear slides down my face and I'm shaking my head, not at what she's saying—because that's how I acted and that's how I made Nina feel—but because it was so wrong.

Brittany and her mom treated Nina differently than they treated me, and I paid no attention to it. And when Nina used to hint at me that she didn't like hanging out at Brittany's house, I didn't even bother to figure out why she felt that way. But I think, really, maybe I was just happy Tara seemed to think I was special. I was too young to put together that Tara was treating me better because of my skin tone, but I *was* old enough to know that her actions were wrong, and I did nothing. When Nina needed me then and every time after, I wasn't there for her.

"I need to say this because you deserve to hear it, Nina. You were my friend." I swallow and wipe my face. "My best friend. And I made you feel like . . . like you were less than . . . like *you didn't matter*. If I hadn't ignored the stupid shit Brittany or her mom said, if I hadn't stood by and watched when they treated me like I was special, like I was different from you . . . if I hadn't let them push you away, maybe you wouldn't have let my grandma finish the job. This . . . it's my fault. I wasn't the friend you deserved."

Nina's throat bobs and she nods. A solitary tear slides down my face painfully slow, and Nina laughs, pushing my shoulder softly. "Don't do that. Don't cry. You're going to make me cry." She looks around awkwardly for a moment, and then hugs me, quickly. I only have a second to feel her bony back as my arms wrap around her, then she pulls away.

My heart pounds as time stretches between us.

"It wasn't just back then. I know I shouldn't have kept going along with Brittany, whenever she said stupid stuff, over the years, even after we weren't friends. I should have said something."

Nina looks at me. "Yeah. You should have," she says. There isn't malice there, or pity. Just a statement, a matter of fact.

I do all I can to keep eye contact, even though it's hard. "I'm sorry. Things are different now. I am. I won't let it happen again."

Nina exhales heavily and gives me a small smile. "Noted. Now, get it together, Ri." She rolls her eyes and smiles, as if we've maxed out on emotional stuff for this conversation.

She starts walking toward the table where everyone else is and beckons me to follow. "Can we talk?" Edgar asks as I squeeze into the seat beside him. "We could meet up after school?" Still out of sorts from everything Nina and I just talked about, I take a breath, but that doesn't keep my stomach from clenching at Edgar's serious demeanor. I've had a suspicion that he noticed

I was acting differently at Cassie's party, and it looks like he wants to talk to me about it.

Nina turns to us. "Actually, I have an idea." She smiles at Edgar. "Didn't you say you want to shoot photos of me painting for your website? And Ri, you would make a great model!"

"Are you still painting?" I ask Nina. "You were always so good at it when we were kids." *I have the paintings you made for me in my closet to prove it.*

"She's amazing," Edgar says. Nina grins appreciatively at him, and I do too. Edgar smiles at my smile, and I feel lighter.

"Ortega Park, four o'clock. That work for you guys?" Nina asks.

Miguel faux scoffs. "What about me? I'm not cool enough to get an invite?"

Nina bumps shoulders with him. "Nope," she says, looking at me. "I work better without an audience. Necessary personnel only."

Miguel opens his mouth and widens his eyes dramatically, putting his hand to his chest as if he just got shot in the heart.

"Boy, you know she's doing us a favor," Cassie says. "Nina would have us posing for her or would boss us around to move props the whole time." Cassie tilts her head in my direction and laughs. "But you have fun."

The bell rings. Edgar, Cassie, and Miguel dump the trash from their lunches as I grab my backpack.

Edgar and I lag behind the others. He walks a little closer

to me, unless I'm imagining it. "See you at four. I'll bring my camera."

Nina takes Miguel's hand. "I'll bring my painting stuff."

I smile, look back and forth. "And I'll bring . . . me."

I wave goodbye to everyone but Edgar as they pass our lockers, my heart happy. I actually get to hang out with Nina this afternoon, on purpose. Because she wants to.

But then Brittany catches my eye from her locker. I turn away. Can't stand to look at her. All I see is my grandma and how she makes choices *for* me. I won't let Brittany do that too.

FOURTEEN

Brittany texts me the next day, basically popping the happy bubble I've been in since hanging out with Nina and Edgar at the park.

> Ri, I know you're mad at me, but I love you. Don't let this
> get between us.

What does she mean by *this*? Brittany's trying to play it like she got mad at me because I did drugs, but we both know the real problem is how she's been acting.

My phone dings and I'm about to tell Brittany off when I see it's not her. It's Mom. Asking if we can meet at Jack in the Box instead of the library. Jack in the Box isn't far from my house, so I walk there after school. I open the door and see a family eating on the other side of the restaurant. No one else is here except a couple of middle school kids.

I slide into a booth in the back, facing the entrance so I can see Mom when she arrives. Tap my fingers on the table.

I look at my cell phone. No messages. I text her, I'm here, in the back. No answer.

Fifteen minutes later my mom, windswept, opens the

door along with John, who has his arm wrapped around her. We haven't talked about him much. All I know really is that they've been together for a few years and John is helping my mom get on her feet while she looks for work. The owner of the bar my mom used to work for fired her when she rebuffed his advances. She hasn't been able to find another job, or at least one where she says she'd be working for anyone less sleazy. I'm glad my mom has John to help her. But he works as a salesman at a cell phone store so I'm guessing money must still be tight.

John leads her to my table. "Good seeing you again, Ri."

He takes a seat across from me and Mom slides into the booth next to him, setting car keys on the table.

"Same." I smile at John. She didn't tell me he was coming. But I'm glad he did. It would be nice to get to know the man my mom loves.

"So, I never asked," I begin, looking at my mom, whose head full of curly hair bounces as she squirms in her seat. "How did you two meet?"

John laughs and Mom blushes. "Oh, we don't need to tell that—"

"Oh yes, we do," John interrupts. He chuckles again, grinning at me, his eyes shining. "Your mom here was a cocktail waitress in a casino in Vegas. I was working security in one of the clubs inside. On my break, I decided to meet my boys for some food, but one of 'em had his eye on this beautiful woman and wanted to stop by the tables to say hello."

Mom bounces in her seat, grinning. She seems giddy. Maybe John brings that out of her.

John continues, "So, he struts up to your mom, looking like a fool." He mimes by pushing his chest forward. "He opens his mouth, right, and before he even gets a word out your mom says—"

"Nope," Mom interrupts. "Nope, nope, nope."

John and Mom are both laughing now.

"And she straight up walks away. Leaving him red-faced in front of his boys. So, I knew I had to introduce myself then. And you know what?"

Mom is beaming at the story. I lean forward. "What?"

"After I say hello and chat with your beautiful mother for a few minutes, real respectful, not creepy at all, I swear—"

"Yeah, yeah, yeah," Mom says. "*I* gave *him* my number."

John nods with a huge smile on his face. "Yep. You know why? Because I got game!"

Mom rolls her eyes at him playfully before looking at me. "Shouldn't we eat something? Ri, are you ready to order?"

I nod, and she slips out of the booth.

I stand, but John holds a hand up to stop me. "What's your order?"

"Oh, um, how about an Ultimate Cheeseburger?"

I unzip my backpack and pull my wallet out.

"Oh no you don't." John says. "My treat. What kind of fries and soda?"

I put my wallet back. "Curly Fries and a Diet Coke. Thanks."

Mom smiles at me, and she and John head to the counter. I pull out my Spanish textbook to keep me busy while I wait, but instead I end up watching them as they order. John is taller than Mom, but only by a hair. His shoulders are broad, his arms muscular. RIP letters with dates are tatted on his right arm. His cargo shorts leave more ink to be spotted, a tattoo of a nautical star on his right calf. He holds Mom around the waist, only removing his arm to reach into his pocket and take out his wallet to pay.

After they come back and pass me my food, John eyes my Spanish textbook. "Your mom's been telling me how good you've been doing in Spanish."

"Thanks to her help." I beam at Mom before digging into my burger.

After swallowing a bite, John shakes his head. "I can't believe those grandparents of yours never taught you. And they think *they* know so much. Or did. May that old grumpy bastard rest in peace."

My mouth falls open. *Those are my grandparents he's talking about.*

"I may not agree with them, but they had their reasons." I look at Mom, who now seems preoccupied with the straw in her soda, and then back at her boyfriend. "My grandpa wasn't perfect, and neither is my grandma, but they've been there for me my whole life."

I swallow, stopping myself. My subtext was clear, even if I didn't mean to say that.

Mom looks back and forth between us, and after a tense moment of silence, I ask, "Aren't you going to eat, John?"

John's food is mostly untouched on the tray in front of him. He takes a slurp from his straw and changes the subject instead. "So, I hear you're a whiz with technology too. You've been making a video for one of your classes?"

After a beat, I tell him about the Multimedia project I'm working on and how I've been filming at Leadbetter and doing the voice-over in class.

"Maybe you'll show it to me when you're finished," Mom says. "I'd love to see it."

Despite myself, I grin. Grandma never asked me to show her the video when I finished it. Speaking of Grandma . . .

I reach for a napkin and wipe my hands, checking my cell phone. "Grandma gets off work early today. She might stop to check in on me before Bible study."

I grab my books and shove them into my bag. "This was really nice."

John grabs the keys off the table and Mom reaches for them. He stares at her for a second. "You know I like driving, baby," Mom says. Before John can reply, she gets to her feet and pulls me into her arms.

The hug ends too soon, but I need to make sure I beat Grandma home. I nod at John. "Thanks for dinner."

He follows Mom out of the booth as I hoist my backpack on. "Text me, Mom, when you're ready to go to the library next." I smile at John, who was mostly nice, except that dig at my grandparents. I try to shake it off, though. He loves my mom, and no one has hurt her more than her parents. It makes sense that he wouldn't be their biggest fan.

Mom tells me she loves me and says goodbye. I turn back to see her watching me as I walk out the door.

When Carlos walks into Spanish class, in an attempt to be civil, I nod at him. I didn't respond to his text the day after the party when he asked if I was okay. Hearing about him hooking up with Tasha was still too fresh. But I know he didn't do anything *really* wrong other than lead me on. Still, it's hard to act like nothing ever happened between us. As I open my textbook and get everything else ready for the start of class, Carlos leans in to whisper in my ear. "Hey, we haven't talked since the party. You good, Ri?"

Before I can respond, Nina, Cassie, and Edgar stride into the classroom. Nina holds a big canvas painting, which she attempts to tuck closer to her side as she approaches us. But Miguel appears behind her and slips the painting out from under her arm. "Don't be so shy, Neen!"

He lifts it up for Carlos, Edgar, and me to see. It's a beautiful portrayal of the harbor at sunset. The waves reflect a purple sky over rows of boats, from tiny fishing vessels to humongous yachts.

Miguel makes his voice high-pitched, impersonating Nina—badly, I might add. "Not until it's finished, not until it's finished!" He holds the painting high, his voice dropping back to normal. "Well, this one is finished, so I'm doing everyone a favor. Showing off your talent!"

Nina's face flushes. "This is why I didn't want to bring it. He wanted to show you guys. It's my anniversary gift to him."

I stifle a laugh at Miguel's unexpected sweetness before looking again at the painting. "It's amazing, Nina. Really." I nod enthusiastically.

Edgar leans over for a closer look at the painting. Nina scrunches her nose as though she's uncomfortable with the attention before handing it to Miguel. They and Cassie make their way to their seats behinds us.

"Glad to see everyone getting along so well," Carlos says, awkwardly. "Ri, wanna hang out after school today?"

"You know, I think I'll pass."

Edgar's gaze shoots to mine but I quickly look back to Carlos. "You seem busy enough with Tasha, from what I heard, and I'd rather not complicate things."

Realization dawns on Carlos's face. He looks at me and then Cassie, who rolls her eyes at him dramatically.

Carlos has the decency to appear sheepish for a second, and I find myself very interested in inspecting my nails. Nina tsks and shakes her head.

Miguel laughs. "They done with your ass!"

Carlos scoffs. "Come on, güey, you're gonna give me a hard time too?"

When Miguel doesn't back him up, Carlos sighs. "I'm not hooking up with friends who are girls anymore—you two have proven it's too messy. I'm sorry, okay? Will you be done icing me out now?"

Cassie lifts an eyebrow. "Like any of us would ever want to again."

At that, I'm really laughing. Carlos puts his hands up in the air, as if in surrender. "I get it. I need to think with my brain more and not other," his lips turn up slightly, almost wistfully, "body parts."

Miguel puts a hand on Carlos's shoulder. "Took you long enough, my man."

Carlos may be fine and all, but he's not for me. And I'm okay with that.

Señora Almanza hands each of us our latest quiz, and I have a big red A on mine. I show Edgar, grinning. Immediately, I think about showing Grandma. Or putting my test on the fridge. But then I'd probably have to talk to her, something I've avoided since Nina told me about Grandma blackmailing her.

"That's awesome, Ri!" He high-fives me, and I see on his desk that he got an A too.

When the bell rings later, I gather my stuff quickly. "Edgar, walk with me to my locker?"

Sitting next to us, Carlos gives me a knowing look and a smile. He nods at me before walking away.

Edgar and I stop at my locker. I put my Spanish stuff in and grab the books I need for next period.

"There's something I still want to talk to you about,

actually . . . about the party the other night. We didn't have a chance to get into it the other day at the park," Edgar says. "But you were different at Cassie's."

Immediately, I can tell I was right before. Edgar has suspicions about the cocaine. I try to think of a response that won't be a lie but also won't give away what I was up to that night.

"You were up there with Amy, right?" Edgar continues, looking uneasy. "You can take care of yourself, I'm sure, but I just don't get a good feeling about her."

I stare at my textbooks in my locker and consider what he's saying. I didn't think Amy or Stephanie had a reputation for trouble. But I guess I was wrong. Even still, I tried coke once. Sure, I'd like to try it again, but it's not going to be something I do all the time.

I shrug. "I hung out with Amy and Stephanie for a bit, but it's not like we're actually friends."

Edgar opens his mouth but then closes it. My shoulders tighten a bit at the awkwardness between us.

"You ready for lunch?" I say, shutting my locker.

Edgar blinks and then opens his locker to grab something. We start walking together, and, yes, that could have gone better just now. But it's not what I want to focus on. Instead, I think of the way Edgar looked at me when I told Carlos I'd pass on hanging out with him. And I smile.

Chapter

FIFTEEN

Grandma is sitting at the kitchen table when I get home. Her hands grasp a coffee mug. The door clangs against the wall, since I flung it open, thinking I was alone.

"Grandma! I didn't know you would be home so early. Did Bible study change days again?"

Grandma's face is stern and tired, the lines around her mouth accentuating her frown. "Sit."

My gut tightens at her coldness. And then I remember how she threatened Nina to keep her away from me. The nerve of Grandma to be mad at me *for anything*, after she's done all that she has. I eye the seat next to her for a second before I choose the chair farthest away.

"I was at the store getting groceries for Mrs. Reynolds this afternoon, and I saw Brittany there with her mother." Grandma pulls her coffee mug toward her but doesn't lift it to her lips. Her eyes narrow, and I swallow, dread coursing through me.

"I asked Brittany how she was doing, of course," Grandma continues. "I told her I am glad you have her to keep you company with me working overtime so much." Her face is hard, almost like she's daring me to lie here.

Which is really something, coming from her.

I speak slowly but try to think fast. "Brittany and I have been seeing each other less." I shrug, though my shoulders and chest feel tight. "We've grown apart, made a few new friends."

Grandma slaps her hand down on the table, and I flinch at the resounding thud of the wood. "She said you've been hanging out with the sort of kids who would land you in trouble!"

Collecting myself, I try another tactic. "She would say that, wouldn't she? It wouldn't sound as good to say that she ditched me as soon as she got a boyfriend."

Grandma's features soften into confusion. "I'm sure that's not true."

I stare at her without budging.

Grandma sighs. "Well, Brittany will come around," Grandma looks as though she's conflicted between anger and feeling bad for me. "And Tara told me she already paid for the golf lesson she hoped you would attend, so maybe that will help you two make up."

I scoff, and Grandma rushes to keep talking. "I expect you to be gracious and go, regardless. I will call Tara to check that you do."

I give in. There's no use arguing. I don't even know why I bother anymore.

The house is quiet when I wake up the next morning. Per usual, I'm alone. I spent all night seething at Grandma and Brittany. I text the latter, Judas herself, before class. *What the hell were you thinking saying that crap to my grandma?*

Brittany has the audacity to respond, *What was I supposed to say? That we aren't talking because you've been getting high?!!*

I want to throw my phone against the wall. Scream. Text all the terrible things I want to say to Brittany right now. But I don't. I won't give her that much. I won't give her any of me anymore.

At lunch, I see Brittany and Finn head for the parking lot, hand in hand.

Cassie watches them go, sitting next to Nina on the other side of the patio table from Edgar and me. "What's the deal with your friends? They're not talking to you now that you're hanging out with us?"

I cringe. It's true, sort of.

"Maybe it's the other way around." I force a smile. "I think I'm the one who's upgraded here."

Cassie laughs like she doesn't believe me, but she doesn't press me further. Her eyes fall on Carlos across the lawn, talking to Miguel and Amy, along with a few girls from leadership. No Stephanie or Tasha in sight. "I'm glad you dropped *him*. Saying you could do better would be the understatement of the year."

I stare at Amy. Her hair, rather than curled into soft waves, per usual, is pulled back in a messy bun. But not the kind that looks like you've put a lot of effort into looking like you don't care. Just sloppy, pieces falling out haphazardly. And instead of one of her usual stylish outfits, she's wearing sweats.

I feel a tinge of some emotion I can't name as my eyes linger on Amy.

Nina looks to the group over there too. "You know, I think I'll go see what's taking Miguel so long." She heads in their direction.

Edgar turns to me. "What are you doing after school today, Ri?"

It takes me a moment to pull my eyes from Amy. "Nothing much, what about you?"

Edgar fiddles with the edge of the fraying paint on the bench table. "I was thinking we could study together, if you want."

Cassie pauses mid-bite in her sandwich to give me a knowing grin behind Edgar's back. I ignore her.

"That would be great."

"Pssh," Cassie interjects. "I have to be at home for family game night today, but can I get in on this study action some other time? My parents said if I get straight As this semester, they'll consider giving me their car instead of just trading it in when they buy a new one soon. And I didn't do so great on the last homework assignment."

My eyebrows lift. "Oh? How come?"

"Because, *apparently*, you all study without me."

I blink several times and look back and forth between Edgar and Cassie.

Edgar cocks his head with a smile.

Cassie laughs loudly. "Wait, what? Girl, please tell me you

didn't think you were the only Latina who doesn't know Spanish?"

My face warms and I blink quickly as I try to gather my thoughts.

"Oh, um, sorry. I just . . ."

"I'm a fourth generation Santa Barbaran," Cassie says, and I look up to see her shaking her head. "My grandparents haven't even been to Mexico, no less me."

I look at Edgar, who's giving me an *I told you so* kind of look. But he didn't. Tell me, that is, when I was nervous about oral presentations.

It's like Edgar reads my mind. "When you were worried about talking in front of everyone in class, *I told you* that we knew a lot of people who don't speak Spanish."

I think back to Cassie's presentation. I didn't even register anything about hers because it went so seamlessly. It's easy to not realize how many of my assumptions are still sticking around— because of my own insecurities—that I need to unlearn.

"Sorry, Cassie." I look at her sheepishly. "My bad."

Cassie laughs. "It's fine." She takes another bite of her sandwich and then gives us a playful glare. "But go on, you two. Keep making your plans without me."

"So, uh, next time for sure you should come," I tell her before looking at Edgar. "But today, can we go somewhere other than my house? My grandma might come home from work early, and I don't want to deal with her bugging us."

"We can go to my house," Edgar says. "My mom and aunt should still be at work, if we go right after school, and my brother has plans too."

I try to keep my smile in check at the thought of spending time alone with Edgar again. I shrug. "That would be great. I'll walk with you after school."

Edgar nods, and Miguel and Nina approach us, ending the conversation.

Edgar lives in an apartment complex off of Upper State Street, but we bypass the shops and restaurants by walking on cross streets. I wonder what he thinks of me, especially now that I'm not hanging out with Carlos. I kissed Carlos, several times, and I wanted more. Thankfully, we didn't go all the way, and I know Edgar heard me tell Carlos I wanted to just be friends but I hope Edgar doesn't think I'm a homie hopper or something.

"There's something I've being wanting to talk to you about," I begin, keeping my eyes forward rather than looking at Edgar as we walk. "The other night, at Cassie's party, with Carlos—"

Edgar interrupts, "You don't owe me an explanation."

My lips part and I force myself to look at him. "Right, but I want to tell you. We didn't . . . he and I didn't . . ."

"Got it, good to know." My cheeks flame, and Edgar gives me an awkward smile before maneuvering around a pothole on the street we're crossing. Our steps slow as he directs me into a gas station parking lot.

I follow him, stepping inside after he opens the door for me. Edgar waves at the cashier, who smiles at us, his cheeks wrinkling as he does. "Edgar, my man!"

"¿Qué onda, güey?" Edgar slaps hands with the guy before he heads for the snack aisle, me trailing behind him. He grabs a bag of barbecue chips, and I take Flamin' Hot Cheetos. We grab a couple of sodas, and Edgar pays up front.

"Luis, this is my friend, Ri."

Luis shuts the cash drawer and grins at me. "Pretty."

I blush. "Thanks, it's short for Maria."

Luis gives Edgar a look and a wink. "Don't get into too much trouble."

Edgar flushes and laughs, but a breath catches in my throat at the thought of *exactly* what kind of trouble we could get into with no one home.

At a small white apartment building, Edgar leads me up the concrete stairs and lets us into his apartment at the top. Inside, two black couches sit adjacent from one another. The one farthest from us has a couple of pillows and a folded blanket on it.

Edgar collects the pillows and blanket and pushes them neatly to the side. "Sorry, the futon's my bed." Edgar gestures to the couch. "I would have cleaned up, if I had known you'd be coming over."

We both seem to avert our eyes from each other. He pulls the wooden coffee table closer to the couch nearest us and sets the bag full of snacks on it.

I sit next to Edgar as he passes me my chips and soda. "It

was getting cramped with Armando and me sharing a room, so I thought I'd take the couch. Mi tía has José's old room, my other brother."

I open my bag of chips. "José's the one who helped you buy your camera, right? I didn't realize you have two brothers."

"Had," Edgar says quietly. He points to a family portrait on the wall behind the TV. In it, there's a woman and three sons, including a preteen-looking Edgar. "I used to have two."

Used to.

We both stare at the photo. My mind reels, so many thoughts, so many questions, but no words.

Edgar inhales deeply. "He died. José got in a car crash when he was seventeen. He'd be twenty-one, if he were still alive."

"I'm so, so sorry," I choke out.

Edgar gives me a sad shrug. "It was four years ago. It nearly killed my mom, when it happened. But we're okay now. Or as okay as a family can be after something like that. Like I said, one of my aunts lives here now. It helps my mom having her around."

"I . . ." I catch my breath. "I can't even imagine . . . I—"

"I know," Edgar says. "So, yeah. Anyway, now it's just me and Armando."

I grasp for something to say, something, anything. "How old is Armando?"

"Nineteen," Edgar says. "I could have stayed sharing a room with him, but it was cramped, and we fought all the time over the dumbest stuff. I could tell it was driving my mom nuts. She and my aunt were going to share a room at first, but . . . I just couldn't be the reason for her to have one more thing taken from her."

My throat dries and I take a drink. "That was really nice of you."

Edgar shrugs. Like it was nothing. I imagine Edgar moving his stuff out of his old room, him offering up the space to his older brother. Never trying to take for himself. He's lost so much, and he gives so much. To his family, to me.

I look around again. Besides the family photo, there are more pictures on the walls in the living room—gorgeous scenic photos that I have no doubt Edgar took himself, always able to capture beauty and portray it for all to see.

I spot a picture collage on the wall nearest the kitchen. I stand, without thinking, and walk closer. In the center is a group photo with more than a dozen people in it. Edgar walks to me.

"That's a family picture from the last time we were all together in Mexico." He points to a preteen version of himself, his curly hair longer and unruly. "There I am."

Next to him, I see younger versions of José and Armando on one side, and then a couple teenage girls on the other. As I look at everyone in the picture, I see that that there must be over twenty people photographed, all of varying shades. There are a few who have skin like mine. "Your family is so big. For me, I've only ever known my grandparents and mom."

"We're usually a little more spread out, but we had a reunion to celebrate my great grandmother's ninety-ninth birthday. It was really nice to have everyone together . . . well, for most of the time."

"What do you mean?"

"You know how awful old school Latinos can be about skin color, thinking lighter is best." Edgar says. "One side of the family has indigenous roots. My great grandma sometimes called them prietos and teased them for their dark skin."

I pull my head back in surprise.

Edgar sighs heavily. "Mis primas Isabelle y Camila hated it. It made them self-conscious. They thought she was calling them ugly, basically. And my great grandma was in rare form that day, with all of her comments. José noticed, though—he was always good at that kind of thing. So he rounded up all the cousins and snuck us out of the birthday party to play some soccer on the beach. My great grandma would have hated that too—girls shouldn't run around kicking a ball, not very *ladylike*."

"José sounds like a really great guy." I watch Edgar's face, his sad smile as he remembers his brother.

"The best," Edgar replies, a hint of nostalgia in his voice. "He was really good at making people smile like that, getting them to have fun or to feel better if they were having a hard time."

"Sounds like you," I say quietly.

Edgar's breath hitches. "Thanks."

I swallow, feeling my heart in my throat, and then I look back at his family photo. His cousins. They're beautiful. My mind drifts to Grandma and Mom. I wonder if anyone ever made them feel less than beautiful.

Edgar looks behind us to his book on the table. "So, Spanish?"

I nod and we head back over and study. Sometimes our knees touch, and neither of us pull them away.

About an hour later, keys jangle on the other side of the door right before it opens, revealing a petite woman weighed down with several bags full of groceries.

Edgar rushes over to take a couple bags out of the woman's hands. "Mom, you're home early. This is my friend Ri." He gestures to me on the couch, and I stand and make a move to help with the groceries.

"Ri, this is my mom, Catalina."

Catalina's round face illuminates with a grin. She shoos me away from helping as she makes her way to the kitchen. "So nice to meet you. Edgar has told me wonderful things!"

My face flushes and I look at my feet to hide my smile.

"I switched days with Susan for tutoring last week, when she needed the time off to help her mom after surgery," Catalina explains to Edgar. "So I have the night off."

I follow them into the kitchen, where they begin unloading food into the fridge and cabinets. "Ri, would you like to stay for dinner?" Catalina asks.

Edgar looks at me hopefully. Grandma's not working tonight, so as much as I don't want to be home, I know she'll want me to be. But there's no harm in asking, so I pull out my phone. "Let me just check with my—"

I see a text from Grandma, saying she ended up having to work tonight. Figures.

"I can stay."

"Great," Catalina says. "¿Me puedes pasar el pollo? Wait, you're not a vegetarian, are you? Instead, I could make—"

"I'm not a vegetarian, and I love chicken." I grin as I hand her the package, feeling a blush creep into my cheeks. Who says they *love* chicken? But really, I'm just thrilled I understood her when she asked me to pass it to her.

Catalina smiles at me before putting the chicken on the side of the sink. She pulls her long, wavy black hair into a bun and washes her hands. "Mijo, can you wash these and cut the fat off?"

Catalina starts shredding cheese as Edgar gets to work. "Ri, you can sit at the table," he says. "If you want, I can keep quizzing you on Spanish from here."

I shake my head. "I feel like we're in a good stopping place. I can help."

Catalina smiles before instructing me on how to make the sauce.

The three of us work together in the small kitchen. I remember Edgar telling me his mom loves corgis, so I ask Catalina about them.

Her eyes light up as she stops stirring the rice to show me her phone. "This is from Corgi Beach Day in Long Beach. I went last year." I stop cutting the onion to look at the picture of

Catalina, Edgar, and Armando on a beach, surrounded by hundreds of corgi dogs wearing costumes of everything you could imagine. Corgis wearing shark fins, superhero outfits, and one is even dressed as a banana. Behind them, a corgi stands on a surfboard, apparently riding a wave.

My eyes pop. "Is that dog *surfing*?"

"Yep!" Catalina exclaims. "And he's really good!" She swipes to show me a photo of her posing with the corgi.

Edgar laughs. "She's obsessed with this dog. She follows him on Instagram and likes all of his posts."

Catalina nods and smiles at Edgar before putting chicken in the oven to bake and covering the rice. She grabs a pitcher of lemonade and sets it on the table. Edgar grabs three glasses and we join her.

As she begins to pour us each a glass, Catalina glances at me. "So Ri, Edgar tells me your family is from Mexico too. Which part?"

My eyes widen. I have no idea. "I . . . uh . . . " I mumble, before Edgar furrows his eyebrows. I'm sure he can tell that I'm uncomfortable, which is so embarrassing to begin with, but does he know why?

Edgar jumps in and saves me from answering. "My grandparents on both sides are Santa Barbarans, but my mom's grandparents—"

"Are from Teacapán," Catalina finishes.

Catalina looks wistful, for a moment, and a little sad. "It's this tiny, fishing village a couple of hours away from Mazatlán, in Sinaloa." Catalina runs a manicured finger down her glass. "We used to go there once every few years when the boys were little."

It takes me a moment to realize she must be remembering having José there on those trips too.

Catalina takes a deep breath before continuing, "I miss it. Santa Barbara beaches are wonderful but there is nothing like eating fresh totopos under una palapa by the beach."

I look at Edgar. "You haven't been back in a while?"

Edgar shakes his head. "No, but we should. And I've told my mom I could get a summer job to help pay for it."

Catalina gives her son a warm smile. "Maybe one day soon, mijo. In the meantime, I have many good memories. Of the food, the singing and dancing at night with all my family around. But we can make memories here, too, sí?"

"She doesn't need to be in Mexico for the dancing, that's for sure." Edgar chuckles and then he turns to me with a bright smile. "Mom volunteers sometimes at the nearby senior center, where they have a lot of Mexican seniors. She, my aunt, and a bunch of their friends did a performance for the center's Día de la Independencia celebration a while back. Me and Armando helped the cooks make pozole."

My eyes widen. *He cooks too?* Of course, he does.

Catalina grins. "Only because you boys wanted to have an excuse not to dance!"

Edgar widens his eyes in faux exasperation. "I'm just a simple guy. All I want to do is enjoy mi pozole and wait for el presidente to come on the television and lead El Grito." Edgar pauses when he sees I'm confused. He gives me a silly smile and then pumps his fist in the air. "¡Viva México! ¡Viva!"

He's adorable. When I catch Catalina watching me watch Edgar, I quickly look back down to my glass.

"I swear you get all los viejitos riled up—it's like being en el medio de un zócalo. All I'm saying is that I would still love to see my handsome sons dance with me again, like when they were little boys. Maybe next year we'll finally get Edgar, at least, to join us if you come?"

An invitation! And suddenly a new connection to my culture opens up. "I'd like that."

Chapter

SIXTEEN

I busy myself with my locker as I see Brittany heading toward me. As angry as I've been, I still miss her. I've caught my hand twitching toward my phone when I wish I could tell her some cute thing Edgar said to me. Or when I've wanted to talk about how things have been progressing with my mom.

But before I feel sentimental enough to act, I remember. My stomach actually hurts when I think about everything Brittany's said and done.

After setting my stuff inside, I slam the locker shut. Then I hear Brittany's voice, soft and uncertain.

"Ri, can we talk?" Brittany's arms cross in front of her, and she's looking at my shoulder rather than at my face.

My tone is indifferent. "About?"

"Us. I hate this."

For a second, I feel like telling her I agree, but I can't shake off all the crap Brittany has pulled.

"I've got nothing to say."

Brittany's eyes cast down. "Okay, I guess I'll leave you alone, then." She takes a step before turning slightly. "I'll tell my mom to cancel our golf lesson. It was stupid anyway."

Unbelievable.

"Great, so your mom can tell my grandma I bailed on that too? You plan on telling her about the party, Brittany? Would that make your self-righteous garbage feel deserved?"

Brittany looks back at me sadly. "I'd never say anything." And then she walks away.

I huff. I wasn't ready for the conversation, one-sided as it might have been, to be over yet. Despite how I acted. Without thinking, I grab my phone and text Brittany. I'll go with you to the stupid club to golf. I'm not giving my grandma another reason to come after me.

Brittany pulls into my driveway later that week to pick me up for the golf lesson. We're to meet her mom at the club, keep up appearances like everything is fine between us and act like what Brittany said to Grandma at the store was just the result of a petty squabble that we already resolved. That's what I told Brittany and what I expect her to tell her mom, who will report to my grandma if asked.

The second I open her car door, my eyes widen at her outfit. A short, pale pink pleated skirt with a white top, and a thick white headband holding her ponytail back. "My mom made me wear this," Brittany says as I settle in beside her.

I look down at my old tennis shoes, leggings, and T-shirt I got from T.J. Maxx probably three years ago. On clearance.

"You look great," Brittany says. But when she sees the look

on my face, she nods over her shoulder at a duffel bag in the back seat. "But I have a change of clothes for you, another golf outfit, if you'd be more comfortable."

Brittany leans back to unzip the bag and I see a white skirt, much like hers, and a black polo with some golf shoes. She looks at me, almost fearfully. "We're the same size, so . . ."

I grab the bag and change quickly inside my house, leaving Brittany in the car. When I'm back, I ask, "Why didn't you just tell me you had clothes for me in the first place?"

Brittany looks away from me, out her window. "We're not really talking . . ."

My lips are a hard line. *Because whose fault is that?*

Brittany continues, "And I didn't want you to feel like . . . like you had to, like there was anything wrong with whatever you chose to wear."

Brittany stares at me and I stare back, and I know we're both thinking about our fight, and everything that has happened between us. "Thanks," I mutter. But that's it.

We drive in an uncomfortable silence, up the hills overlooking Santa Barbara. The car pulls up to acres of pristine grass surrounded by lush trees and greenery leading to several red-roofed stucco buildings. I've heard Brittany complain enough about Riviera Country Club that I've imagined it many times, but as she pulls into the parking lot, I realize it's the first time I've ever seen it.

A valet takes Brittany's car keys, and another uniformed employee grabs her golf bag and escorts us into the main building. Brittany thanks them profusely. There's a lobby and I look around, noticing the people walking through.

There are several perfectly coiffed, probably Botoxed women near Brittany's mom's age wearing similar tennis outfits as us. To be expected. But also a few younger women with small children in swimsuits, running in their bare feet toward the floor-to-ceiling glass doors.

Brittany heads for a room that says "Lockers." The man who walked us in lets Brittany know he'll bring the clubs to our caddy when we meet her mother at the cart outside.

I follow Brittany and watch her fidget with a lock outside what must be her locker. She puts her bag at the bottom and leads me out. "We can cut through the clubhouse," she says, gesturing to a restaurant full of round tables covered with thick white tablecloths. "It's quicker this way."

Just a few seconds later, I stop in my tracks. At the pickup area for food stands Grandma, wearing her usual work uniform. Sensible black shoes, black slacks, and a plain white shirt. She's talking to a young Latina who's wearing an airy scarf over a simple white blouse and a pair of dark jeans.

I walk toward them.

Brittany follows me. "Hi, Mrs. Fernández."

Grandma blinks several times, looking surprised. The woman she was talking with smiles at us before turning to the counter and answering a question a server asked her.

"What are you doing here?" I ask.

"Hello, girls." Grandma uses her warmest, most pleasant tone to greet Brittany. "Brittany, so good to see you. I am happy that you two have made up. Best friends are very important."

Brittany nods slowly before looking at me and then plastering on a big smile.

"I didn't realize you would be here today," Grandma says to me.

"You left for work so early I didn't get the chance to tell you." Not that I need to make an excuse. The smile on her face shows that she's thrilled that I'm here with Brittany. Figures.

"How wonderful," Grandma says.

Grandma looks behind her, at the counter where take-out orders are delivered. "My boss sent me here to pick up her usual Cobb salad. Once a week at least she has to have me get her one."

I remember the many times Grandma has complained about Mrs. Reynolds making her pick up takeout from the country club rather than somewhere easier to get to.

"Those must be some Cobb salads," I mutter.

After her order is complete, the woman behind us takes her sandwiches and turns back toward our group. She grins at us before looking at Grandma.

Grandma chuckles. "Forgive me, this is Yesenia." Grandma nods at the woman. "She's new to Santa Barbara and just joined the club."

Yesenia smiles warmly and says hello before something behind us catches her eye. "I better get going, actually," she says. "My husband will be signing us up for every activity imaginable if I don't rein him in. Mucho gusto, ladies."

She waves goodbye before heading out toward the pool.

One of the little kids from earlier, a boy who's maybe eight years old and is wearing American flag–decorated swim shorts, flies past us. His feet pattering on the tile, leaving little wet footprints in our wake, he's running from a girl who must be his little sister. A young white woman with light-brown hair and a sun-kissed nose dotted with freckles chases after them.

"Chaise! Alexandra!" she calls. "Stop running right now." She swoops both children in her arms and wraps them both in the same towel.

She looks at Brittany and me. "I'm so sorry about that."

Brittany shakes her head and smiles at the kids. "No worries."

The woman takes the towel off her children and folds it before looking at my grandma. "You'll put this in the laundry, won't you?" Before Grandma gets the chance to respond, the woman hands her the towel. Grandma takes it from her without a word, but by the way she averts her eyes from me, I can tell she is embarrassed.

Brittany stammers, looking horrified at my crumpling face.

"Oh, I'm sorry, honey," the woman says to Brittany—to *Brittany*—and not Grandma, who lowers her head, her shoulders slouching.

The woman smiles sweetly at Brittany and me as her children take off again, probably running back to the pool.

"I didn't realize she was with you. I just assumed she was

staff. I saw her talking to that other employee." She indicates Yesenia on the other side of the glass wall, chatting with a man by the pool.

I blink several times. "That's Yesenia, and she doesn't work here either, she . . ." I trail off.

Is a Latina, like Grandma. Is this woman for real?

Grandma takes a step back.

Brittany's head jerks quickly as though she's shaking off a fly. "This is Mrs. Fernández; she doesn't work for me. Mrs. Fernández is—"

I cut her off. "My grandma, she's my grandma," I say, glaring at the woman.

The woman blanches, noticeably uncomfortable.

I snatch the towel out of Grandma's hands and shove it at the woman, whose mouth falls open in shock. "I'm sure you can figure out how to get to the laundry area yourself."

Before the woman has the chance to say anything, a bell dings and a cook from the other side of the counter calls, "Cobb salad."

Grandma grabs the bag and lowers her voice so only I can hear. "Enough, Ri. Don't make this . . . please don't." Her chin twitches, and I know it's because she's trying not to cry.

I take Grandma's hand and hold it tight, feeling shame and anger all at once. I give the most cutting look I can manage to the woman.

She stammers. "Oh, well, of course. Diversity is so important to the club and our community. You know, I'm actually on the board for the Boys and Girls Club and—"

"We. Don't. Care," I force out, stopping the woman in her tracks. "Come on, Grandma."

As I push past her, with Grandma and Brittany following me, the woman mutters something about "an honest mistake."

Tears sting my eyes as we walk Grandma to her beat-up car in the sea of luxury vehicles in the parking lot. Brittany notices I'm crying and stammers something I don't catch.

Grandma turns to unlock her car. "Don't think anything of it, Brittany. It happens."

"It shouldn't," I hiss. The sad look in Grandma's eyes reminds me of when she told me about how people treat her because of the color of her skin. And that's the only reason that woman didn't make an assumption about me too, because of the lightness of mine.

Grandma sighs heavily before appraising me. "Don't let it bother you, Ri. Go have a fun time today, you girls."

I'm shaking mad, adrenaline pumping. "I'm not . . . I—" I turn to look at Brittany. "I want to go home."

"I . . . I'm sure that woman didn't mean—"

I rear around to face Brittany, seeing red. "She didn't mean *what*?" I shout in Brittany's face. She flinches but I keep yelling. "She didn't mean that because my grandma is Mexican, she couldn't have the money to be a country club member? Or even a guest? She must be working here?"

Brittany gapes at me.

Grandma's stern voice rings out. "Stop it, Ri. Brittany didn't know—"

"How could she, Grandma?" I snap. "When she refuses to see?"

"Get in the car. Now."

I ignore Grandma's command and glare at Brittany. "If you don't see how seriously messed up that was, after everything I've tried to tell you already, then I don't know how you think I could ever call you my friend again."

I get in the car and slam the door behind me.

Grandma pulls out of the lot, driving out of the long driveway, and I see red stucco roofs and beyond, the ocean peeking around the hill.

"Grandma, I'm so sorry," I finally say. "That lady—"

"No," Grandma interrupts, her voice cutting. "No, you don't apologize for her, you apologize for yourself. Talking to Brittany that way."

"What? No, that was bullshit."

"Language!" Grandma roars.

I stare at my grandma, lines drawn around her tightened expression, eyes focused ahead, both hands on the wheel. And I finally see the rage in her eyes, how everything that just happened has affected her, even if she won't admit it. My voice softens. "She assumed that you worked at the club, and then she talked about you like you weren't even there. Like you weren't a person, just a servant or something."

"I *am* a servant, in a way," Grandma tells me, eyes still on the winding road. "I serve in my job for Mrs. Reynolds."

I scoff. "But you're a person, you're not, you're not . . ." I stammer, unable to find the words to describe how small that woman made me feel. Like Grandma didn't matter. Like she was only there to wait on her.

Grandma turns the car, the side of the road overlooking the many beautiful Spanish-style homes dotting the hill below. "That's why you have to earn good grades, Ri, and go to a good university, become something respectable like an engineer or a nurse or a doctor, so people don't treat you like that."

Tears fall down my cheeks. "Grandma, how would that woman know you weren't a nurse or a doctor? You were in the same country club as she was. Yesenia too."

"Well, lucky for you you'll never have to worry about that," Grandma replies. "It is exactly what I have been trying so hard to get you to understand. You can take advantage of the way you look, and then work extra hard so that you can have a better life. You'll thank me when you're a doctor."

"Grandma!" Tears drip into my mouth as I shout at her. How can she act like everything that happened is something we have to accept or fight against only by playing by their rules? "I don't want to be a doctor. I don't want to spend my life doing something that isn't what I'm passionate about. And the sight of blood makes me want to vomit!"

Grandma gives me the side-eye as we pause at a stop sign near our house. "Fine. You say you like writing so much, you can go to business school, become a marketing manager or—"

"Grandma, just stop. Please!" I'm sobbing uncontrollably now. Angry and sad and frustrated and done with this same argument that we have practically every time we speak. "I told you I want to be a writer. I want to tell stories about people, and I want to travel the world."

Grandma's laugh stops me short. She pulls into our driveway.

"Don't be ridiculous. How can you make a living doing that?" She shakes her head. "I hoped you would see when I told you about my dreams. We can't always have what we want. You are a smart girl, but you aren't thinking straight."

My throat throbs, and I sniff back the tears. Grandma thinks my dream is *ridiculous*. She doesn't take me seriously, and she never will.

"That's exactly why I don't talk to you about this, because you don't care," I snap. "But it's what I want, Grandma. I want to be a writer, not an engineer or a marketing manager or a doctor. And even if I were one of those things, that wouldn't stop people like that woman from assuming—"

Grandma scoffs. "What would that woman assume about you if she hadn't seen you with me?"

My stomach feels like it drops from my body. Grandma raises her eyebrows at me, triumphantly turning to face our house in front of us. "When you are not so angry, you'll see that I'm right. I need to get back to work. Mrs. Reynolds is waiting for her lunch. Now that you have the afternoon free, you can study."

I don't move. We can't keep doing this. I can't take another minute of being told what to do, without having any say. I can't take any more of Grandma's backward thinking. I force the conversation where Grandma doesn't want to go.

"You know, you think Brittany is perfect, but what she does is the same kind of crap that happened right now at the country club." I stare at Grandma and watch for a reaction. None comes.

Grandma hesitates. Finally, she doesn't have a canned response. Finally, maybe she'll see.

"Well, Ri, Brittany is a good friend, and I know she didn't mean what you think she was saying. I'm sure she—"

"Nina told me about what you did," I interrupt, unable to bear another word. "I know you threatened her to get her to stop being my friend."

Grandma's eyes flash. "I don't know what you're talking about."

"Liar." The word comes out cold.

Grandma's mouth falls open. We may have had our differences, but I would never, ever call her a name like that to her face. Until now.

Grandma stammers. "Ri, I think if you calm down and think from my side, you'll see that I was doing what I thought was best for you."

"Bullshit."

"Watch your mouth, Maria," Grandma shouts. "It was a long time ago. I . . . Nina is probably remembering it differently than how I do."

"Let me refresh your memory. You threatened Nina to get her to stay away from me!" I'm yelling now, so loud that I can feel the veins in my neck bulge. So loud that if anyone were to walk by us on the sidewalk behind our driveway, they would hear. But I don't care. "You told her I'd be better off without her!"

"It wasn't like that—"

"Nina was my best friend! You took years of friendship away from us! You took so much away from *me*!"

Grandma's eyes dart from left to right as if she's thinking of what to say. But her jaw remains set, her lips pursed.

Suddenly I don't see Grandma sitting next to me in the car. I see a younger version of me, sobbing, alone in her bedroom, after she calls Nina with no answer for the umpteenth time. She is confused and depressed, walking to the wharf alone, staring at the spot where Nina and she bought their friendship bracelets. And I can't go back and tell her the truth.

Grandma sits up in her seat and smooths her blouse. "I thought it was best. I was trying to—"

"YOU THREATENED A CHILD, GRANDMA!" I bellow, and Grandma flinches, her eyes widening. "She was my best friend. I loved her, I needed her. It was wrong!"

Grandma's eyes soften. "I hurt you and I am sorry for that. But you don't understand. You don't like the choices I've made but they are always to protect you. Nina was hanging out with older boys, with troublemakers. Pero no me hacías caso."

"You were protecting me, Grandma? From what, exactly?

Kids like Nina who act like other kids but don't have rich parents to fix everything for them when they slip up?" Once the words are coming, I can't stop myself. "Ones like my friend Edgar? He knows how embarrassed I was that I don't speak Spanish, so he helps me practice. Do you think I need protecting from him too?"

Grandma's nostrils flare. "You told me you have excellent grades in Spanish."

Of course, that's the part that she would hear.

So I laugh loudly, angrily. "Why would I tell you anything about my Spanish class when I know you don't want me taking it? Why would I tell you about Edgar? You hardly know anything about me anymore, because you're never around." My voice breaks as I shout. "I basically live alone, but who cares? That's the way it's has to be since no one is good enough to meet your approval process."

Our car is still running. Grandma needs to get back to work, but I can't let this go. We need to settle this.

I look Grandma straight in the eye as my voice shakes and I sputter. "You drove Mom away too. Didn't you?"

Grandma jerks her head to look out the window. "That. Is. Not. True." She huffs. "Your mom left because she was a drunk, because she was caught up with one bad man after another. She left because she wouldn't give up that life, Ri, and you are better off for it."

I slam my hand on the car dashboard. "You're lying!"

Grandma flinches but quickly regains her composure. "I

wish that were true. But your mother wouldn't do what was right. She wanted to spend her time running around with whatever man would pay attention to her. She'd stay out all night and leave your grandfather and me to take care of you."

I almost can't take it anymore as Grandma keeps rattling out her accusations, with conviction, as though she's persuaded even herself of her lies. "We wouldn't allow her to bring men home, so she stopped coming, for days or weeks at a time. Then, she would return, and everything would be fine for a while, until she'd go on another bender. When she started drinking while she was supposed to be taking care of you when we were at work, we couldn't allow it anymore. We told her to choose. She could stay if she gave up drinking, started to go to AA meetings, and tried to be the mother you needed. We would help her and she agreed, but your grandfather warned her that if she left again, we wouldn't let her come back."

Grandma shakes her head and her voice rises, like she's angry. As if she has any right to be. "It took less than a month for her to give up! If it weren't for me, she would have had you both living God knows where. She couldn't hold a job down. She—"

"Stop it!" I scream. I follow Grandma's panicked stare to look behind me, where an old man walks by with a bag of groceries. Of course, Grandma would care more about what we look like in here, rather than the truth of what she's done. All the ways her lies have hurt me, have hurt Mom.

"No wonder Mom left," I hiss.

Grandma's head jerks to look at me.

Mom said Grandpa and Grandma were just being strict, controlling, and I know better than anyone how true that can be. Even if my mom *used* to make bad choices, Grandma is the one who lied to me. Grandma is the one who kept me from Nina, who kept me from pretty much anyone else who shared our culture, and she's got excuse after excuse for that too.

If Grandma did this to me, there's no telling how bad it was for Mom. Never the "good girl" that Grandma wants us to be. Never "American" enough in her eyes. No, if Grandma is this bad with me, she must have been so much worse to Mom. There's nothing she can say that will make any of it okay.

"Maybe Mom wasn't really leaving *me* but only trying to get away from you! *You* are a controlling liar who does nothing but make people feel terrible about themselves. But you know what?" I laugh coldly. "Soon enough I'll be eighteen and I'll be able to do whatever I want and see whoever I want, and at this rate, that probably won't be you!"

I slam the car door closed behind me and walk inside without a word. Grandma drives away, to bring Mrs. Reynolds her precious Cobb salad and to work late, like always.

Grandma's lying, and I can prove it. As soon as I'm in my room, I unlock my phone and google *alcoholism*.

Symptoms to look for include broken capillaries—blood vessels pretty much—on your face or nose. *Nope.* Drinking in inappropriate situations. Never seen my mom drunk. *Nope.* Weight loss due to lack of eating in favor of drinking. Mom is just skinny, like me and Grandma. It runs in the family.

Most of the rest of the signs, other than poor hygiene and smelling like booze, have to do with drinking interfering with work and relationships. Well, if you ask my grandma, she'd say that about anything she doesn't want Mom or me doing. It says that many alcohol abusers start out experimenting in high school. *Big surprise there.* Practically everyone drinks in high school.

I scroll through the website before searching *signs of addiction*. There's more stuff about damaged relationships, but also about how biology can play a factor. Some people are more predisposed to addiction than others. So while someone can drink or even use drugs in moderation, others aren't able to. They might start to feel like the *only* way they can feel good is if they're using their substance of choice.

Though none of this reminds me of Mom, my thoughts do turn to Amy and how she's been looking pretty rough lately. Last time I got close to her in the hallway, her eyes were bloodshot. Maybe that's what's happening to her. . . .

Luckily, *I* don't feel that way. I tried coke with her for just a little fun, to forget my feelings of embarrassment and anger in the moment. And, if I'm being honest, I wanted to feel good. For once, I didn't want to worry about what Brittany or my grandma wanted from me.

So, yeah, addiction isn't a problem for me, but maybe I should reach out to Amy and make sure she's okay. I save the URL for the website, along with a phone number for a hotline to call for help with substance abuse. Amy and I sit next to each other during English—I can ask her how she's been feeling there, just in case.

My phone buzzes in my hand. Brittany's calling.

I don't answer.

I grab my headphones and blast music, not because Grandma's home to complain about it being too loud, but because I need to drown everything else out. But I can't stop my mind from going back to what happened this afternoon at the club. I screamed at Brittany for refusing to see what was right in front of her, but haven't I been doing the same? What I saw with Grandma and Yesenia is how people are treated every single day. And Grandma is right about one thing: it's something I don't have to deal with.

I plop onto my bed, open my journal, and start to write. I've been focused on finding connections to my culture. Because of Grandma's choices and some of my own. But I don't have to suffer from racism like she does and so many others do. I finally see what Grandma has been trying to protect me from. But she was wrong to teach me that it's better to abandon our heritage and associate ourselves with whiteness. Just because I understand why she feels that way doesn't make it okay.

I push my pencil down so hard on the page that it breaks. I squeeze it in my hands. I have nowhere else to go with all that I feel right now. I don't know one person who is a harder worker than Grandma. But I can't *not* be mad at her either. All the things she taught me about turning my back on being Mexican were wrong. And she laughed, actually *laughed*, at my dreams of being a writer. She doesn't want to see the real me. Not to mention she's been keeping Mom away for years and will never admit it. She would rather lie about it, *again*.

I can't keep living in secrets like this. If I do, I'm going to explode.

I text Mom and ask her to come pick me up. We need to make a plan to tell Grandma the truth, to show her that she can't stop us from being together anymore.

Chapter
SEVENTEEN

I pull a kitchen chair to the living room window to watch and wait for Mom to come get me. I see her arrive from out the window, driving a rusty-looking brown Dodge Neon. As she steps out of the car, I open the front door.

Once closer, Mom peeks behind me. Her eyes dart back and forth as if Grandma is going to pop out from a corner and yell, "Boo!"

She sighs sadly, probably remembering when this was her home.

"You haven't been here in years," I say. "Want to come in?"

Mom takes a step forward, her eyes landing on the framed picture of her father on the mantel. She walks toward it and runs her finger along a small Mexican worry doll that Grandma has kept next to the picture as long as I can remember. She touches the doll's red hair and the fraying edges of its pink dress, before running her finger along the edge of Grandpa's picture. She stares at the gray urn holding his ashes for what feels like a long time.

"I never meant for any of this to happen," she says.

"What do you mean?"

Mom's lip trembles. "Nothing." She closes her eyes for a moment. "We better get going."

I follow her to the car.

The passenger door squeaks open and the stench of concentrated cigarette smoke overwhelms me. I roll the window down before pushing a stack of grocery store ads out of the way with my foot.

"Sorry about that," Mom says. "You can throw it all back here." She leans over my knees and grabs some of the papers in front, crumpling them slightly before tossing them behind us.

"Do you mind if I smoke?" Mom takes a cigarette out from its box in the center console. I know she smokes because I always smell it on her, but that doesn't mean I want to be stuck in a car with it. I nod slowly and Mom lights up.

"I'm trying to quit," Mom says after she takes a drag. "I smoke less than I used to, but what is it they say? Rome wasn't built in a day."

Once on the freeway, I look out my open window. I want to tell Mom about the argument I had with Grandma, but the words aren't coming out just yet. Instead, I stare at the Pacific Ocean on the other side of the fence. Waves lap over rocks on the shore. Purple and pink streams of light streak through the bright orange sunset, glistening over the water, as we cruise on.

Mom pulls off the freeway and in a few minutes we're walking from the parking lot to her apartment. A couple of kids on bikes pass us, their red safety lights glittering in the twilight, as Mom enters her apartment.

She flips on a light and hangs her keys on a hook by the door. I look around. We're in a small living room, with a brown recliner plopped in front of a big flat screen. A tan couch sits on the other side, across from a black wooden coffee table. Instead of family pictures like at Edgar's house, or a makeshift memorial of my grandpa like we have at ours, the walls here are bare. A tinge of sadness hits me. By looking around, you wouldn't even know my mom has a daughter.

Mom smiles, not noticing my turn in mood, and holds an arm to the couch in front of her and I sit down.

She hurries to the kitchen, on the other side of the wall behind the TV, and starts fumbling around in the fridge. "You hungry, baby?"

"No, thanks, but can I have some water, please?"

Mom sets a glass of water on the table in front of me.

Mom joins me on the couch and looks around her apartment. "It's not much, but it's home."

Her home. Without me.

I run my finger along the rim of my glass. "Where's John?"

"Out." She twists her hands in her lap. "He should be back any minute."

I sip on my water, unable to stop myself from thinking of Grandma. If not for her, I wouldn't feel so weird sitting in my mom's apartment. I wouldn't feel like I'm a visitor in her life.

Mom scoots closer to me. "So, how's Spanish class going this week? You seem to be a lot more confident about speaking it in front of me."

I blink, bringing myself out of my thoughts.

"I feel like I'm getting better." *Think about Spanish. Think about normal stuff.* "Thanks to my friend Edgar."

Mom gives me a knowing look. "Hmmm." She lets the word hang between us.

"Edgar's been helping me study," I offer. "He's been really great. Making flash cards for me, asking me questions and having me answer like you do. He says my accent is improving a lot too."

"He sounds like a nice boy." Mom smiles. "They're few and far between, so be good to him. You learn that as you get older."

Before I get the chance to ask her what she means by that, or to tell her about my argument with Grandma for that matter, I hear keys jangling from the other side of the front door, right before it opens. John walks in wearing his usual uniform of baggy pants and a jersey.

"Sorry I'm late," he mutters. "My manager was all over my ass about my sales last month."

I give a little wave as Mom rises from the couch. "I'll fix you a plate. We have some leftover pasta in the fridge."

"I'm good," John says. "Spend time with your daughter." He scowls as he sits on the couch and starts scrolling on his phone.

John is clearly in a mood, so I decide not to press him for conversation. I finish drinking my water and take the glass to the kitchen to wash it, despite Mom's protests.

Looking around, I notice their kitchen's small, but it doesn't give the feel of being well-used like ours. Where Grandma has decorations for even the unlikeliest thing, like a dress cover for the dishwashing soap, Mom has plain bottles and only a few dishes and utensils. My eyes fall on the trash can against the wall, overflowing with large, empty liquor bottles. My stomach clenches. It could have been a while since they took the trash out, but that doesn't explain why there was any booze in the house in the first place. Unless it was John's.

As I turn off the faucet, I flinch, feeling someone behind me. My mom's throaty laugh puts me at ease. "It's just me, baby." She reaches to the cabinet overhead and pulls out a large bottle of Smirnoff vodka and sets it on the cabinet.

My mouth dries as I watch her put ice in a glass and then mix in the liquor. "Oh, it's not for me," Mom says, as if reading my mind. "John had a hard day at work. This'll help take the edge off."

I nod. Exactly what I thought, it's for John. Sure, Grandma said Mom and the guys she dated drank and partied too much but it's just a drink, not a big deal. And it's late afternoon now, not like he's drinking in the middle of the morning or something.

I follow Mom to the living room, and she hands John his drink. He gulps a few times and half the glass, which Mom filled pretty generously, is already gone. My throat practically burns as I remember the times I've had vodka at Brody's and imagine how smooth that must have *not* gone down.

"Where's yours?" John looks at Mom as she sits next to him. I freeze, like I'm a tree that's grown roots right where I stand in the middle of the room.

"Oh, well, you know me . . . I don't really—"

John snaps his head toward her. "Really, Marisol? Your mom still in your head after all of these years? You want to know your daughter," John glances at me and then back to her. "Then she should know us, and the truth is, ain't nothing wrong with a couple of grown adults who enjoy a drink after work."

Mom's voice comes out quieter, softer. "Of course not, John."

My hands are cold yet slick with sweat. Mom won't even look me in the eyes.

John waves his arm out in front of him. "Why are you just standing there? Come on over already."

My feet feel like they are carrying cement as I take the few heavy, slow steps back toward the couch.

"Sit down already," John barks.

I flinch. Mom doesn't react as I sit on the other side of her, so she's in between John and me.

John downs the rest of his drink and then raises an eyebrow at Mom. "Go ahead and pour yourself one, too, Marisol."

I leap to my feet. "I'll come with you," I say to Mom. She rises and I follow her into the kitchen.

I force myself to take a deep breath as Mom refills John's glass and fixes herself one too. "I thought . . ." I lower my voice to a whisper. "I thought you said you didn't drink anymore, Mom."

A hand on each glass, Mom lifts her chin but speaks quietly. "John's right, Ri. I'm a grown woman and there's nothing wrong with me having a drink when I want to," Mom says with a matter-of-fact tone. "I've gone too long letting your grandma use guilt to control me. You should understand that better than anyone."

My stomach tightens. Mom has a point. I do understand that better than anyone. *But then why does this still feel so wrong?*

I press on. "You said it wasn't a big deal when you were a teenager, that Grandpa and Grandma were just being too strict, but after everything you gave it up anyway. So, if it's not a big deal, why did you . . ." I don't say lie, because I can't form the words. "Why did you keep this from me?"

"What's all that whispering?" John calls from the living room. "You girls talking about me?"

John grabs his glass from Mom when we return from the kitchen. "Don't think I don't know what you're doing in there. You gonna blame this on me, Marisol? Act like I'm some kind of bad influence?"

"No, no, no," Mom says quickly. "*Never.* You're right, John. I shouldn't feel like I have to hide this from my daughter. My mother kept me from her before because she said I was trouble. And fine, I was around bad men who did bad things. I got caught up, got in fights, stole, but only ever to make them happy. I was young and stupid."

Mom takes a drink of vodka and sets the cup on the table, before she puts a hand on John's knee. "The men I saw *before*. The men I dated were often in and out of jail, Ri." Mom looks at me. "But not John, he's responsible, always holds down a job— he helps me. Neither of us have anything to be ashamed of."

At the compliments, John leans back to the couch, seemingly calming down. "Yeah, I'm no deadbeat. I pay my rent. I pay *our* bills." He gives my mom a look.

Mom nods and then, eying John the whole time, takes another drink. Like she's doing it to appease him. My stomach lurches. I feel like I'm going to be sick. John lifts his drink in the air in my direction. "How about you, little Ri? Want some?"

Mom stiffens beside me. "Baby," she says, and it takes me a second to realize she's talking to John and not me. I look at her as she's looking at him.

"I don't think that's the best idea," she says. "She's underage."

I'm struck by the intense urge to laugh. Mom's loser boyfriend offers me booze; my mom says no because I'm too young. I've done *drugs* before. Cocaine. I thought it was fun, it wasn't a big deal. Like Mom and her boyfriend are saying about their drinking.

John is saying something, but I'm no longer listening to him. He goes to the kitchen and comes back with the whole bottle of vodka, pouring himself and my mom another drink. It's like he's trying to make a point or something. To me or to my mom.

In my mind, I see this scene as though I'm someone else. It *feels* like I'm someone else. I'm not here, sitting on the couch in this apartment while my mom and her boyfriend get wasted in front of me. I don't know what to do. I hold myself upright, clench my fists, keep control. If I let go, if I allow myself to feel, I'll break.

Time passes.

John turns on the TV, to a rerun of the show *Cops*. As a man is chased out of an alleyway, thrown to the ground and cuffed, John barks with laughter. "Damn! Shoulda run faster!"

The sound of Mom's slurring words pulls me out of my thoughts. "I'll be right back, mija. I have to use the bathroom."

Sitting on the couch, alone with John in the living room, I realize I need to get out of here. I don't want to be here. I text Nina and ask if she's busy.

A screech comes from the TV as a police car skids to a stop, the flashing red and blue lights holding my gaze for a moment. Even though there's a couple of feet between me and John on the couch, I scoot to the farthest edge away from him.

My phone buzzes. Hopefully, it's Nina. But I can't check because John's scooting closer. He leisurely throws his arm around me. His hand feels heavy around my shoulder.

I need to move, start to, but John's hand holds me steady. "Relax, Ri. Why are you so uptight?"

I try to take a steadying breath. But it comes in short, jagged.

My phone buzzes again. I move to check it but John grabs my hand tightly. "Who are you texting, your boyfriend?"

"Uh, yeah," I lie. "Actually, I'm supposed to meet up with him soon so—"

John scoots closer and breathes his sour breath in my face. I look away, anywhere but at him. The apartment is tiny, too tiny, and the walls are trapping me here with John. This is how he and Mom spend most of their time, getting drunk. I can feel it.

John pushes a strand of hair away from my eye. "You look a little like her, you know. Beautiful. And all grown up."

Mom opens the bathroom door just as I jerk my face out of his grasp. Mom stops for a second when she sees John has his arm around me, but she recovers quickly and strides over, sitting on the other side.

She saw my face, she saw him touching me, and she's doing nothing about it. I want to scream at her, to shake her, to make her see that this is seriously messed up. Finally, I find my voice as I shove John's arm completely off me. "Don't touch me."

John smirks. "Got a little bite to you, don't you? I like that in a woman." He leans toward me, and I can feel his hot breath on my face. "But you are in *my* house. You might think about showing me some respect."

I want to stand, to run, but something about John's glower, the tone of his voice, makes me realize I have to be still.

I look back at Mom as her eyes widen. She finally shows a little sign of the panic I feel. She reaches for my hand. Clasps it tightly.

"John," she says, her voice calm, low, soothing, "let it go.

We're all having a good time. Why ruin it?"

John glares at me for a second, and I scoot away from him.

"I need to go to the bathroom," I practically shout as I leap to my feet. Once the bathroom door shuts behind me, I call Nina and get voicemail. My heart beats faster than I feel like it ever has. Panic, I'm panicking. I have to calm down, I have to think. I look around. The trash is overflowing with tissues and plastic cigarette wrappers. There's a brown rim inside the toilet bowel.

I push the overflowing ashtray aside, hold the sink, and breathe. I cough as I inhale the stench of old cigarettes. Drop to my knees in front of the toilet, heave like I'm going to puke but don't.

Close the lid.

Sit.

I have to get out of here. But I can't ask Mom to take me home; she's drunk.

I text Nina.

> I need help. I can't explain everything that's happened right now, but I'm at my mom's. She's drunk, her boyfriend's drunk, and he made a move on me when she was in the bathroom. I can't be here anymore. Please, can you borrow your mom's car and come get me?

I text her the address and choke on a sob when my phone dies immediately after. I hadn't even realized the battery was low. I close my eyes and try to remain calm. I stay in the bathroom for what feels like a long time, but better in here than out there with John. Eventually, there's a rap on the door.

"You okay in there, baby?"

It's Mom. I hear John yell from the living room. "She fell in the toilet or something?" He barks laughing.

I open the door. "I'm fine." My voice shakes.

A piece of my hair falls in front of my face, and Mom reaches for it. I recoil.

"I'm sorry about that, mija." She sighs. "He's just a little tipsy. I promise you he's harmless."

I seriously doubt that. I watch my mom, feeling like I'm seeing her for the first time. Seeing her like Grandma does. *Bad men. Trouble. Lies.* I feel myself shaking, feel the tears that I try to blink away.

Mom gasps. "Baby! Don't cry." She pulls me into a hug as a sob rises in my throat. "Everything's okay."

Tears fall from my eyes as Mom holds me close. Everything is *not* okay.

Grandma would never bring me around someone like John. She'd be livid if she knew.

My gut sinks as I accept the feeling I've been pushing away since Mom blew me off the first time we agreed to meet.

Grandma knew something about Mom I didn't at the time. She was right to keep her away, right about her. Not about Nina, not about everything else, but about her.

I believed Mom, and I shouldn't have. I *see* Mom for the addict she really is. But what's worse is how am I any better? I've lied to Grandma about so much. I've done coke for God's sake. I could be in Mom's exact shoes in a couple of years, addicted to something even more dangerous than alcohol.

I pull myself away from her.

"Why are you with him, Mom?" I whisper so John won't hear from the living room. "What you said about Grandma and Grandpa, was it all a lie?"

Mom's face falls. "Baby, it's not like this all the time. You don't understand. You don't know him like I do."

There's a knock at the front door, and I sprint toward it. "I called a friend to pick me up," I yell behind me as I cross the living room and swing the door open before John can react.

Then I gasp because it's not Nina I see.

Grandma's hard eyes land on me, her hand clutching her cell phone at her side. Fear crosses her features as she takes in my tear-soaked face. Then Grandma's eyes dart to Mom. Grandma's free hand shoots out to my arm, grabbing it tightly. She steps forward, shielding me.

"Mamá!" Mom says, her voice high-pitched and small, like a child's.

I hear loud footsteps behind me.

"Who the hell are you? What are you doing here?" John glowers at Grandma, as my mom rushes forward. She puts a hand on John, as if she's steadying him.

"Mamá," she pleads, "let me explain."

Grandma looks at Mom in disgust. "I'm not interested in your excuses, Marisol."

"What an entrance, Carmen." John laughs. "Nice to meet you too."

Mom looks at me, her chin twitching like mine and Grandma's do when we're trying not to cry. "You called my mother, Ri? You told her about us?"

I start to shake my head no when Grandma answers. "She didn't need to. Her friend told me where Ri was."

Nina.

Grandma grips her phone tight and glares at John. "I told her I'd get my granddaughter myself, but her friends are waiting for us nearby and if we don't come"—Grandma pauses to look at the phone—"within twenty minutes, they will call the police. I will tell the police all about this *man* putting his hands on my granddaughter!"

"I didn't touch her!"

"Do you think I can't smell the alcohol in this house? What was the plan, to get my underaged granddaughter drunk and take advantage of her? I know exactly what kind of men Marisol surrounds herself with and the types of records they have. And I'd bet anything that one call to the police about a forty-year-old man and a mother with terminated parental rights *kidnapping* a minor would prove me right. How do you think the police will react to such a serious allegation toward people with a prior record?"

"You don't know what you're talking about," John shouts, but the way his eyes widen with fear makes me wonder how close to the truth my grandma is.

"We are leaving now, and you will stay away from my granddaughter or I will make sure the police know all about you both."

Grandma pulls me farther behind her, so I have a foot outside the door.

Mom takes a step forward and puts her hands up toward Grandma. "We don't want any trouble. There's no reason to call the police on John. His name shouldn't be mixed up in all of this."

John's eyes narrow at my mom as she pleads.

"Go 'head, call the cops, Carmen," John says. "They won't find a damn thing by the time they get here."

"It shouldn't be like this," Mom's eyes are red and watery and they are shooting daggers at Grandma. "Talk to me, Mamá! All this time and you won't say a kind word to me now? You haven't seen me in years. The daughter you gave birth to, raised, but now have forgotten about."

Grandma nudges me another step back with her hip. "Go wait in the car, Ri. I'll be right there."

I hold my footing. No way I'm leaving Grandma with John. Grandma glances at me and seems to understand. She touches her phone screen, so the blackness turns to light again. She pushes the phone into my hand, positioning my finger over the call button. "Take this."

Then Grandma looks at Mom, her face a mixture of sadness and another emotion I can't place.

"How could I forget you, Marisol, when I raised the daughter you left behind?" she asks. "When I see her beautiful face every day and know that I would move heaven and earth to keep her safe, but you wouldn't?"

Mom's face contorts, her tears starting to spill. She tugs out of John's grip. "You. Don't. Know. Anything," she spits.

Grandma blows out a breath and shakes her head.

"You don't know what I would and wouldn't do for *my daughter*. My daughter, Mamá!" Mom's voice is shaking, and her hands are too. "She's mine!"

I step back, but Grandma holds her footing.

"You had a choice! Stop the drinking, stop it with the bad men, and be in your daughter's life," Grandma shouts at Mom. "I should have told Ri who you were from the beginning, but now she has seen it for herself." She squeezes my hand. "Now she sees who you really choose to be."

John stomps toward us, and I don't know if he's going to push us out the door or grab Grandma. He raises his hand and I flinch. Mom grabs him by his shirt and yanks him back as he shouts, "Get out of here already!"

We should go. We have to. But watching Mom pull John away from us, I feel my heart breaking. We can't leave her. Mom needs to come too. I love her. *I need her.*

"Mom, please," I say, my voice weak and pleading. "You shouldn't be living like this."

"You have some nerve coming in here running your mouth about my business," John snarls. "I'm done with this shit. Get the hell out!"

But then Mom steps into the opening, and he freezes. Her eyes are wide. She's torn.

"Come with us," I say. Grandma's hand stiffens in mine, but she stays quiet.

Mom looks at John and then back to me. "Just go, baby. I'll call you later."

For a second, I thought we had her. I thought *I* had her. She's supposed to be mine. My mom.

"You don't need him." I can't help but shout. "Just come with me."

John smirks and opens the door as wide as it will go. "Go ahead, Marisol." He takes a step back, and then another, until he plops down on the couch, feet outstretched in front of him. "You wanna leave too? Go right ahead."

He's not even worried.

I want to throw something at him. Make him hurt, like I do. *I hate him.*

Mom shakes her head quickly. "You need to go now, Ri. I'll talk to you later, I promise."

Her face blurs before me. "Mom," I plead. "Please. I'm asking you, *begging* you. Just come with us, and we can figure it all out." I grasp Grandma's hand tighter. "Together."

Mom stands up straighter and lifts her chin as if she's looking down on me. "I'm not going anywhere."

"Goodbye, Marisol." Grandma tugs on my hand.

But I don't move.

"I'm your family, not him!" My chest feels hot and tight.

John's smiling on the couch and Mom's looking at me like she doesn't know me. I want to scream. So, I do. "He's just some creep! He doesn't even care about you. He's—"

"That's enough!" Mom roars. She lunges forward and pushes me completely outside. I tumble into Grandma's arms and the door slams in our faces. The lock clicks on the other side.

I tear out of Grandma's grip, lunging at the door. "Mom! MOM!" Tears are pouring now, and my fists are beating on the wooden door. "Please! Come with me! Don't choose him! Mom!"

Then soft hands are on my back and gently pulling me away.

"It's okay, Ri," Grandma whispers into my hair. "Come on, let's go." She puts her arms around my shoulders and pulls me to the car, my body rocking with sobs.

Grandma clicks the doors locked and drives us through the parking lot. In the rearview mirror, I spot Brittany in her Mercedes, Nina in the front seat.

I turn around so I can see them. "What the . . ."

Grandma's eyes flit to the center mirror. "Brittany called me. She and Nina were planning to come get you, but I said no. It wasn't safe." Grandma gives me a knowing yet sad smile. "Your friends didn't listen to me when I told them to stay home and wait for my call."

I wipe the tears from my face and give a pathetic wave. Nina waves back as Brittany clutches the wheel. They follow us onto the street toward the freeway.

I plug my phone into the car charger. After a few moments, I text Nina Thank you.

Instantly, I see the bubbles showing a reply.

Are you ok? What happened?

I look back at Nina and Brittany's worried faces in the car behind us.

I'm fine. I'll explain everything later.

Nina's next text comes almost immediately.

Please don't be mad. I didn't have my mom's car today and I needed Brittany to take me. And we called your grandma because we thought it could be dangerous. We weren't sure if we should call the police, so we called her instead.

I tell Nina I'm not mad, and then I set my phone down. That's all I say, all I can manage right now.

I look at Grandma, her stoic face. Lips pursed into a thin line, eyes set on the road. My voice pleads. "I never meant—" I stop myself, realizing my excuses are hollow. Just like Mom's.

Grandma doesn't say anything. Her silence scares me.

I clutch my hands tight on either side of the front seat as I start to feel stabbing pains in my stomach. I choke on my tears. *Mom.*

Grandma puts a hand on my leg and squeezes it. "I'm so, so sorry, baby." Her voice is quiet, low. Sad.

I look outside the window at the ocean and night sky, the moon reflecting only a touch of light at the otherwise dark waves flitting in the wind. Driving home now, it feels like giving up. I can't do that.

Maybe Grandpa and Grandma never gave Mom a real second chance. Maybe they didn't spell it out. Maybe Mom didn't really *get* what was at stake. I stab the words into my phone. You have to choose. John and the drinking, or me.

I hold my finger over the send button for a moment before I swallow and push down.

I watch the screen for what feels like a long time, until I start to feel queasy with motion sickness. Mom doesn't respond. I call her and it rings and rings.

Grandma looks from the road to me and my phone but says nothing. I hang up, look at my texts to Mom again. *Text me back*, I beg silently. *Please, Mom.*

Please.

EIGHTEEN

I call my mom again as Grandma pulls off at our exit. It goes straight to voicemail. Either her phone died, or she turned it off. I hold my arms around myself.

Once we're outside our house, I realize how weak I feel. Everything hurts. My throbbing head. My stuffy nose. My sore throat. But mostly it's my heart that's broken. Torn out and cast aside by Mom.

Grandma walks ahead of me, opens the front door, and hangs her keys and purse up. We sit together at the dining room table.

Grandma stares at me, looking as broken as I feel. She closes her eyes and puts her head in her hands.

"I'm so sorry," I whimper.

Grandma holds her head in one hand but reaches for me with the other.

Finally, she lifts her head and looks at me. "Tell me everything."

Inside I feel like shattered glass, stabbed, broken, bleeding. But it's nothing compared to how I feel seeing the way Grandma looks at me. Her *disappointment*.

I close my eyes. I keep them shut, even as I start talking. "I found Mom. I've been seeing her for more than a month." I open my eyes as Grandma inhales deeply, her cross swinging over her chest as she sits up.

"I found her letter, the one you hid from me under your bed."

My hand shakes, but Grandma doesn't let it go. I sniff, try to breathe in through my stuffy nose.

"I got Mom's address from that letter. We started seeing each other, and she told me you and Grandpa kept her away from me." *And I hated you for it.*

I stare at Grandma's blouse, splotchy from me crying on her.

I tell Grandma about everything. Studying Spanish at the library with Mom, our ice cream date, Jack in the Box, what happened tonight with John. All of it bursts out of me, like a tornado, and it's as though I can see the words whirling around Grandma, stabbing her like loose debris as they hit. When I'm out of words and out of breath from rushing it all out, Grandma rubs her eyes and slowly stands. She looks at the wall behind me, rather than at my face. "Why don't you go to bed? We can talk more tomorrow."

My throat constricts. I wish Grandma would yell at me, scream and rage about how I've let her down. I'd rather hear anything instead of this devasted quiet that's come over her. I watch Grandma turn away from me and my heart breaks for the second time tonight.

The next day, I don't go to school. Grandma said I should stay home and rest. I clutch my phone as I lie in bed, hoping to feel it vibrate with a text from Mom.

Edgar messages me in between classes to ask if I'm okay. He says Nina told him I was going through a hard time and needed the day to process. I'm not mad at her for telling him that—I'm glad, actually. Happy he cares. I reply that some family stuff went down and I'm struggling. He says he's here for me anytime if I ever need to talk.

I believe him.

But I'm not ready to do anything more than stare at my phone and wait for Mom to call back.

At a few minutes past noon, there's a knock outside. When I open the front door to see Brittany and Nina, my shoulders sag. A small, desperate part of me was hoping it was Mom.

Brittany's first to swoop in with a hug, and I hesitate, after everything that's happened between us. She lets go and Nina hugs me so quickly after that I don't have enough time to think about it much.

I drag a kitchen chair to sit across from the two of them on my couch.

"Have you heard from your mom?" Brittany asks softly.

I shake my head no, stare at my socked feet.

"It's a good thing you called Ri's badass grandma," Nina says to Brittany, in what I think is an attempt at lightening the mood. "I mean, seriously, if that pinche pendejo John woulda tried anything, I'd put my money on Carmen. She's one scary old lady, skinny or not. I bet she could take him."

It's really something that Nina is complimenting my grandma, and I'm grateful. That reminds me, I told Grandma I'd check in with her while she was at work. I send her a quick text to tell her I'm out of bed and that Brittany and Nina are here during their lunch break.

"Thank you for coming yesterday, for calling my grandma. For everything." My chin twitches and I will myself not to cry. That's all I do lately, it feels like.

Nina gives me a sad smile. "I just wish we could have . . ." She trails off. "I wish things were different."

I look at Brittany and Nina, sitting side by side here in my house. Something I thought I'd never see. Especially after the last time Brittany and I saw each other at the club. After I screamed at her.

Even though I know she deserved everything I said, I can't bring myself to hate her. Not after what we've been through together. Not when I still hope things could be different than they've been.

"It's good having you *both* here."

Brittany twists her hands in her lap, her eyebrows furrowed. "About that."

I hold my breath.

Brittany turns to Nina. "There's something I need to say,"

she begins. "I've been pretty awful with dumb stuff that I say to . . . I don't know, feel better about myself. Trying to keep Ri from you because of my insecurities."

Nina's eyebrows shoot to the top of her head, and I get it. I wasn't expecting this either.

Brittany looks at me and then back to Nina. "And not just lately, but back when we were younger too. I wanted to feel needed, and I pushed you out, Nina. Or I tried to." Brittany swallows, visibly nervous. "And I only recently realized how messed up it all was, that I was using more than just manipulation, but like microaggressions, being shitty toward Latinos, to get what I wanted. I'm sorry."

Nina stares at Brittany for a moment, no movement on her face except a blink. And then another. She lets out a long sigh.

"Okay," Nina says. "Thanks for saying that." Her words turn up almost as if she's asking a question. "As long as you cut that shit out—like immediately—we're good."

It's so quiet you could hear a pin drop, if I had a pin or that was actually something that happens rather than just a weird thing people say.

"And since we're all sharing," Nina adds, "I prefer the term Latinx, since it's gender inclusive. Not Latino."

Brittany nods aggressively. "Got it."

Nina cracks a smile. My room is back to being eerily quiet. "Well, this got weird," Nina says.

The three of us start laughing. So hard I have to clutch my

side. Tears stream down my face, not sad ones, but good ones.

The doorknob turns, and I hear keys jingling on the other side. I stand as Grandma walks in.

"Grandma, what are you doing here? Shouldn't you be at work?"

Grandma sets her keys on the table beside the door. "I thought I'd come check in on you." She looks at Brittany and Nina and smiles. "I'm glad to see your friends came by."

Grandma lowers her chin as her gaze homes in on Nina. "Actually, Nina, would it be all right with you if we talk? In private?"

I hold my breath as Nina slowly nods her head yes. No one moves until Grandma finally looks at me. "Ri, Brittany, could you girls give us a moment?"

"Oh!" I look at Brittany. "Let's go to my room, I guess."

Once the door is closed behind us, Brittany and I look at each other and without saying a word, crouch down and push our ears against the door so we can try to hear.

It sounds like Grandma leads Nina to the kitchen, where they presumably sit at the table.

"What are they talking about?" Brittany whispers.

"Shhh!" I push the side of my face closer to the door.

There's some garbled talk for a moment, but then Grandma's voice rings out.

"It was wrong and there is no excuse. You were a child and I am the adult, and I am so sorry, Nina."

I accidentally bump my shoulder against the door and

Grandma's voice outside lowers. Too quiet to hear. Brittany tucks her feet underneath her legs as we both sit on my bedroom floor. She looks like she's pulling herself together to say something.

I watch her apprehensively, waiting for her to speak. Brittany apologized to Nina, and I'm glad she did, but that doesn't undo everything she's done.

"I know I've been awful, not just to Nina but to you. I've been a terrible friend." Brittany hangs her head. "I shouldn't have made assumptions at Cassie's party."

I lean my back against the door, facing my bed rather than Brittany. "You were right to be worried about me trying drugs, but everything else? Who I am isn't centered on your definition of me. Maybe I was someone else all along, and you just didn't see it. Or didn't want to."

"I don't believe that. At least not entirely," Brittany says. "People change, that's fine, but when I was trying to warn you about Carlos—"

I blow air through my nose. "Just forget about Carlos. He was dating other people but let's not pretend like you knew or that was the only reason you didn't like being around him. And yeah, you apologized to Nina, but what about Edgar, Cassie, and Miguel?" I swallow, closing my eyes. "And me? Because I'm like them too, even if I don't look like it."

I open my eyes to see Brittany nod. For once, she doesn't rush to defend herself.

Brittany's voice comes out softer. "I guess I wanted you to

see yourself as more like me, so that you wouldn't leave me for them. But"—she takes a deep breath—"I was wrong. Just because I was uncomfortable doesn't give me a pass. To act like someone I'd never want to be. It's not a good excuse . . . it's not, I know." She wipes off the tears that have started falling. "I get it now."

I hear Grandma's voice murmuring something to Nina in the other room. This moment doesn't feel real.

"It wasn't just you. Not now, and not back when we hung out with Nina. Your mom said stuff too." My chest tightens. Because now I'm not just calling out Brittany. And though Brittany doesn't get along with Tara a lot, she's still her mom. "It didn't just affect Nina back then. It hurt me too, even though I couldn't admit it to myself at the time."

Brittany goes still, almost as though she's frozen. I don't know how she's taking what I'm saying, but I can't stop now. I force myself to keep eye contact with her. Force myself to tell the truth, *the whole truth*. For once.

"I thought you only liked me if I acted the way you wanted, if I was who you wanted me to be. And because . . ." I pause, keeping my voice even as much as I can. "Because I don't look like them. Because I'm white-passing."

Brittany looks down. "You're right—"

At that, my eyes widen.

She quickly adds, "About part of it. I mean, first thing is, yeah, about my mom saying stuff that wasn't cool, I believe you." She looks at me and her throat bobs. "I'll talk to her."

I inhale sharply, too nervous to speak.

"But about everything else, I mean for sure I wasn't used to hanging out with people who grew up differently from me and who . . . who are Latinx. That's messed up. I . . . I mean, even saying it out loud makes me feel wrong. Like, I never thought I would do anything racist before, but now I see that I was. Even if I didn't know it." She shakes her head, blinking quickly. "But mostly, I wanted to control things, to control you, I guess."

I don't say anything. Even though Brittany said as much to Nina, in a way, it still feels important hearing it from her.

She looks up at me. "I felt like I was losing you."

I don't know what I'd do without you. How many times has Brittany said that to me? My shoulders sag as I realize how heavily this fight must have weighed on her too.

"I remember how sad you were when Nina stopped hanging around. But I never thought she liked me. It was like she only put up with me for you. And then, when you started hanging out with Carlos and Edgar, I thought you'd ditch me for them." Brittany twists her hands in her lap. "It seemed like you were embarrassed of me, like you didn't want them to see me with you."

"I wasn't embarrassed of *you*. I was embarrassed and angry and upset by how you were acting. And that's only part of the real problem," I say slowly as I work out the thought. "I was ashamed of myself."

Brittany gives me a confused look.

"I kept myself away from something in me for so long, like I was trying to erase it," I continue. "I didn't realize until recently that it meant I was erasing myself too, if that makes sense."

Something clangs and whistles from the kitchen. The sound of a teapot, I think. Nina's still out there with Grandma. I should probably go save her soon, but something keeps me tethered here, in this moment, with Brittany.

"Yeah, I get it," Brittany says. "I mean, no I don't *really* get it because I can't, but I think I understand how you were hiding your true self. And I hate that I'm part of the reason you felt you had to."

The old Ri would tell Brittany it's okay, she didn't mean to, what she did wasn't that bad. Or something like that. But none of that's true. It's not okay, and it was bad. So I hold my tongue, and as I let Brittany sit with her choices and her guilt, I feel stronger. More like *me*. Or the me I want to be.

"Look, I promise I'm not trying to be a . . ." Brittany hesitates. "A white savior or anything. But, about the other day . . . since my parents are members of the club, I wanted to ask you if it's okay that my mom and I report that woman to the board."

"White savior?" I lift my eyebrows. "You've been doing your homework."

"Google has a lot to say on the matter. Who knew?"

For that, Brittany gets a smile.

She continues, "I know it's your fight, not mine. But if I don't say anything, I would be complicit, right? So, I found out the woman's name, Lisa Williamson, and asked my mom how to file a complaint. So at least other people at the club will know they can't get away with crap like that. If it's okay with you, that is."

"Yes," I croak, surprised by the emotion I feel. "You should file a complaint. And thanks."

"You don't have to thank me; it's what anyone would . . . well, a decent person *should* do. I'll try . . ."

I put my hand on Brittany's shoulder and she exhales heavily.

She finally says, "I'm trying to be better, Ri. I promise."

Relief floods through me. *Trying.* From both of us. The truth, from both of us. Finally.

Steps sound in the hallway. Brittany and I both practically throw ourselves toward my bed and do our best to act natural as Nina appears in the doorway.

"Everything okay?" I ask, my voice coming out much higher than intended.

"Yeah," Nina says, heading toward us. She gives us a smile that says she knows we were eavesdropping. "Couldn't be better."

Chapter

NINETEEN

After Grandma's off work later that day, she finds me in bed. Staring at my phone, waiting, hoping, praying Mom will call.

"Let's go," Grandma says. "I have something I need to show you."

Before I get a chance to respond, she walks past me toward the door.

I follow Grandma to the car. She doesn't say anything as we each buckle up. She doesn't say anything as she pulls off our street, or when she gets onto the freeway, heading south.

"Where are we going?" I stare at Grandma's face, her brow furrowed, her lips pursed.

"To your mother's apartment."

"What?" I choke out. "Why?"

"I need you to see for yourself, baby," she says. But that's it. Nothing else.

This can't be a good idea—John might be there—but Grandma's mind seems to be made up. And I really want to see my mom.

When we pull into visitor parking at the apartment complex,

I feel like I'm about to explode from all the nerves. Grandma kills the engine and marches to the front door, with me trailing behind her. She doesn't even knock, just grabs the doorknob and twists it open.

No.

It's like the air has been knocked out of me. I stumble back, and Grandma catches me in her arms.

The apartment is empty, cleaned out completely, aside from an overflowing garbage bag in the living room.

A sob bubbles out of me. "They're *gone.*"

Grandma holds me tight as I cry into her shoulder. She rubs my head softly. "Shh. Shh," she whispers.

Tears pour down my face, wetting Grandma's shirt. I hold her tight, feel the bones in her back and cry harder.

I don't know how long we stand there in that empty apartment. When I finally take my head off Grandma's shoulder, I see pain etched all over her tired face. She takes my hand and kisses it softly. "Let's go."

The car chugs to life and Grandma puts her hand on my knee as she drives us out of the parking lot and onto the street.

"I came here earlier today. To see your mom, to tell her she had no right . . ." Grandma hesitates, and her voice softens. "She was gone already."

My throat is throbbing, my head is pounding, but neither compares to the way my chest feels, like it's closing in on itself. Mom couldn't get away from me fast enough.

Grandma looks back at the road as her voice breaks. "I didn't know how to tell you. She's your mother, and I can see how much you love her."

A tear trickles down Grandma's face.

"It's okay, baby," she says. "It's going to be okay."

I cry the whole ride home, and Grandma cries too. She says we are going to be all right, but after this, after Mom left us again, how can we ever be?

Grandma flicks on the lights as we walk into our house.

My mind flashes to Mom's empty apartment, and I feel a hole growing in my stomach. I made such a mess of everything. And for what? For nothing. Because Mom left me again.

Grandma looks at me as though she's trying to figure something out. She walks to the table and sits. "Come over here, Ri. It's time we talk."

I sit across from Grandma, at this tiny table where we share our meals and our arguments.

Grandma sighs heavily. "Baby, I should have told you more about your mother. I should have seen how desperate you were to know. If you knew more, this wouldn't have happened."

I watch Grandma's face crumple. I've blamed her all along, but now . . . I don't know. Everything is different.

"Maybe it wasn't just for your safety that I kept the truth from you." Grandma looks down at her fingernails, laid against the wood. "Sometimes the stories we tell ourselves, sometimes they aren't exactly real. It felt easier to think that you couldn't handle the truth about your mom than it would be to tell you.

It felt easier for me, because I was ashamed."

I scoot closer to Grandma, hanging on her every word.

"I thought you'd hate me if you knew I turned away my own daughter, my own flesh and blood," she says. "But I was so worried that if you knew her, she'd have an influence on you. And I couldn't bear to think that I'd lose you too, after I already lost both my daughter and my husband. I was afraid."

I can't stand the way she looks, like she's breaking. "Grandma, I . . ." I don't know what to say.

Grandma's eyebrows knit together, and her eyes seem far away, as if she's lost in thought. "I'll be right back," she says, before disappearing down the hallway and into her room.

Grandma returns with the box that she kept Mom's letter hidden inside before all this started. I hold my breath as she opens it. She holds the fraying picture of Mom, when she was pregnant with me. Grandma looks at the picture, her face contorted with grief, before handing it over.

This young girl with the curly hair and a round belly is the same woman who grew up to leave me. I put the photo on the table. Grandma lifts a stack of envelopes—some look like bills and others like important documents—and sets them aside along with Mom's letter, revealing a stack of photos I've never seen. She begins thumbing through them, smiling sadly. "I hold pictures like I hold memories, secret."

Grandma shows me one of her and Grandpa holding a baby in between them. "I keep them to myself because of the pain I worry they will cause you, but not only that." Grandma looks at me as she hands me the photo. "It's because of the pain remembering causes me. That changes now—I think, for you to understand what happened with your mom, first you need to understand your grandpa and me."

I stare at the picture. Grandpa looks so young and dapper, his dark hair slicked back. He's wearing a white dress shirt, tucked into jeans. Grandma is young and beautiful, her hair longer, curling down toward her chin. She's wearing a billowing blouse with long sleeves and cuffs that circle the wrists she uses to hold my mother.

"His parents did not want us to marry, they . . . they . . ." Grandma lifts her chin and stares at me. "They didn't think we were a good match. They thought your grandfather could find someone better, someone prettier."

I scoff, having never heard this before.

"Someone lighter," Grandma adds.

My mouth drops open.

Grandma breathes deeply. "In Mexico, and even here with a lot of people from my country and Latin America, many people think you are attractive only if your skin is light. If you are dark, you are ugly. Your grandfather's family had some Spanish roots. They were light and beautiful. I was not."

My eyebrows furrow in shock. "Grandma, I'm so sorry that happened to you. But you *are* beautiful—"

"What you say doesn't matter," Grandma cuts me off. "It is not how people saw me when I was young. They called me fea in school." Her tone softens. "But your grandpa never saw me like that. He loved me."

My heart breaks for Grandma as she remembers, her voice full of emotion. "But his family forbade us to marry. They said he should focus on getting an education instead. My parents were poor, too, and I couldn't offer anything in a marriage, nothing to make me more of an attractive wife. Because being darker in Mexico made everything harder. People would laugh at you. It could make it more difficult to get a job. And our children would be more likely to be dark, like me, his parents said."

I realize with a pang in my gut that every time I tried to make her acknowledge me as someone like her, someone who is part Mexican, Grandma saw me as taking for granted a privilege she doesn't have. Something that would have kept her from being bullied in school, something that would have made her husband's family more likely to accept her.

Everything makes sense now. But it shouldn't. It shouldn't be this way.

"Do you think Brittany is better than I am?"

Grandma blinks several times. "Of course not," she says quickly, taken aback by my question. "I think highly of Brittany, of course, but you are my granddaughter. I love you more than I love anything or anyone in the world."

My words come out softly. "Right, but other than me being your granddaughter, like objectively, is Brittany more important than me? Does she matter more?"

Grandma cocks her head, like she's confused. "Why are you saying such ridiculous things?"

I push harder. "Is Brittany a better student? A better kid?" I tamp down my anger at my grandpa's family who I'll never know. "Prettier?

"Ri, why would you—" Grandma stops abruptly. "Oh, I see."

"Brittany's skin is lighter than mine. Does that make her better than me?"

Grandma's eyes water. "No one is better than you, baby. No one."

Tears fall down Grandma's cheeks. I wipe my own eyes. I never knew my grandma was rejected and treated badly, for something that wasn't her fault, by our own people. It's not fair.

"You are right." Grandma looks down at her dark hands on the table. "There is nothing wrong with your skin."

We are both quiet as I watch Grandma stare intently at her hands. Her lower lip trembles. "Just like there is nothing wrong with mine."

I hesitate because I know this is difficult for Grandma. And I don't want to push her when I finally have a chance to know *why* all I have left of Mom is her empty apartment. But this moment feels so big, and I can't let it end here. We have a chance to make things better. "You had all these experiences I never knew of, and I've been oblivious to you being judged and treated badly, but that's not a reason to do everything you've done, to keep me away from my heritage."

Grandma sucks in a breath quickly.

"You wanted me around Brittany, and I love Brittany, I really do. But you made me feel like she was better than Nina, *better than me*, because she's white." My words come out faster. "It made me so confused. It made me feel like I wasn't good enough, like I'd never *truly be good enough*, exactly as I am, everything within and in between."

Grandma's shoulders slump and I hate that what I'm saying is hurting her, but she needs to know. She needs to finally see.

"Learning Spanish made me feel closer to Mom, yeah, but that's not all our culture means to me." I lean closer to my Grandma and stare at her intently. "It's who I am, where my family is from, and it makes me feel like I'm a part of something. I want to do things like celebrate Día de la Independencia by cooking up a storm of our favorite food and honor Grandpa's memory on Día de los Muertos. I want to learn Spanish, but I also want to do things like that, and I want to do them with you. But if you won't, then you shouldn't try to stop me."

I exhale, let go of so much. So much that has been holding me back. Holding *us* back.

Grandma tilts her head at me, and she blinks a couple of times. Finally, she nods. "I'm so sorry, Ri. I'm so sorry that I haven't listened. That I've made you feel so alone. That I've made you feel that you're not good enough, not perfect, just as you are. There is no excuse."

My eyebrows shoot to the top of my head. Grandma may have apologized for keeping me from Mom but this I didn't expect. We stare at each other quietly, and Grandma takes a tissue out of her pocket, handing it to me. I dab at my eyes.

"From now on, I will share with you whatever you want to know about my life back in Mexico."

Grandma gives me a small smile. "And we can work on your Spanish together. Would you like that? I think I would."

My mouth falls open and I stare at her in disbelief. Grandma nods, affirming what she just said.

Grandma tilts her head and stares at me for a moment. "I am lucky to have such a wonderful granddaughter. I wish Grandpa were here to see what a special young woman you've become."

I smile at her, really smile. For a moment, I'm happy. This is what I've wanted so badly. But then I remember Mom and everything that brought this on. I slump back in my seat.

I look down at the picture of my family; it hasn't left my hand. "Do you think you're still up for telling me more about you and Grandpa . . . and Mom?" I tentatively ask, hoping that she'll say yes.

"Of course, baby," she lifts her chin. "What your grandfather and I had was special. I never knew love, not really, until I met him. My parents were always busy with my brothers—they didn't seem to have time for a daughter. And part of me wondered if I was prettier—" Grandma stops herself. "But after we fell in love, your grandfather and I married in a small ceremony, rented a tiny apartment, and worked very hard to save all we could as we started the process to get our green cards in America."

I stare at the picture. Grandma must have been devastated after Grandpa died. She loved him so much.

"Your grandfather had an aunt and uncle who lived in California. They were not like the rest of his family; they were kind to me. His uncle died before your mother was born and his aunt died when your mom was very young, but they helped us with the process. Soon after we moved to California, we learned we were going to be parents." Grandma's eyes water as she smiles. "I'd never been happier in my life."

Grandma flips through the pictures until she lands on one that makes her laugh. Her smile is so big, I peek over to see what she's looking at. A picture of a toddler with black pigtails, sitting on a bicycle with training wheels and a pink bow on the handlebars.

"Your mother loved this bike." Grandma hands me the picture. "Grandpa and I saved and saved to get it for her for Christmas that year. Back then we couldn't get a job that could even cover all our bills."

Grandma smiles, pride lighting up her face. "But your grandpa took night classes to learn English, and then picked up extra work, after he quit his job picking strawberries in the fields. Even after he started working as a janitor, he continued to put together furniture with some of his friends. They would stand outside the stores and wait until someone would pick them up from the parking lots to hire them for furniture assembly or yard work. I've told you about that, yes?"

Only vaguely, but I nod.

"We worked so hard back then. He always did." Grandma heaves a deep sigh as she flips through more pictures before landing on one of Mom, where she looked around fourteen or so.

"That is why it was so difficult, for your grandfather especially, when your mother started to act out. He had sacrificed so much for our family. Once we married, his parents cut him off financially and mostly stopped speaking to him. And when we arrived here, we endured how so many people in this country thought they were better than us. Though it wasn't the same as it was for me in Mexico, in a way, I was used to it. Your grandfather was not.

"Slowly, all we wanted was to be seen as 'American'—like we belonged here just as much as everyone else—so we pushed our past behind us. Now, I see how what Grandpa and I did must have hurt your mom like it hurt you. Though when she was a teenager, she always seemed like she knew exactly who she was."

Grandma hands me another photo. My mom is wearing a low-cut shirt and tight jeans. She's got several silver bracelets on each wrist and a look of defiance on her smirking face.

"After your grandfather passed, I see that I became even more set on becoming what I considered to be 'American.' I am not defending my actions, only explaining them to you. I stopped talking to people in our neighborhood as much, like you pointed out, and I switched churches." Grandma frowns, looking down. "It felt like it was what your grandfather would have wanted. I had lost so much already and so I held on to our dream even more tightly."

I gnaw on my lip, holding back the emotion as I stare at Mom's picture. If I focus on who my mom was then, maybe I won't have to think about who she is now. "What was she like?"

Grandma closes her eyes. "Oh, she was smart, so smart that she always had a retort when someone gave her a hard time." Grandma smiles sadly. "She was sweet. If I was having a bad day, she'd pull me in a big hug, kiss me on the cheek, and tell me she loved me so much."

I wrap my arms around myself. Hearing Grandma talk about Mom this way hurts. It hurts because I can see my grandma's pain in her pinched expression. Grandma opens her eyes.

"She got into trouble with her friends. First, she was thrown out of places for being too rowdy. I thought she was just being a teenager. A regular rebellious teenager." Grandma looks at me. "That's what I told your grandfather. It wasn't your mother's fault or concern that we had given up so much to be here with her. She wanted to be like her friends—to go to the movies and stay out late. She didn't want a lecture every night about how she was throwing her life away. She just wanted to have fun."

My mouth parts. Grandma, saying all those things? I can hardly imagine it.

"I know, I know what you're thinking. Your grandfather

and I argued so much about your mother, me telling him to go easier on her. But their fights were worse. He would scream at her, and she would scream back telling him she hated him. There were times when they wouldn't speak for days. This house often felt like a war zone."

Grandma looks at me pointedly. "Sound familiar?"

"So, what changed then?"

"Your mom got in with the wrong crowd. Once it was clear she wouldn't stop drinking on her own, we scrounged every penny, swallowed our pride and even accepted money from some friends from church, and sent her to rehab. She came out of the program saying she'd learned so much. Promising she'd stay sober. But it didn't last. When we found the empty bottles in her closet, your grandfather screamed and screamed. He told your mom what a disappointment she was, and she ran away. When she eventually came home, I was afraid we'd lose her to foster care if things went back to how they were before. Or worse, that she'd run again and never come back. Every time your grandfather was tough on your mom, I comforted her, tried to give her a break."

Grandma pulls the memory box toward her, leaving her hands on the metal as she says, "But Marisol got worse and worse. She dated older men who were nothing but trouble. She fought other girls while drunk in public. When she got pregnant at only seventeen, I believed she'd turn her life around. For you. The nine months you were in her belly was the longest time I had seen her sober, and I hoped she would be able to keep going after you were born. But your mom . . ." Grandma looks down at the box.

"She couldn't."

Grandma nods solemnly. "I used to disagree with your grandfather about keeping your mom away. She's my daughter, and I thought she needed help. But every time I tried, she'd lie."

I imagine a younger Grandma spending her nights worrying about Mom. Wondering where she was. What would happen to her.

Grandma's chin quivers and her voice comes out forceful, like she's trying to be strong. "Let me tell you one thing, Ri. Some people say addiction is a disease that the person can't help, and others say it's just someone who isn't strong or smart enough to make the right choices. I used to think, your grandpa thought, it was the weak person. It was a stupid person who would choose to wreck their body, who would risk everything to chase a feeling that would not last."

Guilt twists my insides up, my secret eats at me. Hearing Grandma say all this about alcohol, I can only imagine what she'd say if she knew I've tried cocaine.

Grandma's eyes well. "I don't know that I believe that anymore. Maybe it is both, bad choices *and* a disease. But I have to believe we have some say in the matter. We always have a choice, even if it's a hard one. Even sometimes when choosing right seems impossible."

I blink several times. I liked coke so much after trying it just once. Maybe I don't feel like I *need* it, but it could only be a matter of time. Maybe you never truly know what you're predisposed to until it's too late. And now that I know addiction runs in my family, the stakes seem even higher.

After seeing the truth of Mom with my own eyes, I know that I can't do what she did. I won't hurt people I care about like she has. I'll have to stay away from cocaine, completely, and watch my drinking habits to be safe. Still, I keep my mouth closed.

Grandma's face twists as she remembers. "We'd struggled for years with her. We'd tried everything, but already we were seeing how her choices were hurting you. Eventually, your grandpa was convinced your mom wouldn't change unless we gave her an ultimatum. He told her to leave you with us, for her own good. And yours. He told her to only come back when she was sober."

Grandma sniffs. "It broke my heart to send her away, but we hoped she would get her life together for you. Once your grandpa knew he was going to die, he made me promise I'd honor his memory by keeping you safe, and that meant keeping you away from your mother. He said we, *you and me*, would be all we had now."

Grandma closes her eyes, her voice guttural. "I couldn't lose you too."

Every fight I've ever had with Grandma about my future and what I need to do to achieve it—college, grades, extracurriculars—seems different to me now. She thought she went too easy on my mom and look what happened to her.

Grandma didn't want the same thing to happen to me.

"I made a lot of mistakes, Ri," she says, "with you."

My throat constricts. I'm getting the apologies, the truth, and everything I've ever wanted from Grandma. But she doesn't know what I've done. No matter how hard fessing up will be, I won't keep this a secret any longer.

"I've been lying to you about more than just Mom." I say quickly, before I lose my nerve. "I've been lost. I was lying, not only to you, but to myself too. I've been trying so hard to figure out who I am, and I just wanted to feel okay in my own skin for once. To have fun. To feel free." I stop because even though all of these things are true, I don't want to make excuses. "I tried cocaine at a party recently."

At the word cocaine, Grandma's head whips up, her eyes wide with shock.

I rush to keep talking. "I thought it wasn't a big deal. I thought it was just me having fun. But after seeing Mom, after hearing all her excuses, all her lies . . ." I'm unable to finish the thought.

Grandma stares up at the ceiling for a few beats, and then she lowers her face slowly to meet my eye. I will never, for as long as I live, forget the way she looks at me.

Grandma's eyes are wild with pain. Her lips tremble. "Drugs? Drugs, Ri? How could you be so . . ." Grandma heaves, tears finally falling from her eyes and sliding down her cheeks. She looks toward the hall. She can't even look at me.

I inhale so fast it hurts.

I knew telling Grandma would be hard. I knew she'd be crushed. But I had no idea how much seeing how I've hurt her would hurt me.

"I'm so sorry, Grandma," I croak. "Please. Please. I'm so sorry."

Grandma stands and turns her back toward me. She starts toward the hall.

A sob crashes out of me. "Don't, Grandma. Don't shut me out. Please don't . . ." I choke on my tears.

Grandma whips around and rushes toward me. She sits back down beside me and takes my hands into hers.

"You can't become like her, baby." She holds my hands so tight it hurts. "You can't . . . you can't throw everything away. What I've worked for—" Grandma stops abruptly. "*No*, not what I've worked for. Who *you are*. Our family. You are all I have."

I flinch as Grandma's hold on my hands tightens even more. Her grip loosens and her voice softens. "We are all we have. And I won't lose you. I *can't* lose you, like I lost your mother."

I launch myself into her arms. "Can you forgive me, Grandma?" I ask, my voice coming out as small as I feel.

Grandma holds my shaking body and caresses my hair. "Of course, baby." She pulls away from me and tucks a piece of my hair behind my ear. "Of course, I will forgive you, so long as you never, ever, so long as you live, touch drugs again."

I nod, over and over. "Never again."

"Good. And I think, I should be asking for forgiveness too. I tried to do everything right." Grandma sighs. "I was terrified of you becoming your mother, but what I didn't see is that I pushed you away like your grandfather and I pushed her away. I made our sacrifices the reason for everything, rather than seeing you for who you are. I didn't listen. Not just about your mom and everything you wanted to learn from me. I have tried to force you to do things my way, when I can see now how much that has been hurting you."

I wipe my face and take a deep breath, exhausted from all the feeling, the pain, and the relief. Grandma sits up straighter "I see now. I see what my interfering in your life has cost you, and I'm so sorry. You choose your friends, as long as they don't do drugs. You do have to go to university," Grandma smiles wryly at that, "no exception. But maybe you choose where, and what you want to study. That should be your choice too."

I sit up, almost afraid to believe, and nod vigorously. "Agreed."

"Good." Grandma leans over and wraps me in another hug. So much has passed between us— frustration, anger, lies, and betrayal. But here, at our table in our home, the place where she and I tore everything down but have begun to build it back up, I have hope. Hope that we can make our relationship better. Hope that she and I can see who each other are for real and love one another even more for it. Minutes pass by as she holds me and I listen to the comforting sounds of her heartbeat, strong and steady.

I'm not sure how much time has passed, but my stomach interrupts with a loud grumble.

Grandma laughs, "I think that is a sign that I should get dinner started. Why don't I make your favorite? It's been that kind of day."

I lean my arms back on the table after she leaves our embrace. Grandma reaches over to close the memory box.

"Wait." I look down at the photo of my young mom for another moment before stacking it on top of the ones of my grandparents and her as a baby. I slide them back to Grandma but keep close the one of her pregnant with me. "I think you should hold on to these two, for now. But can I keep this one?"

Grandma nods. "Of course, baby."

She puts the other two photos inside the box and closes it. But I don't want that to be the end of this conversation.

"She left me." My voice suddenly breaks, and I suck in, clench my jaw. I'm so *tired* of crying, of feeling this way. I'm emotionally wrung out, and I'd rather be angry if I have to feel anything at all. I'd rather throw things or break stuff.

"I told her to choose me or her boyfriend, me or drinking, and she left me."

"It's not your fault she left, Ri," Grandma says seriously. My head jerks. It might not be my fault, but I still wasn't enough for my own mother. And that makes me mad at her, but also, in a way, at myself.

Grandma stands. "I have an idea." Before I get the chance to respond, she heads back to her bedroom, leaving the memory box behind. She returns with a notepad and a pen.

"You are my writer. Tell her." Grandma slides the pen and paper toward me.

My mouth falls open. "Mom's gone. Tell her what? And how?"

"This isn't for her, not really." Grandma looks at the blank yellow page. "It's for you. Tell her how you feel."

I'm angry at Mom; that's how I feel. She lied to me, or at least kept the whole truth from me. She put herself first.

But Mom's not the only one who lied. I lied to myself, too, when I pretended what I was doing was okay. Lying to Grandma, sneaking around with Mom, doing drugs. I told myself doing all those things was the only way I could be my own person, step outside of Grandma's control. Blamed her, rather than taking a good, hard look in the mirror and admitting I was behind the choices I was making.

I squeeze my hands, remember what it felt like to hold Mom's. To sit with her at the beach. To know I was hers, and she was mine.

I blink back a few tears and stare at the notepad. I could write a letter telling Mom the truth. Maybe she'll see it someday. If we find her address and mail it. What if she begs me to forgive her? What if she tells me she never wants to see me again?

I miss her so much.

I swallow. I won't cry anymore. I look up at Grandma, who's watching me. I nod and take the pen.

Grandma leans down and kisses my cheek. "I love you, baby. So much. So very, very much." She looks down at the paper and then back at me. "I'll leave you to it."

As Grandma disappears down the hallway, I clutch the pen in my fingertips and begin.

Chapter
TWENTY
Six months later

The smell of the huevos rancheros Grandma cooked for breakfast still wafts through the kitchen, even though I already stuffed myself full twenty minutes ago. I duck under Grandma's arm and take her place in front of the sink.

"Disculpe," I tell Grandma, nudging her out of the way with my hip and taking the dirty plate from her hands. "Puedo limpiarlo."

Grandma laughs and pretends to scoff. "Con permiso."

I smile and make room for her beside me. "Tu lavas. Yo seco." I don't try to say the words extra fast. I let them linger in the air. Even if my pronunciation isn't perfect, it doesn't matter. Because Grandma can understand me, and I can understand her. Plus, necessito la práctica.

"¿Pero no vas a llegar tarde para ver a tus amigos?" She takes a plate from me and then dries it with the dish towel, setting it aside.

I glance at the wall clock. "Oh shoot." I correct myself. "¡Me voy"—I dash to grab my backpack from the dining room table—"ahora! ¡Lo siento!"

Grandma chuckles. I rush to her and let her envelop me in a hug, the dish towel against my back as she says, "Te quiero mucho, Ri."

"Te quiero mucho, Abuelita." I pull away with a smile, swinging my backpack up off the ground as I head for the door.

Grandma calls out to me. "Dile a Nina y Brittany que vengan a cenar esta semana. ¡Puedo preparar sus enchiladas favoritas!"

"Sí, Abuela."

I rush through the living room—past Grandma's overflowing box of knitting and crocheting projects. She's been creating new stuff all the time, ever since she made my navy-and-gold scarf. When she gave it to me months ago, I looked at her in shock, almost not daring to believe. "For UCSB school colors," Grandma said with a smile, before pumping her fist in the air comically. "Go, Gauchos!"

I love the scarf so much that I wore it all winter, including when I got Grandma to visit the Art Walk with Nina and me. We took Grandma to a booth where a woman sells her sewing work and after I showed off my scarf, the two of them became fast friends. She's been asking Grandma to make things for her to sell in the fall. And now the knitting box is overflowing with Grandma's new projects.

"¡Hasta luego!" I call to Grandma, smiling as I head out the door.

I drop my backpack on the park bench as soon as I arrive. Cassie and Brittany are laughing at something Nina is saying.

"Nice of you to show up." Nina smiles at me. "I was just telling Brittany that she better not tell Miguel she considers herself a DDR expert."

I laugh, remembering my and Miguel's dance off at Nina's house last week. "I would have never guessed that your boyfriend is so good at *Dance Dance Revolution*."

Suddenly, I feel someone jump from behind me. Miguel yells, "Boo!" Nina and Brittany laugh as I practically fall off the bench.

Miguel is beside himself with laughter as I softly push his shoulder. Edgar's camera bounces off his back as he jogs to catch up, Carlos trailing behind. Miguel must have run over when he realized we were talking about him.

"Oh, I'd say her boyfriend is muy bueno at a lot of things!" Miguel sets the basketball he's holding on the ground, wiggles his eyebrows at us before leaning in and planting a sloppy kiss on Nina's lips.

"Ew!" Cassie and Brittany say in unison as Carlos reaches us. He types something in his phone before pocketing it.

I step around Nina and Miguel so that I'm standing in front of Edgar.

"Cool camera," I say. "Do you take all the girls' pictures?"

Edgar grins at me and lifts the camera, snapping one of me. "Only the most beautiful ones."

Cassie turns to Brittany. "I can't even with them."

Brittany rolls her eyes faux dramatically. "Barf."

Edgar steps back, looking down at the ground as if in serious thought. "They're right. We better stop. If my girlfriend were to see—"

I launch myself into Edgar's arms, unable to stay away any longer. "I can take her," I say. And then I kiss Edgar, ignoring the gag noises coming from Miguel and Nina behind me.

Carlos chuckles at us. "I think those were some of the corniest lines I've ever heard."

"I thought Miguel was bad," Nina says, talking over him, "but these two are the actual worst."

I laugh at my friends, not caring that my and Edgar's PDA is the butt of the joke. Because we're all here, together.

It's been months since that day at my mom's, when Nina and Brittany followed Grandma to come to my rescue. Months since Grandma and I went back and I saw Mom's abandoned apartment. When I realized she left me again.

I remember how awful that felt, but Grandma and I picked up the pieces of our broken hearts and started to rebuild. Together. Working on trust. Working on allowing each other in. Telling the truth. No more secrets.

I look around at my friends sitting on a park bench in front of a blacktop basketball court, and I smile. Even without my mom, I'm not alone.

Cassie grabs a bag of Doritos out of her backpack and pops it open. "Well, as fun as it is watching the four of you make out, Brittany and I were thinking it's time for a girls' night. We can watch a movie or something at my place later?"

Brittany beams and I put my arm around her.

"What?" Miguel sputters. "No fair, you can invite your girl-friend to girls' night, but we can't come?" He looks at Carlos, as if in search of backup. Carlos shrugs. He does *not* care about missing girls' night. Miguel returns his scandalized gaze to Cassie. "Why don't you bring Mia around more, anyway? You're afraid we're going to steal her from you or something?"

Cassie rolls her eyes dramatically, swatting Miguel's hand away from her Doritos. "No!" She laughs. "I actually *like* Mia and don't want you, fool, to embarrass me!"

Miguel cradles his hand like Cassie has wounded him severely.

Edgar gives Cassie a winning smile. "So, I guess that means I'm not invited? You're looping me in with Miguel and Carlos?"

Nina raises an eyebrow at Edgar, ignoring Miguel's affronted scoffs. She walks to the side of the bench that Brittany and I are sitting on and bumps her shoulder against mine. "If you're there, we won't be able to talk about you."

Edgar laughs and my chest flutters.

Cassie crumples her empty bag of chips. "So, are we going to just sit around, or are we going to finally play?"

"I call first in," Carlos says quickly. "Just because we have an odd number, how is it that I'm always the last to play?"

Cassie and I look at each other and smile. He might not be in the doghouse anymore, but it's still fun to give Carlos a hard time.

Miguel grabs the basketball off the ground. "Fine, but Nina

and Cassie can't be on the same team because—"

Cassie snatches the ball out of his hands. "Because you're afraid you'll lose!" She makes a run for the basketball court, bouncing the ball and taunting Miguel as she goes.

The rest of us grab our stuff as we follow them, Edgar and me trailing behind the others. A light breeze blows my hair, and the California sun glistens off the blacktop as we approach.

Edgar takes my hand and I squeeze his. My thoughts return to what Grandma told me after Mom left, what she repeated over and over, so many times that I can almost hear her deep voice whisper it in my ear right now.

"It's going to be okay, Ri. We're going to be okay."

I smile. I believe her.

Dear Mom,

I'll never understand why you left me, not when I was a kid, and not now. You're my mom, and I've always needed you. I wanted to know you so badly. My whole life I've told myself stories about you, who I thought you were, how I thought you wanted me. I told myself you'd be around if you could, that something was keeping you away. And I imagined one day you'd come back for me.

And then when you told me it was Grandma who wouldn't let you be around me, I felt so angry at her, but glad that I was right. You wouldn't leave me by choice. You loved me so much.

Now I know that wasn't true. That was just what I told myself because I couldn't face that you weren't here for me. And now that you've left again, I feel like a huge part of me is missing.

I wish you'd come back. I'm going to learn Spanish, Mom, with or without your help. I'm going to graduate from high school, and I'm going to go to UCSB and study writing. I'm going to become a journalist and travel the world. I'm going to do all these things, even if you aren't here to see them happen. But I hope you will be. You can be, if you leave John, the drinking, and the lies behind. I want you to choose me.

But until you do, I don't want you around.
So, you can hate me like you hate Grandma and
Grandpa, or you could come back.

The choice is yours. I love you.

Ri

ACKNOWLEDGMENTS

It feels like I have been writing this book for many years, long before I started typing Ri and her grandmother's story. Like Ri, I'm biracial and I grew up grappling with many similar challenges when figuring out my identity. Moreover, as I wrote, my heart was full of love for my grandmother.

Grandma, I often think about how you wanted to be a doctor, and you were going to college before you and Grandpa left Mexico and came here. I remember asking if you ever wished you'd stayed, finished college, and had the kind of career you dreamed of, and you told me, very simply, that you didn't. You said that your children had more opportunities in the United States and that to you, that was most important. When I think of you and the mark you've left on me, I remember whenever I visited your job at a nursing home. You worked hard as a cook without complaint. I recall how when nonprofits, churches, or anyone less fortunate asked you for money, you gave it, even when you had so little for yourself, living in a tiny studio apartment. I think of the time you bought me cheesecake from Jack in the Box for my first birthday at the group home, and you brought enough for all the other foster kids. You told them they could call you Grandma too.

Despite the heartbreak you've suffered—the losses of your daughter and then your grandson—you've never become bitter,

Grandma. You've been a wonderful example of faith, generosity, and love. In many ways, you are the reason I made it out of a childhood full of darkness. That is why this book is dedicated to you, Maria del Carmen Almanza. I even named both main characters, as well as Señora Almanza, in this book after you! Te quiero mucho, abuelita bonita. Thank you for calling me every day, without fail, to tell me that you love me, and for always believing in me.

I have many other people to thank, starting with my most wonderful literary agent and agency, Sarah Gerton and the rest of the Curtis Brown team. Sarah, your enthusiasm for this story, and for my reasons for wanting to write it, gave me the support I needed to make it happen. I truly couldn't ask for a better partner, cheerleader, and friend. Every day, I'm grateful for what you've done for me and my career. Thank you!

Next up, I want to thank my incomparable editor, Carolina Ortiz. Carolina, from our first phone call, it was clear that you had the vision *Everything Within and In Between* needed. You got what I was trying to say, and you had the empathy and skill to guide me and my characters on the journeys we needed to go on. ¡Muchas gracias y abrazos, Carolina!

My sincerest gratitude goes to Nicole Moreno, Cara Norris-Ramirez, Gweneth Morton, Jessie Gang, Lisa Calcasola, Sean Cavanagh, and the rest of the wonderful team at HarperTeen for making this beautiful book the absolute best it could be. Thank you to Carina Guevara for illustrating the cover of my dreams!

I am indebted to the sensitivity readers who helped me to

write and revise this story with the cultural care necessary, as well as to my Las Musas friends who have been so supportive and helpful in this endeavor.

Thank you to Rachel Breithaupt for helping me with the Spanish in the classroom and for being an amazing friend. Adriana Esparza, I can't thank you enough for sharing with me about your family's traditions, listening to mine, and inviting me to start some of our own with our daughters together. All my thanks to Paulina Batani Cooke for letting me practice Spanish with you. I'm also grateful to Hannah Rael, Rita Chang, and Talisa Hail-Hoover for talking with me about the feelings I've had that made me want to write this book. Evergreen thanks to Katie Watson and Carolyn Bolton for cheering me and my writing on. I'm so lucky to be friends with all of you!

Thank you to Autumn Krause and to Kathleen Chappel for critiquing an early draft, and to Drew Hoover, Amy Albano, Michael Tachco, Devlin Durkin, and Ruth Rowe for the overall encouragement as I wrote this book.

Nikki Grimes, I will always be grateful to you for believing in and mentoring me.

In addition to my grandmother, I'm grateful to the rest of my Almanza family, especially Aunt Diane, Uncle Rudy, and Yvonne, for their support of my writing.

To my sister Rachelle, I've enjoyed the conversations we've had about this book's subject matter and learning about some of our shared feelings or experiences that I didn't realize we had when we were growing up. Thanks for being my sister and friend.

Big thanks to my adoptive mom Barb for the steadfast encouragement. I'm also grateful to my aunt Luann for reading my work and cheering me on.

To my in-laws, I couldn't have asked for you to be more enthusiastic about my writing! Thank you to the Gs, Aunt Sue and Uncle Tom, as well as Aunt Tina. DeeDee, I'm glad you've started "shipping" my characters—that's the kind of investment I like to see! Don, thank you for the Clorox wipes. Please see Don Abrams in chapter twelve for your payment in full. Carol, I've said before that you do more to publicize my books than anyone who doesn't get paid to work on them. I am honored and truthfully very proud that you are always eager to read my writing. Your support always makes me smile. Thank you.

Corgus, I appreciate you staring lovingly at me while I write. Hadley, I wrote the earliest version of this book years before you were born, and, since then, you've gone from sleeping beside me as I typed to screaming whenever I got my laptop out and trying to bite it. I can't tell you how much I love when you sit beside me when I work and you hit the keys next to me on your toy computer. I hope one day you'll read my books and will be proud of me. Robby, thank you for sharing Santa Barbara with me and in some ways inspiring parts of this book. And thanks for reading it and making sure I got the landmarks right, as well as helping with all the camera stuff! I'm able to live this dream because you support me in doing so. I am grateful for every sacrifice you make and every word of encouragement. I love you!

As always, I'm thankful to God for giving me this life, for every good thing.